JAYNE FAITH

Reign of the Stone Queen

First published by Andara Publishers 2020

This novel is entirely a work of fiction. The names, characters and incidents portrayed in it are the work of the author's imagination. Any resemblance to actual persons, living or dead, events or localities is entirely coincidental.

First edition

ISBN: 978-1-952156-07-6

Cover art by Deranged Doctor Design

This book was professionally typeset on Reedsy.
Find out more at reedsy.com

Contents

Chapter 1

THE MORNING AFTER King Oberon named me the Queen of the Carraig Sidhe, I woke to the jarring sound of insistent knocking. My eyes popped open, and I took in the unfamiliar canopy above the large bed I was sprawled across. I pushed up to sitting, my pulse speeding to an alarmed sprint as I swung my gaze around wildly, seeking anything familiar. It took me a few seconds to remember I was still in the castle of the Summerlands, the realm of Oberon and Titania.

Flopping back and hoping whoever was at the door had given up and left, I groaned long and loud. I'd probably only slept an hour or two, and at that moment, it almost felt worse than no sleep at all.

The knocking started up again, more rapid now, like a woodpecker demanding entrance.

I pushed stiffly up to my feet and looked down at my wrinkled clothes. Apparently, I'd collapsed across the bed still fully dressed.

"Your Majesty!" came a loud, too cheerful female voice from the corridor outside my quarters. "Your Majesty!"

I almost shouted that she had the wrong room, that there was no monarch to be addressed as Majesty in these quarters, but I couldn't hide from my new status.

More knocking.

Swearing under my breath, I went to see who it was.

"Queen Petra!" a plump woman with the feathery lashes of a Sylph exclaimed. "Top of the morning to you. I've come to bathe and dress you."

I winced as she bellowed each sentence. The woman must have been hard of hearing. She bustled past me, and a tiny, meek little mouse of a girl followed, straining to tug a rolling trunk along behind her. They both turned to me, stopped, and dropped into curtsies.

I just stared at them dumbly for a few seconds. When the Sylph woman peeked up at me with an expectant look, I gave my head a shake. Right. They were waiting for me to say something.

"Please rise," I said, feeling ridiculous.

"Your Majesty! I am Claudine." The plump woman placed her hand on her chest. "And I am happy to be at your service, at the behest of the lovely High Queen Titania who sent me to dress you for the day. She and the regal High King Oberon have requested your presence at half past the hour. As I said, I'm here to bathe and dress you."

Oh gods, why did royals think anyone needed help with things such as washing themselves and putting on clothes? I'd been doing both just fine without assistance since I was a child.

I informed Claudine as politely as I could that I'd bathe and dress on my own and to please just leave my fresh clothes. She complied, though I could tell she was scandalized by my refusal of her services.

I quickly bathed and dressed in the clothes the servant had left. As I put on the faux leather riding pants, white tunic blouse, jacket, and boots, the wisps of a dream I'd had flashed through my mind. The rolling green hills in the dream reminded me of the strange hallucination that'd happened when I'd killed Marisol Lothlorien. Just before I'd run my sword into her, both of us had seemed to transport into a different place and into different bodies that wore ancient armor.

I still didn't know what the strange vision had meant, if anything, but my stomach twisted at the thought of the former Stone Order monarch. She'd sent assassins to kill me and my twin sister Nicole, and Marisol wouldn't have stopped until we were dead. In spite of that, there was no real satisfaction in ending her life, even if it had been necessary to ensure my and my twin's survival. Marisol Lothlorien was the only Fae ruler I'd ever sworn to, her domain the stone fortress was my childhood home, and her son Maxen was my longtime friend. In the whole mess, Maxen was the source of my deepest regret. Marisol was his only family, but in sending assassins after me and Nicole, she'd also tried to kill the woman he loved. I'd only just learned that Nicole was pregnant with Maxen's child. And to add extra stress to the mix, my poor sister was still in the Duergar kingdom, captive of our blood father Kind Periclase. Maxen's feelings on all of this had to be in turmoil.

The thing was, I didn't want to be hard-hearted about what Maxen was going through, but I needed him to forgive me for killing Marisol. Or at least be able to work with me. I just hoped that for the sake of his unborn child and his love for our people, he'd be able to stand the sight of me. Because whether either of us liked it or not, Oberon had named me the ruler of our people, and I was going to fail spectacularly as Queen without Maxen.

Truth be told, I was dreading having to ask him for anything. But I had no choice.

And running under all of my concerns was the gut-twisting under-current of grief that I was trying hard not to acknowledge. I was almost certain my father, Oliver, was dead. Periclase had threatened to kill Oliver if I didn't cooperate, and I'd had to make a terrible choice.

I smoothed my long hair back into a loose bun, trying my damnedest to focus on my reflection in the vanity mirror rather than on thoughts of my father. I couldn't afford to grieve. With Aurora slung across my back to complete my ensemble, I was off to meet with the Seelie High King and Queen.

I arrived at Oberon's office, which was decorated with heavy furniture, paintings of hunting scenes, and other masculine touches. But it seemed I was late to the party, as there was already a crowd gathered. Titania stood near the fireplace mantle, her peaches-and-cream skin and strawberry-blonde hair looking as fresh and youthful as if she were barely past twenty, though she'd been alive for many generations. Standing next to her was Melusine, a study in contrast to the High Queen's summery beauty. Melusine, the Fae witch, was clad in black satin that matched her dark hair. Her strange orange eyes darted around shrewdly as Titania spoke in her ear.

Melusine and Titania had a falling out long ago, as often happened between Old Ones, but the dire situation with the Summerlands under attack had brought them together. Surprisingly, they didn't seem to be putting on a front only for the sake of the Summerlands and the future of Faerie. They genuinely appeared to have mended their differences, as their heads were bent together, and they whispered back and forth like a couple of school girls.

The rest of the rulers, except for Oberon who stood silently off to the side, were arguing boisterously. I tried to get the gist of the situation as I approached them.

A quick glance around revealed the absence of Jasper Glasgow, the Duergar man I was romantically involved with, which sent a little ping of disappointment through me. It was quickly followed by trepidation as I realized my kingdom was the topic of discussion.

The voice of Moreau Maclean, King of the canine shifter Dobhar Sidhe, boomed above the others. ". . . must aid the efforts of the Carraig Sidhe to establish and maintain their independence. How can you not see that? King Oberon himself said it was foretold that the Carraig must not fall under Unseelie rule."

My senses sharpened at the mention of Carraig. Those were my people, formerly called New Gargoyles of the Stone Order, but now an official kingdom: the Carraig Sidhe. But at this point it was in name only, as the Duergar King Periclase, who also happened to be my blood father, still occupied my people's stone fortress. And that, apparently, was what the kings and queens in Oberon's office were arguing about.

From what I gathered, Moreau was trying to persuade King Lawrence, the stocky, barefoot ruler of the Gnomes, to help me in my efforts to take the stone fortress back from Periclase. My pulse bumped with a little swell of adrenaline. This wasn't the kind of fight I was used to, but it was one I needed to win. I needed to oust Periclase from my realm, but he had the place on lockdown. I wasn't going to be able to force him out unless I had help. But I was among rulers, now, and everything I said carried weight. Missteps could cost my people everything.

Five-foot-tall Lawrence huffed and glared up at the Dobhar king, unintimidated by Moreau's stature. "But if Finvarra takes the Summerlands, it won't matter what happens to the Carraig," the Gnome insisted. "Our forces need to be concentrated here, not in the stone fortress."

Moreau shook his head. "But it *does* matter, that's exactly what I'm trying to say."

Voluptuous and long-lashed Queen Vida, monarch of the Sylphs, stepped in. "Gentlemen, you're both correct. We can't let the Summerlands fall, and we also have to ensure the Carraig Sidhe get out from under Unseelie control."

Several of them spotted me approaching and inclined their heads in acknowledgement. I nearly stumbled, on the verge of dropping into a curtsy, before I remembered that I was one of them.

Moreau flashed me a winning, if slightly wolfish, smile. "Queen Petra," he said. "I was just attempting to gather some support for you."

I glanced at Oberon, trying to gauge where he stood in the argument. But he'd remained on the sidelines, his arms crossed.

"Uh, that's very generous of you, King Moreau," I said, my mind spinning as I tried to work out what I needed, who I might piss off, and what unintended consequences could come out of whatever I said in this room. "I'm going to be frank with you. I need aid. Whatever you can spare. My military people are most likely imprisoned, if not worse, so I have no forces to work with. Even if I had the full might of the Carraig, Periclase has a formidable army many times larger than mine, and it wouldn't be easy to extract him from the stone fortress. That isn't what worries me the most, however. Finvarra and Periclase have the Fae sorcerer Eldon on their side, and he was almost single-handedly responsible for the hostile takeover of the fortress, though of course Periclase took credit."

That set off another round of exclamations through the group.

Oberon had gone to his desk and was scribbling something on a notecard. With practiced movements, he rolled the note, sealed it with wax, and imbued the wax with a bit of magic. A messenger raven appeared at the half-open window behind the desk, and the High King passed the scroll to the bird, who flew away with it.

"Let's allow Petra to speak," the Fae witch Melusine cut in through the din.

Everyone quieted and turned to me. Trying not to fidget under their attention, I recounted how the banished Unseelie High King Finvarra had brought Eldon, a sorcerer, and working with Periclase the three of them had forced me to let them into the stone fortress. There, Eldon had used his unnaturally powerful magic to take control of my body, march me into Marisol Lothlorien's shelter, and murder her.

When the image of Marisol's dead form—her head severed from her body—tried to rise in my mind's eye, I shoved it down. Right behind that memory was the look on Maxen's face after I'd killed his mother. I pushed that away, too.

"So, you see," I said quietly. "It was hardly a true Unseelie victory. With Eldon on their side, they were unbeatable. It should be obvious that I can't go in and take the fortress back on my own. And King Oberon's oracle said that for the sake of keeping Seelie control of Faerie, it's imperative the Carraig remain free of the Unseelie."

There was a long moment of silence. More than one ruler's face had gone stony, clearly not liking the way I'd stated my case.

I didn't enjoy invoking Oberon's oracle in my attempt at persuasion—it made me feel like a child using a "Daddy said you have to" argument—but another part of me was surprised and even a little disgusted that so many of the rulers were so unwilling, watching out for themselves or focusing on the Summerlands, not wanting to commit resources to the Carraig struggle. Didn't they care that it could likely spell doom for all of us?

Melusine snorted.

"Eldon's not *unbeatable*," the Fae witch muttered under her breath, but loud enough for everyone to hear.

In spite of the weight of recent events, Melusine's sulky words brought a ghost of a smile to my lips. She was the only one I knew of who might possibly compete with Eldon in magical skill and sheer power. She clearly didn't like the implication that he had no competition.

"Even more reason to give aid to the Carraig," Moreau said with a charming smile, opening his arms wide as if inviting the other rulers over to his side.

That set off another burst of arguing. My gaze ping-ponged around as I tried to take in what everyone was saying, but the conversation seemed to be spinning out of control.

"Rulers, come now!" Melusine called out, once again forcing the room to quiet. "Let the new queen speak."

I blinked a couple of times and swallowed hard, quickly trying to think of what more I could say to gain support. I desperately needed help taking back the fortress. But as a queen who was literally only a few hours on the throne and ruled the smallest realm in Faerie by at least ten-fold, I couldn't push too far in making demands or sounding entitled.

"I don't want to cause a rift among us," I said, striving to sound diplomatic but internally irritated that I was going to have to take such a soft line. When no one interrupted me, I continued. "We need to stand together. But I can't take the fortress single-handedly. The Carraig will fall to Periclase without your aid. For all I know, my entire military may be slaughtered. I don't even know the state of things in the stone fortress right now, but it would be stupid not to assume the worst."

"There's someone who can help us with *that*, at least," Oberon said.

I looked up at him, surprised. He lifted a muscled arm and pointed at the room's entrance.

I twisted around. Maxen Lothlorien stood in the doorway.

Chapter 2

I SWALLOWED HARD. "Maxen. How did you . . .?"

Maxen's eyes skipped right past me. "King Oberon. I can't stay long, for obvious reasons," he said with a bow.

In spite of Maxen's chilly bearing toward me, I took several steps in his direction, not quite believing he was really there.

"How did you get away?" I asked. Last I knew, Maxen had been imprisoned in the fortress, along with other high-ranking Carraig.

"Like I said when I helped you escape, I know that place better than anyone," he said, meeting my eyes for only a fleeting second. "It's a risk, but I can escape my cell in the fortress jail for short periods without notice. I used a secret doorway to come here."

He brushed past me, and I turned and trailed after him, an unsettling mix of emotions twisting my stomach. Part of me was happy to see him, but I also feared the repercussions if Periclase discovered he'd left. My guilt over killing his mother lodged like a stone in the middle of my chest.

"I summoned Maxen here," Oberon said, moving out from behind his desk with purposeful, swift strides. "We will do this quickly. Please." He gestured for Maxen to take the figurative floor.

Maxen went to stand in front of the dark fireplace. He was pale, his blue eyes red-rimmed with fatigue, and by the slight hollows in his cheeks, I guessed he hadn't been eating much lately.

"Periclase's soldiers are still thick throughout the fortress," Maxen said, speaking with quick, clipped words. "They have the whole place on lockdown, with everyone confined to their rooms. Periclase has pulled out some of the military leaders for meetings, but I haven't been included in any of them. The violence seems to have stopped, but the threat is clear that if anyone steps out of line, there will be bloody repercussions."

"What of Finvarra?" asked tall, leggy King Delun, ruler of the Kelpie kingdom.

"Finvarra is currently in the Duergar palace, though he occasionally comes to the fortress."

There were murmurs, and I heard Oberon say to Moreau that we needed to act fast.

I couldn't imagine how Maxen was getting such detailed information while confined to the fortress jail, even if he was able to sneak out occasionally.

"What about Eldon?" Melusine asked.

Almost reluctantly, Maxen's gaze drifted over to me for a brief moment. "He's been traveling back and forth between the Duergar palace and the stone fortress, as far as I can tell." I thought I saw something in his eyes, something that hinted he understood just how completely Eldon had controlled my actions when I'd stormed the fortress with Periclase's army and killed Marisol. Maybe it was wishful thinking on my part.

The kings and queens exchanged quick glances.

"Has Periclase acknowledged King Oberon's certification of our kingdomhood?" I asked.

Oberon cleared his throat and cut a hard look at me. I stared back blankly for a moment.

Oh, damn. *Damn.*

I'd assumed Oberon had informed Maxen in the summons he'd sent.

But Maxen didn't know. He would have found out soon enough, no doubt, but this wasn't the way I'd wanted it to happen. Not here, with all of these kings and queens staring at him and his emotions still so raw.

"This may seem strange and abrupt," Oberon said, addressing Maxen. "But I've granted your mother's petition. The Stone Order is now the Carraig Sidhe kingdom."

Maxen's mouth fell open, his sapphire blue eyes widening. I thought I saw the faint mist of tears in them. He blinked several times and then swallowed.

"I . . . I don't know what to say," Maxen said, his voice ragged.

I couldn't even imagine the turmoil of emotions he was feeling. Regret that his mother wasn't there. Anger that Oberon hadn't made the move while she was still alive. Maybe confusion about why he'd done it at all.

"You should know that it was a move based on the advice of my oracle," Oberon said. "Otherwise I never would have done it. The Carraig don't have sufficient numbers or land to be a proper kingdom. And you must understand that my decision was no favor to any of you."

Maxen closed his mouth, blinked a few times, and gave a short nod.

"You also should know that I've placed Petra on the Carraig throne," the High King finished. He spoke firmly, but respectfully.

Maxen's head tilted slightly, and then his attention slowly turned to me, confusion turning to anger flashing in his blue eyes. His face had gone hard, his jaw muscles bunching as he clenched his teeth.

"I never would have done it, had the High King not insisted on the condition," I said quietly. "I had no choice. You have to know that."

It wasn't my fault. None of it was truly my fault—not Marisol's death, not the situation in the fortress, not being named Queen of the Carraig Sidhe. I knew all of that, but still, I felt the weight of Maxen's anger and grief so acutely as he glared at me, it was all I could do to steadily

11

hold his gaze. For a split second, I was almost grateful that my father Oliver had likely died in Periclase's custody. At least Maxen would see that I'd sacrificed, too.

"I must get back to the fortress and into my cell before anyone notices I'm missing," Maxen said to Oberon. "I will not be able to leave again for some time, Your Majesty."

"We understand," Oberon said. "Petra will be moving against Periclase very soon. Your confinement will come to an end."

After a curt bow, Maxen turned to go.

"Maxen," Oberon called.

Maxen turned at the doorway.

"You will recover from this. Your people need you. We need you. Faerie needs you."

"Yes, Your Majesty," Maxen said woodenly. Then he was gone.

My entire being longed to slink away, to be away from kings and queens, to try to hide from the image of Maxen's face that was burned into my mind's eye. But I couldn't go. I pulled up to my full height, second shortest in the room to only the Gnome king, on whom I had a scant few inches.

Forcing purpose and confidence I didn't feel, I went to where Maxen had stood only a moment before and faced the rulers who had silently but with keen interest watched the exchange between me, Maxen, and Oberon.

"Now we know Eldon is still there, and that will make things very difficult for us," I said. I looked at Melusine. "Any ideas about what to do?"

She flipped the black-polished fingers of one hand. "Leave that to me."

"But can you maintain the shield that's protecting this castle as well as help us with Eldon back at the fortress?" I asked.

"I wouldn't have said anything if I couldn't," she said, clearly annoyed by my doubt. She gave a loud, surly sniff. I had to give her credit—she seemed thoroughly sure.

Again, the Fae witch nearly made me smile. I nodded at her. "Much appreciated." I turned to the rest of those gathered. "I need whatever forces you can spare, and I can't wait. I have to act."

"Before we do that," Oberon cut in. "We need to go after Finvarra in the Duergar palace. We can't waste the opportunity. Continue your discussions, and I will send an urgent summons to Jasper Glasgow. As soon as he arrives, a small group will set off for the Duergar realm with the mission of killing the so-called Unseelie High King."

I couldn't help flicking a glance around again, as Jasper's absence seemed conspicuous. When we'd all met the previous night, Oberon had revealed that one of Finvarra's own blood would have to take him out. That meant it was up to Jasper, who was Finvarra's blood son, though only a few in Faerie were aware of that fact. Everyone else believed Jasper was a bastard son of King Periclase. For all we knew, Finvarra himself didn't even know the truth.

While Oberon went to his desk to ready a message, we went around the group, and my heart dropped a little lower in my chest with every passing moment. King Moreau and Queen Vida were the only ones who pledged support. The Gnome and Kelpie kings declined, as did Queen Corrain, ruler of the Baen Sidhe. The new Spriggan King Trey, son of recently deceased Sebastian, gave a resounding and ice-cold no. I didn't expect him to come to my aid. He'd been shooting me death stares since I arrived at the Summerlands, obviously blaming me for his father's death. A small number of other Seelie rulers weren't present, but I couldn't hold out hope that they'd help.

Disappointment weighed heavily on me, but I didn't know what else to say to persuade them. At least I had Moreau and Vida on my side. Their aid would have to be enough. I pushed down my bitterness toward the other rulers and my fears for my realm. The state of the Carraig

Sidhe, though closest to my heart, wasn't the only critical thing we had to contend with.

"With that settled, we must put Carraig concerns aside," Oberon said, rejoining us. "Finvarra has the Stone of Fal, and we must kill him before he begins using it."

The Stone was an enchanted gem. It gave the holder the power to force people under his control and could be invoked up to three times by any one individual. We'd only recently learned that Finvarra had it.

"It will be a small, focused mission into the Duergar realm," Oberon continued. "A group of three, perhaps. Jasper Glasgow must go, of course."

Melusine raised her hand. "And me, to keep Eldon in check."

I waited for Oberon to nod his approval.

"And you must go," the High King said to me. "If there's a fight, we need to make sure Glasgow has the best possible backup."

I started to protest, but Oberon gave me a menacing look that clearly said he wasn't in the mood for debate.

"Where is Jasper, Your Highness?" I asked, taking a different tack.

"He's on an assignment," Oberon said. I thought he'd say more, but he didn't elaborate. He scanned the rest of the rulers. "Let's disperse for now. I know some of you need to return to your respective realms."

The others began to move toward the door, but Oberon beckoned at me. I went to the High King, tipping my head back to meet his gaze. He was nearly two feet taller than me, and I felt like a child staring wide-eyed into the face of a larger-than-life, mythical figure.

He watched the others leave and then turned his attention to me. "Jasper is trying to gain information about a magical artifact that might help us level the playing field against Finvarra's Stone of Fal. Our fear is that even if Jasper manages to take him down in your fortress, the Stone will fall into the hands of some other Unseelie."

My brows lifted in surprise. "Does such an object exist?"

"We certainly hope so. The Chalice of Dagda, an object of legend, could help us. We must not allow the Unseelie to discover that we're seeking it."

"Of course," I said.

"He should arrive very shortly," Oberon said. "Be ready to depart for the Duergar realm."

I nodded, trying to imagine what could possibly match the power of the Stone of Fal. The legendary jewel allowed its possessor to almost effortlessly convince people to pledge their allegiance to him, to follow him with single-minded devotion. I couldn't imagine a more dangerous thing for Finvarra to have. By all accounts, he hadn't used it yet, but we all knew it was only a matter of time.

I went out into the hallway where I found Queen Vida speaking to Queen Corrain. Their conversation came to a close, and Vida flipped me a wave and strode over to me, her curvy hips swaying slightly.

"Did you ever imagine it?" she asked.

I peered at her. "Imagine what?"

She gave me a faintly amused smile. "That you would rule a kingdom."

I gave a rueful laugh. "Not in the slightest. It was the furthest thing from my mind when I imagined how my life would unfold."

"Ah well, Oberon certainly had his reasons for appointing you."

When she'd first approached me, I'd been on guard. But it seemed she just wanted to make friendly conversation.

"It could easily turn out to be a huge mistake. In fact, it's very likely," I said with a sigh. "As you've probably already figured out, I'm a fighter, not a diplomat. I've no patience for ceremony, posturing, and negotiation." I'd probably said too much, but I considered Vida an ally. It was too late to take it back, anyway.

"Well, you can't rule by your sword alone. People will never love a ruler they fear, and you need their true loyalty. You'll just have to figure out the ruling style that suits you best, as all kings and queens do. If that means leaving some of the posturing, as you say, up to others who are better suited, then so be it. You're in charge."

"Ceremony and posturing are too tightly intertwined with the crown, I'm afraid," I said. "I'll just have to learn how to do it and enjoy it, I suppose." Or at least fake it really, really well.

Vida bid me goodbye just as a castle messenger came to fetch me. I followed the young man through bustling corridors where all servants and attendants displayed the red, orange, and new-grass green, the colors of the Summerlands realm, in some form, whether a simple vest, full dress, or livery. Fae of all races served Oberon and Titania. I didn't know much about the selection process for such jobs but had heard that swearing blood oaths of some sort were required for serving in the Summerlands.

In the past, I'd had the vague impression that Oberon and Titania lolled around a fair bit, spending much of their time attending and hosting lavish parties and quarreling with each other and other Old Ones, and tearing themselves away from their follies to take care of Faerie business when the occasion called for it. There was a grain of truth to at least some of it, but since I'd spent some time in the castle and in the High King and Queen's presence, I realized that much of my so-called knowledge of their lives might have been more idle gossip than truth. Especially now that the Summerlands was threatened, and all of their efforts were directed at preventing an Unseelie takeover.

The messenger brought me to a small private room, and when I entered, I found Jasper there alone. Warmth flooded through the center of my chest at the sight of him. His clothes were smudged with grime and his hair was a wind-blown mess, but I didn't care. As soon as the messenger closed the door, I practically ran to him, ready to bowl him over.

"Wait," he said with a laugh as I crashed into his chest. "I'm supposed to bow, and you're supposed to—"

I didn't let him finish, instead pressing my lips to his. He hummed low, an expression of his enjoyment that vibrated against my mouth, and wrapped his arms tightly around my waist.

When I pulled back, he looked down at me, his tri-colored eyes glowing.

"You're a queen, now," he said. "I suppose you'll want to upgrade to someone other than a bastard prince."

He said it purely as a tease, with no concern or even flicker of doubt, and my heart bumped as I realized how much I appreciated his strength and confidence. They'd been there all along, I was certain, but recent events had allowed him to begin to show the man he truly was.

I snorted and punched his chest plate lightly. "Even if you were a bastard prince, I'd probably keep you around." I turned serious. "But soon everyone in Faerie will know the truth about you, that you're not just an ordinary soldier."

He pressed his lips together and nodded, inhaling slowly through his nose. "Aye. And I suppose it's time. I can't hide my true identity forever."

I bit my lower lip. Yep. I *really* liked this man.

He arched a brow at me. "What?"

I shook my head. "Nothing, really. I'm . . . just very glad we met."

He chuckled and his arms tightened, pulling me firmly against him. "As am I."

I wanted to say something about Oliver, but if I brought up my father, it would take too much will and energy to compose myself afterward. There was too much work to do, and I didn't have the luxury of such emotions.

A noise at the door sent us springing apart, and the glow of reuniting with Jasper was quickly replaced with a tensing of my insides when Oberon and Melusine entered the room. Oberon held a black velvet drawstring bag in one hand. When he stopped, he cupped the bottom of it protectively with the other hand.

Jasper bowed, and I nearly curtsied before I caught myself and inclined my head instead. Or maybe I should have curtsied. I needed to school myself on basic protocol among kings and queens at some point.

Oberon turned to Jasper and me. "We didn't talk about timing. Do you need the cover of darkness to make your way into the Duergar realm?" I could tell by his expression that he hoped not, as that would significantly delay our mission.

I'd been thinking about the logistics of entering the palace and had formulated a loose plan.

"I don't think that's necessary, Your Majesty," I said, with a quick glance at Jasper. He knew the Duergar palace more intimately than I did, but I had an idea I thought he would approve of. "We can go as soon as you dismiss us."

He gave a quick nod and then began loosening the drawstring of the velvet bag he held.

"You must get safely into the palace on your own," he said, reaching in the bag. "But I can help you get back out."

He extended his palm toward me. In it was a tiny velvet packet, a little envelope made of fabric.

"It's a portal jewel that will bring you back to the Summerlands," he said. "But I can spare only one, so the three of you need to stay together if at all possible."

Then he told me the words to whisper that would unlock a doorway when I tossed the jewel in the air. He made me repeat them twice to ensure I had them memorized correctly.

I held the packet with both hands, feeling the little round lump of the jewel inside. Portal jewels were incredibly rare, powerful, and valuable. Jasper had used one to bring the two of us to the Summerlands after Maxen helped me escape the stone fortress jail.

Oberon turned to Jasper. "I also have something for you."

The High King reached for a knife sheath on his belt and unsnapped the flap. With even more care than he'd used to handle the portal jewel, he withdrew a dagger. It was designed as a simple fighting knife with a slim seven-and-a-half inch blade and a low-profile handle. But it was the pale yellow color of butter and seemed to glow from within. Something about it tickled at my memory.

"Gae Buide," Jasper said, his voice low and thick with his Scottish brogue.

"I hereby pass Gae Buide to you, Jasper Glasgow," Oberon said. Magic glittered around the knife as Oberon turned the blade around to pass Jasper the handle. The magic dispersed as soon as Jasper took it. "Take care not to accidentally nick anyone you don't intend to kill."

Then I remembered. Gae Buide inflicted mortal wounds. Even a small cut would cause rapid death within seconds, and it was said there was no magic that could stop it. It acted like the deadliest poison, but the lethal quality was in the blade itself, and there was no need for the application of any toxin. The knife was now bonded to Jasper, until he decided to pass it sot someone else.

Jasper's lips parted, and he gazed at the dagger in awe as he brought it up to eye level. Tilting it back and forth, he watched light dance across the metal.

"I'm honored to carry this weapon," Jasper said. "I shall wield it in the name of the future peace of Faerie."

Oberon held out the sheath, which he'd removed from his belt, and Jasper carefully slid the knife into it before attaching the leather strap to his own belt.

"Now, I will leave you to organize yourselves, as I have other business to attend to," Oberon said. "Melusine knows the location of the doorway you'll use to leave the Summerlands. Please take care, all of you."

The High King left us.

Melusine let out a little titter once Oberon was gone. "Look at this, the two lovers off on another mission together. Only this time, you've got a third wheel." She said it in a sing-song voice of a mocking child. I wasn't really sure how to respond.

She looked oddly pleased with herself, and then I remembered how she'd said my and Jasper's destinies would be intertwined, and that it was important they were for reasons she claimed she didn't understand at the time.

"I must admit I don't know much about the powers you possess, only that you are extremely strong in magic," I said. "When Periclase's forces stormed the fortress, Eldon used his gloaming magic to obscure us and make it difficult for the New Gar—ah, Carraig Sidhe—to fight back. Do you happen to have any magic that might similarly mask our entry?"

Melusine scowled and muttered something about silly shadow tricks and optical illusions. I waited, hoping she wasn't going to spiral off into one of her moods.

"I have counterpart magic to the gloaming, if that's what you're asking," she said, her orange eyes slanting off to the side as she seemed to become absorbed in her own thoughts for a moment. Then she spoke softly. "It's painfully bright and beautiful. Strong enough to burn away the gloaming as the sun chases away shadows and dispels fog."

Jasper and I exchanged a glance.

"Okay, that sounds interesting," I said carefully. "I'm not sure that will help us sneak into the Duergar palace, though."

Melusine's attention snapped to me. "Of course not, don't be stupid," she said shortly. "What we'll *need* is manifestation transformative magic."

She said it as if it were obvious, but I wasn't certain what she was referring to.

"I believe you call it glamour?" she said, her eyes wide with exasperation.

"Glamour doesn't work on Fae," I said.

I'd used glamour in the Earthly realm, back when I was working as a mercenary. I could change my appearance, even my clothing, and the instant disguises came in very handy. But glamour only fooled humans. Fae could see right through it.

Melusine glared at me, and then her face dissolved into a blur, along with the rest of her, as if I were looking at her through frosted glass. Her features sharpened, and I gasped and drew back a step.

She looked exactly like me.

All I could do was blink and stare for a long moment.

"Can you disguise me and Jasper, as well?" I asked.

She blurred again and then snapped back to her own features. "Obviously."

It was anything but obvious, but I wasn't about to correct her or try to argue. Again, I thought of the shield she'd erected around the Summerlands Castle. She'd said it wouldn't be a problem to keep it in place while she accompanied us to the Duergar palace, but it was difficult to imagine the level of magic needed to do that *and* perform extremely complex glamour magic on the three of us. I couldn't help wondering if Melusine had gone into hiding partly because her power was so enormous. As with great wealth or fame, it was probably difficult to know who wanted to use her for her abilities and who was truly a friend.

Jasper had remained quiet through the demonstration. When we'd visited Melusine at her cottage in the woods, he'd been reluctant to engage her in conversation, and that unease seemed to have resurfaced.

"We are indeed lucky to have you, Melusine," I said. Despite her cranky demeanor, I was determined to treat her with respect and sincere appreciation.

She gave a little shrug and a demure smile.

"I'm was thinking we could go into the palace through a doorway located in a supply storage wing," I said to Jasper. "It's inside a warehouse, tucked among some shelving units, so if there are guards posted there we should be able to overwhelm them before they can signal to others. Do you know the one I mean?"

Jasper nodded. "I do. Sounds like a wise choice."

"Shall we go?" I asked Melusine.

She took the lead, walking swiftly out into the corridor. Like Oberon and Titania, the Fae witch was close to seven feet tall. I had to trot to keep up with her long strides.

The servants roaming the halls startled when they caught sight of her, some of them gasping when they peered into her strange orange eyes. I caught up to walk along beside her and saw her shoot glares here and there. Otherwise, she kept her chin level and her eyes straight ahead. I still wasn't sure if her hostility was part of her true nature, or if it was an artifact of the substantial emotional walls she seemed to have built around her.

She led us to a quiet area of the castle that was detached from the main structure, and when we passed a few dark-robed Druid monks, I guessed we were near a monastery. It was rare to see Druids in Faerie because druidic magic was weak here. It drew its power from the Earthly natural elements.

Melusine ducked into a low alcove that led into a room that was open to the sky. It was actually less a room and more a miniature enclosed arboretum. Two huge, twisted columns of wood rose from the dirt floor. They were so massive at first my brain didn't even register they were living trees. Each one was over thirty feet in diameter, and their lower branches had twined together overhead to form a natural arch between them.

"The Arch of the Summer Queen," Jasper breathed.

We were looking at a doorway of legend. Oberon had planted the two trees when he'd began his rule in the Summerlands. He'd named it in Titania's honor. Golden light filtered down from above, and birds darted here and there, chirping merrily, oblivious to the battle raging just outside the shield that protected the castle. It was so serene I wished I could have lingered there a while.

Melusine didn't appear impressed, as she went up to the doorway and then looked back at us. "Well?"

Jasper stepped ahead of us, and Melusine and I each placed a hand on his shoulder. He began tracing sigils in the air and whispered the words that would take us through the netherwhere to the doorway in the Duergar palace's warehouse. Just before he finished, I drew Aurora.

Together, we stepped into the space under the arch.

Chapter 3

IN THE BRIEF moment when I floated in the void of the netherwhere, it occurred to me that I was about to enter a place where there was likely a bounty on my head. Perhaps it wasn't the wisest move to return to the Duergar realm, but it was the necessary one. I deeply wished I could make rescuing Nicole part of the mission, but I couldn't let thoughts of my twin—or the thin hope that Oliver might still be alive somewhere in the palace—distract me from my mission. If we could take out Finvarra before he invoked the Stone of Fal, that would be worth almost any price.

We stepped out from the void and onto the concrete floor of the warehouse. I crouched and pivoted, grasping Aurora in both hands and taking a defensive stance, my eyes searching wildly in the darkness for Duergar guards.

A small light sprang to life and then another four next to them. Melusine held up her hand, which looked like a candelabra, each finger ending in a flame.

"We're alone," she said. She shooed irritably with her candle-hand at Aurora and shot a glare at Jasper's drawn short sword. "Put those things away before you slice off someone's limb."

"I'd prefer to keep my weapon drawn," I said, peering through the shelving units.

Melusine was moving the fingers of her other hand in motions that reminded me a bit of Eldon. Magic shivered through the air.

"Well, that's going to look suspicious when other people see you," the Fae witch said.

"What do you mean?" Jasper asked.

"Look at yourselves," she said.

Satisfied that no one was going to jump out of the shadows at us, I turned to him and gasped. He looked like a Duergar soldier. Well, technically he already *was* a Duergar soldier and had been for years, but Melusine had completely changed all of his features and clothes. Before me stood a man with light brown skin and close-cropped brown hair who stood about four inches taller than Jasper's height. He was dressed in the standard Duergar light armor. All I could do was blink at him.

When I realized he was staring open-mouthed at me, I glanced down to find I appeared to be wearing the same soldier uniform.

I raised one of my arms and flexed it. A man's thick, hairy forearm moved, and the round bicep bunched just below the sleeve. My eyes whipped to Melusine. "How in the name of Oberon—"

She preened a little, stroking her long black hair with the hand that didn't have flames coming from it. "Terribly impressive, isn't it?"

I pressed a palm to my lower abdomen, suddenly wondering just to what extent she'd transformed me. "Wait, you didn't . . .?"

She rolled her orange eyes. "Don't be stupid. You're still a woman. It's an *illusion*."

I brushed my hands over my arms and then touched the chest plate of my armor. It all felt completely real. What she'd done was far more than simple glamour. It was an actual manifestation of the garb and physical changes.

"Think of it as wearing a costume, just one that's made of magic," she said. "But it's still your body and clothing underneath."

That actually helped quite a lot. I looked up and staggered back a little. In the seconds I'd been distracted by my own transformation, she'd changed herself into a stocky Duergar soldier with a blond crewcut, heavy brow, and beefy fists.

"Ready?" she asked crisply.

I almost nodded but then held up a hand. "Wait, I still sound like me. You sound like you, too."

"We'll have to let Jasper do the talking, obviously," she said.

Okay, then. The fancy Fae witch glamour didn't extend to disguising our voices.

I turned to Jasper. "I guess you'll have to get someone to tell us where Finvarra is."

"Probably better, anyway," he said. "I know the men and women in the Duergar military, and I know how to speak to them. I can help us blend in."

Our disguises were convincing. We had someone who could navigate any run-ins with Periclase's people. I suddenly felt a hell of a lot more confident about our chances of negotiating the fortress without giving ourselves away.

We just had to hope Finvarra was on site and we could get to him and allow Jasper the opportunity to use Gae Buide, the dagger of fatal wounds that Oberon had loaned him. And quickly. I desperately needed to get back to my own people and kingdom. If not for Oberon's order that I go on this mission, I'd already be back in the fortress trying to reclaim it.

I blew out a breath, steeling my nerves, and turned to go as Jasper began to lead us out of the bowels of the palace.

He took us toward the big swinging double doors that spilled into a service hallway. It was empty, giving us a moment to collect ourselves. I let Jasper go ahead a bit, as he was the one who knew the layout of the place best.

"No, walk three abreast," Jasper whispered to us. "Low-level soldiers such as us move about as equals."

We arranged ourselves as he directed and made a couple of turns through the corridors before we ran into anyone. My pulse kicked up a notch as a pair of Duergar soldiers came into view. For a moment, I panicked, thinking the soldiers would know we were strangers—fakes.

But Jasper spoke up. "Ho, men," he called to them. "Any news?"

The soldiers stopped in front of us and seemed to relax after quick scans of the patches on our armor indicated we were all the same rank.

"Mostly quiet," one of them said, showing a gap in his top teeth.

"Ah, come on," Jasper said. "You must have something of interest to share to entertain some fresh recruits such as us. What of the son of the dead New Garg matriarch? He giving our comrades any trouble at the stone fortress?"

The other soldier, a beefy-armed, stocky fellow with dark brown skin shook his head. "Nah, he's been locked up since our victory."

Jasper and the two men made low, guttural growling cheers of conquest. I put on a grin, hoping it wasn't strange that I remained silent.

"Our King?" Jasper pressed. "I suppose His Majesty is reveling in triumph?"

Gap Tooth shrugged a shoulder. "Haven't seen him of late. He and the General left the King's brother to command us." His top lip lifted briefly in a slight sneer, an indication of what he thought about Periclase's brother, Darion.

"And what of our Exalted One?" Jasper asked.

I nearly cut him a quick glance. Exalted One?

The two men looked at each other and let out lascivious chuckles. "Word is, the Unseelie High King is here in the luxury military guest quarters, and he's been entertaining. Three whores at once, we heard."

Beef Arms held out his hands and made thrusting motions with his hips.

I perked up, ignoring the crude noises of the soldiers. Finvarra was here. And if he was, uh, *occupied*, we might be able to catch him off guard.

We were saved from further inane conversation when someone else rounded the corner into our hallway.

"You two! Back to your posts," barked a lone Duergar officer. "You're not supposed to be here. You're in deep shit."

Beef Arms and Gap Tooth whirled and scuttled away.

The officer stalked toward us. "And you three, what are you—"

Swirls of magic streamed through the air toward him, surrounding his head. He froze mid-sentence, and then his eyes rolled back and he collapsed onto the tiles.

I turned to look questioningly at Melusine.

"We don't have time for him," she said crisply. "He'll wake up eventually with a bad headache."

I gave her a quick nod, wheeled around, and followed Jasper to the nearest staircase with the Fae witch on my heels.

"The luxury military quarters are on the third floor, almost directly above us," Jasper whispered as we took the stairs two at a time.

At the top of the third flight, Jasper stopped and allowed me and Melusine to catch up.

"Straight ahead a hundred yards, and then right," he said, and took off.

When we made the turn, the activity picked up considerably. Foot soldiers like us were streaming in and out of some of the doorways farther down bearing food and drink, most likely serving some of the higher-ranking officers.

"Not sure how we're going to get in," Jasper muttered.

"Periclase will get us in," Melusine mumbled without really moving her lips.

I looked at her, confused, and she tipped her head, indicating I should look the other way.

When I saw the Duergar King Periclase marching next to me, I stumbled and nearly fell flat on my face.

"It's me," Periclase whispered in Jasper's voice. He was looking down at himself, obviously trying to orient to his new appearance.

I swallowed hard and nodded. If we pulled this off, it was going to be a fricking miracle.

Jasper, in the Periclase glamour, walked up to the guards posted. They wore Duergar armor.

One of them, a black-haired guy with impossibly wide shoulders, blinked. "Ah, we were given strict orders not to disturb him, Your Majesty. He has a . . . guest."

"I don't care," Jasper snarled. "Open this door now, or I'll do it myself and make sure you never work in Faerie again."

He was laying it on a little thick, but we needed to work fast.

Jasper leaned into the man. "I am your King, and you occupy this post at my command. I now command you to stand aside." He said it rapidly, but with a deadly calm.

A sworn subject could not deny a direct order from his or her ruler.

Looking decidedly conflicted, the guard reached for the door, opened it, and hastily went in first. "Your Majesty, let me at least inform His Highness that—"

Jasper elbowed past him, and I hurried along behind. A woman's high-pitched sounds of lusty excitement were coming from a short hallway to our left.

The guards followed us inside and pushed ahead. He stood in front of the bedroom door and pushed his palm out at us.

"Your Majesty, I must insist that you wait," he said. Red splotches flushed his cheeks. "Give the Exalted One a few moments to collect himself."

"Oh, for the love of Maeve," Melusine muttered behind me.

Magic punched through the air like a sonic wave. Green and red strands of it zipped past me and around the black-haired guard like lightning bolts. It slammed into the door, which disintegrated with a deafening crack of wood blasting into a hundred pieces. I drew magic to form stone armor, squeezed my eyelids closed, and threw up my hands to protect my eyes and face from the debris. When I raised my eyelids, I found the hallway filled with thick white smoke.

Jasper sprinted past me, Gae Buide in his hand. I ran through the doorway after him, nearly reaching for Aurora. I made a fist instead, not wanting to blow my cover quite yet. Melusine's glamour couldn't disguise my sword, and if anyone saw it, they'd know immediately who I really was.

The smoke was beginning to clear. Shrill screams cut through the air, coming from a woman pressed to the wall with a sheet partially covering her nude body.

"Shush!" I hissed at her. Her eyes popped wide, and she stopped shrieking.

Jasper lunged at Finvarra, who'd sprang from the bed, the yellow blade drawn back. The Unseelie High King was naked. All Jasper had to do was nick Finvarra's skin. I wanted to help, but if I got in the way, Jasper might accidentally cut me.

Magic flashed at my back, and I whirled to find Melusine creating a blockade across the open doorway. There was a crash behind me. The two struggling men had fallen to the floor, Jasper on top. The hand holding Gae Buide was raised, but Finvarra had a hold of Jasper's wrist. Finvarra wasn't an Old One, but he was very old. Age meant strength in Faerie.

Deciding it was more important to try to finish the job than keep my cover, I drew Aurora and moved closer to the fight. If I could injure Finvarra, it would make Jasper's job easier.

"Drop the knife on him!" I said to Jasper. "You only need a small cut."

Following my suggestion, Jasper let the knife go. I froze, watching as the blade left his hand. It was point-down, heading for Finvarra's upper chest.

Just as the blade would have made contact, a nearby window shattered inward and a dark shroud of shadow rushed in and surrounded Finvarra. And then the shadow disappeared, Finvarra along with it. Jasper fell forward, catching himself on his hands. The dagger had clattered to the floor.

I whirled. "Where the hell did he go?" I shouted.

A familiar prickling began to creep into my skin and work its way deeper. Jasper's glamour was gone. A glance down told me mine had dissolved, too.

"Melusine, it's Eldon," I said, turning to the Fae witch. Her disguise had disappeared as well. "He's trying to take control of me."

I managed to get the words out just before magic sealed my lips. My gaze swung to the window as Eldon appeared there, standing on the sill and nearly filling the space.

I saw his face as he caught sight of Melusine. His eyes widened, and then the strangest expression swept over his face. For a split second, his normally stoic demeanor cracked. He looked oddly captivated.

"My lady Fae witch," he said, one corner of his mouth quirking.

I could only see Melusine's disguise, but Eldon must have been able to see through it.

Then his hands whipped up, palms out, and the gloaming began streaming toward us. Dark as the deepest forest shadows, it surrounded me, blinding me and choking off my air.

Melusine cackled from somewhere off to my left. "Oh Eldon, you and your ridiculous shadows."

A blinding flash cut through the gloaming. Moisture and the smell of singing mold billowed up my nostrils as the darkness began to retract in curling tendrils. My eyes watering from the bright light and offending scent, I backpedaled to get out of the way of the magic hurling through the air.

From Melusine's hands, pure yellow-white light flooded into the room, driving back the gloaming. Eldon was still standing in the window, and in a break in the shadows, I saw a small smile curling his mouth. His lips moved as he whispered chants, and his fingers flicked through the air so fast they nearly blurred.

It was a clash of Old Ones, Melusine's light power against Eldon's shadow magic. The air seemed to electrify, saturated and alive with magic. Pressing my back against the wall, I could only watch, open-mouthed for a second or two.

"Are we going to die?"

I looked to my right, where the woman who'd been keeping Finvarra company cowered against the wall. Her green eyes were wide with terror, and she clutched the bedsheet against her chest in a white-knuckled grip. I'd never seen her before we'd burst into the room.

"I sure as hell hope not," I said. I slid down the wall into a crouch, just in case any stray magic came flying my way. The woman did the same.

Holding up a hand to shade my eyes, I squinted through the room, looking for Jasper. He'd ended up on the other side of the four-poster bed but was military-crawling under it toward me.

He stood and brushed himself off, watching first Melusine and then Eldon.

"She's losing," he said, kneeling next to me. His face was tight with anger, but I knew it had nothing to do with the magical battle that was waging in front of us. Finvarra was gone. We'd lost our chance.

I frowned. I thought Melusine had been holding her own just fine against the Fae sorcerer. If anything, she seemed to be genuinely enjoying the battle, tittering to herself every few seconds.

"Petra, get that portal jewel ready." Jasper's voice was thick with warning.

"No, she's doing okay," I said. But I dug into my pocket and my hand closed around the pouch, just in case Jasper knew something I didn't. "We need to find Finvarra. What'd Eldon do with him?"

His brow wrinkled in confusion, and he flicked a quick glance at me. "Eldon only provided the cover. Finvarra shifted into a very small bird. Maybe a hummingbird. I couldn't see very well through the gloaming. He escaped out the window." His face darkened in frustration, and he pounded a fist against his thigh. "Gods damn it, he's gone. I had my chance, and I lost it."

I swore under my breath. I wanted to say something comforting, to make a joke about how we'd reduced the Unseelie High King to a barely more than a moth, but Jasper was right. We probably wouldn't get a shot like that again, and that was very, very bad. But it was done, and I needed to get on with the business of saving my own realm. First, we had to make it out alive. My gaze fixed on Melusine.

"She's tiring," I said tightly. "She's holding the shield back at the Summerlands, too."

Jasper gave his head a shake. "Damn, that's right. We need to get her out of here. Let's get closer."

Jasper and I began crawling toward Melusine, but I wasn't sure she even noticed us. She had begun gleefully shouting insults at Eldon.

"White-haired mushroom eater!" she hollered. "Fern sniffing grub lover!"

Her name-calling seemed to have a theme. For four hundred, what are things you find in dark pockets of the forest, Alex?

We got behind her and gingerly rose. I stuck my fingers into the velvet envelope and plucked out the jewel and was just about to try to get her attention when a shrieking form came running at us.

"Don't leave me here!" the woman in the sheet pleaded. "He thinks I aided you. He'll kill me!"

She crashed into me, and the jewel went flying up into the air.

"Say the words, quick," Jasper bellowed.

I gasped and then began chanting. Light was already bursting from the jewel.

He grabbed my hand and dove at Melusine, grasping her wrist with his other hand. We all had to be in contact in order to go through the jewel's doorway together. His impact interrupted her magic, and the gloaming rushed in. A jet of it, meant for Melusine, pummeled against Jasper's temple. His head jerked to one side, and then I lost my sight in the brightness of the jewel.

Something clipped my ankle, and I stumbled. I couldn't see a thing. I only felt Jasper's hand in mine, and something tugging at my foot, and then I lost all physical sense as we fell into the void of the netherwhere.

We reentered the world in a tangle, tumbling and separating onto the grass of the Summerlands grounds. I jumped to my feet. Melusine rose and began brushing green blades off her dress. The woman from Finvarra's room had somehow become rolled up in her sheet.

Wait, what?

"What the hell are you doing here?" I demanded.

But I forgot all about the hitchhiker when I caught sight of Jasper's still form sprawled on the other side of the woman.

I rushed to him and landed next to his shoulder. His face was pale and slack, his eyelids half closed. He wasn't breathing. I pressed my fingers to the side of his neck.

Nothing. My heart tumbled.

"No, no, no," I whispered.

Fear seared through me in a bolt of lightning, and I realized that I could lose both my father and Jasper. I was fairly certain Oliver was dead, though I'd done my damnedest to not allow myself to think about it. If Jasper died, if I lost both him and my father, I would never, ever recover.

Tipping Jasper's head back, I frantically tried to remember the correct steps for CPR. I pinched his nose and lowered my mouth to his and began rescue breathing.

Chapter 4

MELUSINE SNORTED DERISIVELY behind me, and anger laced my veins.

I glared up at her through tears as I stacked my hands and began chest compressions on Jasper's sternum.

"Move," she commanded.

Her fingers made nimble gestures, and jets of sunlight shot from her fingertips. Heat singed my arm as it zipped past me.

I slapped my hand over the slice in my shirt and fell back on my butt. "Ow."

"Told you to move."

Melusine's magic split into tendrils that wound to Jasper's head, entering his nostrils, mouth, ears, and even his eyes. Just like Eldon had done with his shadow magic when he'd tried to revive King Sebastian. That hadn't worked, though.

I sat perfectly still, my breath dead in my dry throat and my eyes glued to Jasper's chest.

Seconds ticked by, but he didn't move.

"Please," I exhaled, slumping. "Please, wake up."

"Hush," Melusine hissed irritably.

Magic like ribbons of sunlight continued to stream from the Fae witch to Jasper.

I started to shake my head and sucked in a breath that was more of a sob. It'd been too long. It wasn't going to work. Jasper was gone, and—

His eyes popped wide, his back arched in an impossible angle, and he drank a loud lungful of air through his mouth. His body went limp, and he lay staring up at the sky, breathing hard. I crawled over to him, let my forehead fall to his chest, and lost it for a few seconds as I felt the glorious rise and fall of his breastbone and the thump of his heart.

His hand found my hair. "Hey. Why are you crying?"

I lifted my head and looked into his tri-colored eyes. "Because you were dead for about five minutes." I swiped the backs of my hands across my cheeks, but a fresh wave of tears filled my eyes. "I was sure I'd lost . . ."

I couldn't finish the sentence. Jasper sat up and folded me into his arms.

A ground-shaking blast jolted me from my misery. I looked up just in time to see a giant flaming ball of neon-yellow spitfire land only about ten yards away.

"Up with you," Melusine barked, already gathering her skirts in her hands. "I didn't bring you back from death only to have you die by spitfire."

She lifted her hem and ran ahead of us toward the white castle of the Summerlands. Jasper and I scrambled to our feet and took off after Melusine. Finvarra's lover abandoned modesty and joined us, sprinting naked with her sheet trailing behind her like a banner. She let out little shrieks each time a boom erupted through the air.

The portal jewel had brought us to the unprotected grounds surrounding Oberon and Titania's stronghold, and we had about a quarter of a mile to go to reach the drawbridge that would take us into safety.

I stayed close to Jasper, fearing that after his ordeal this sudden strenuous burst might cause him to collapse. But he seemed as strong as ever. I wanted so badly to reach for his hand, but it would have slowed us down.

I kept Jasper in my line of vision while shouting over at the naked woman running next to me. "What's your name?"

I flicked a glance at her when she didn't respond. She looked wild-eyed and pale, her attention fully on the drawbridge ahead.

"Hey," I said. "You're going to be okay."

She tore her gaze from the lowering doorway of salvation long enough to lock eyes with me. "Eunice."

"Well, it's your lucky day, Eunice," I said, breathing hard. "You're about to enter the protection of the High King Oberon."

She let out a little relieved sob.

Avian screeches sounded overhead, and I looked up to find an impossibly huge hawk circling directly above us. I drew Aurora and pushed magic over my skin and into my weapon. Violet flames of power lit my fist, and the sword's sunrise colors swelled. It wasn't the same kind of connection I had with Mort, but pushing magic into Aurora seemed to heighten my strength and reflexes when I wielded it. The great sword almost seemed to anticipate my actions. I looked up again and stumbled. The hawk was at least twice as large as any Great Raven I'd ever seen. And its predatory, beady eyes were trained on us.

"What the hell *is* that?" I shouted.

Jasper had twisted to look up at the bird. His eyes narrowed.

"It's Finvarra," he said, his voice low. "He must have somehow figured out we came here. He's coming for me."

We'd lost our disguises at the hands of Eldon's magic. Finvarra knew who we were. All of the terror I'd felt while Jasper had lay dead in the grass flooded through me anew, but now I transformed it into fury and focus.

"Oh no he's not," I growled.

The bird folded its wings against its body and dove, a feathered missile aiming straight for us.

All of the emotions I'd shoved down over the past several days seemed to spring to life and pour into my veins. Mentally calculating the hawk's trajectory, I sped up, darting ahead toward one of the many small rises that formed a field of little hills on the grounds. I let my armor fall away so I'd be lighter for a jump. I raced up the hill, and with a wild yell, I hurled off the top, using all of my inborn stone blood strength to gain unnatural height in the air.

For a couple of seconds, I flew, hurtling over Jasper and the woman as they ran past, ready to meet Finvarra in the air. The wind kicked up by the bird's huge wings snatched at my clothes and hair. Everything seemed to slow as my sword appeared to be on a perfectly calculated collision course with the bird's neck. At the last second, the hawk realized it was headed straight for my blade and wildly dipped one wing, trying to avoid me. I brought Aurora down like a hammer anyway.

The sword flared with orange light and sliced through the wing, hitting about a third of the way from the end. The hawk let out a deafening shriek of fury. Feathers spewed everywhere.

I fell, managing a clumsy roll to distribute the impact when I hit the ground. Aurora tore from my grasp. Pain screamed through my arm. In spite of my rolling landing, I still hit my shoulder hard enough to dislocate it.

Muffling a screech behind pursed lips, I scrambled after my sword, scooped it up, and raced to catch up with the others.

Jasper had skidded to a halt and was starting to run back toward me.

"Go, go." I waved my sword at him.

He waited for me anyway.

"Are you all right?" I asked through gritted teeth.

He flashed me a tight smile, his tri-colored eyes sparking. "Aye, never better, Your Majesty."

I looked over my shoulder to see the hawk making a lopsided retreat. The severed piece of wing lay on the grass where it'd fallen. It wasn't a mortal wound—only Jasper could have killed Finvarra—but it was serious enough to give us a chance to make it into the castle.

Every step was jarring agony on my shoulder. I locked my eyes on the drawbridge and tried to block out everything else.

The guards at the gate must have been expecting us. Either that, or they recognized Melusine, who'd pulled ahead by about twenty yards. The drawbridge lowered rapidly, making crashing contact with the cobblestones just as we reached the moat.

Melusine and the Eunice made it into the castle first. Jasper and I crossed the bridge together. Once inside, I collapsed to my knees and let out an agonized cry through my teeth. Aurora fell from my hand.

Jasper knelt next to me. "What? What's wrong?"

I cradled my damaged arm. "Dislocation."

He quickly shifted around to that side, braced one hand against my shoulder, and grabbed my dislocated arm above the elbow. Without hesitation, he yanked.

I screamed and whacked him in the breastplate with my free fist. It hurt my knuckles enough to momentarily distract me from my shoulder. With heaving, ragged breaths, I folded over on myself and squeezed my eyes closed. The pain was already retreating.

"Sorry I punched you," I mumbled.

He chuckled. "It hurt you more than it hurt me."

With an arm slung around my lower back, he gently helped me stand.

I took a long, shuddering breath and tipped my gaze up to meet his.

"Don't you ever, *ever* die on me again," I said fiercely, my voice ragged with emotion.

He lowered his head and covered my mouth with his. The warmth of his lips on mine was exactly the reassurance I needed.

He pulled back, his golden eyes inches from mine. "I don't plan to."

King Oberon was sweeping into the grand entry, so Jasper stepped away from me so he could bend at the waist in a bow.

I swayed a little, feeling weak and lightheaded, but forced my spine straight. For gods' sake, it was just a dislocated shoulder. Jasper was the one who'd come back from death.

"Your Majesty," I greeted Oberon.

He looked grim. His gazes shifted to Eunice, and his eyes pinched with irritation. "Who is this? We cannot allow strangers within these walls." He turned and beckoned to one of the guards. "Take her to the dungeon."

"No," I said, skirting a glance at Eunice. I hoped she appreciated what I was about to do. "She was an innocent bystander. I've promised her protection."

He narrowed his eyes at me and brandished his index finger. "Then she is your responsibility. She will not be allowed to wander."

I nodded.

"King Oberon, I regret that I failed in my mission to—" Jasper began.

"I know," Oberon said, cutting him off. "We don't have time. I've news of more Unseelie forces on the move and heading here." He looked at me. "You must go to the fortress and take the throne. You can't wait any longer. It's time to oust Periclase from your kingdom."

I inclined my head. I certainly couldn't argue, though I didn't have a plan for exactly how I would make things work back home.

The High King turned his attention to Jasper. "You must continue the search for a weapon that can help us against Finvarra's Stone of Fal."

Jasper's jaw tightened, and I knew at that moment the only thing he wanted in the world was to make amends for his failure to kill Finvarra. The assassination mission had been a long shot, and we all knew it. But it was obvious to me that the outcome was eating at Jasper, and he couldn't rest until he'd redeemed himself. That was the kind of man he was, and my heart ached as I realized it meant he and I might not see much of each other for a while.

"Do we know why he hasn't invoked the Stone's power?" I asked.

"We know he only gets three chances to use it. We believe he may be saving it for later, perhaps thinking that once the Summerlands has fallen and he's taken the throne here, he'll use it to force all of Faerie to be loyal to him," Oberon said. His face turned darkly fierce. "Not that we have any intention of letting that happen."

"I just need to gather some supplies, and I can depart," Jasper said.

Oberon nodded. To me, he said, "Queen Vida and King Moreau are still here, but not for long. You should catch them to discuss the backup forces they promised you. I'll leave you to your duties."

I wanted to sit down, take a breath, and convince myself that Jasper was indeed alive and out of danger. But there was no time. And at that moment, Jasper and I didn't have the luxury of privacy for a lingering goodbye.

He kissed me quickly. "Your people *will* accept you, Petra. But it may take time. In the meantime, watch your back."

I clutched at his shirtsleeve, balling the fabric in my fist. "If you get hurt, I'll kill you," I said.

He quirked a small half-grin at me, and then I let go and he turned and strode away. I didn't watch him go. I couldn't stand to see him disappear around a corner.

Drawing a deep breath, I faced Melusine. I knew I needed to catch Vida and Moreau, but I had one problem that outweighed any need for brute force at my back.

"I can't beat Eldon," I said. "As long as Periclase has him there, I have no chance of ousting the Duergar from the fortress. I have no chance of anything at all if I go back in there. Eldon controlled me completely with his magic, so skillfully that no one could likely even tell that my actions weren't my own. He moved my body, forced me to say words I never would have said. His magic was so perfect and so powerful I couldn't imagine anything that might work against it. Until I saw you battling him. But I'm honestly not certain your power is enough against him, even if you weren't holding the wards here." I ended with a slight lift, implying a question.

And then I paused for effect. I was purposely trying to tap into her apparent need to compete with and better Eldon, sensing that might motivate her more than the idea of helping me. I frankly didn't care what it took.

Her dark brows furrowed over her orange eyes, and for a second I thought she was going to be angry, finding insult in what I'd said. But when there was no outburst, I realized she might have taken my bait.

"I know you can't leave the Summerlands for long," I ventured. "I know that you need to use your energy to maintain the shields around this castle, but is there anything at all you can do to give me an edge against the Fae sorcerer's enormous power?"

I wasn't above begging. I would have granted any request that was within my power to grant. A blood oath. Whatever she wanted. Just about any price would be worth it.

Her face turned thoughtful. "You go and meet with your little king and queen friends. After, come to me."

My lips parted. I wanted to ask for details but then thought better of it. I nodded and then turned and scurried away before I could accidentally do or say anything that might piss her off and make her change her mind.

Once I rounded a corner, I pumped my fist and let out a quiet, victorious, "Yes!"

"Your Majesty!" called a male voice behind me.

I turned to find two people running after me. One was a castle page trying to flag me down, a young man wearing the Summerlands livery. The other was the naked woman who'd come through the portal jewel's doorway. She wasn't naked, but the poor woman still had only the sheet to cover herself.

I bit back a groan. I'd completely forgotten about Eunice and frankly didn't have time to deal with her.

"Your Majesty," the page said, breathless from hauling ass down the hallway. "Let me take you to your quarters. You can quickly freshen up before your meeting with Queen Vida and King Moreau."

He looked pointedly at my clothes. A glance down showed a ripped sleeve, a neat slice in my shirt, mud and grass caked onto the shoulder I'd dislocated, and dirt-stained knees on my pants. I didn't even have to lift a hand to my hair to know it was a wind-whipped mess.

"Are you positive they they're able to wait while I change?" I asked.

I was all for being presentable, but not if it cost me an important meeting.

He nodded vigorously. "Yes, Your Majesty. They aren't due to depart for another hour, and they both want to speak to you."

He stepped in front of Eunice, who'd been standing nearby listening to our exchange. She'd let out a little gasp when he'd addressed me as a ruler.

"Wait," I said. "I need to speak to this woman. I'll be quick."

She tried to perform a clumsy curtsy, the sheet wrapped around her body and slung around one shoulder like a toga.

"I didn't know you were royalty, Your Highness," she said, her eyes fearful. She curtsied again. "My deepest apologies, Your Highness."

I held up a hand, irritated that no one had come to take care of her. "It's okay. We'll get you some clothes and food, and then you can go home. Where are you from?"

Even in disarray, she was quite lovely, with golden skin, a slim waist, an ample bust, and a sculpted face. But I couldn't guess her bloodlines in her features, as there was nothing terribly distinct in them, despite her beauty.

She began to shake her head. "No, Your Majesty," she whispered. "Please, I beg you, don't send me away. The Unseelie High King will kill me. He'll find me and kill me."

I'd forgotten her pleas back in the fortress. I didn't think she was trying to take advantage of me. Real fear filled her wide, violet eyes.

The page shifted his weight impatiently, but I suddenly realized that not only might this woman genuinely need protection, but she also might be able to help us, if she'd been close to Finvarra for any length of time.

"Why do you believe he'll kill you?" I asked. "You did nothing wrong."

"Because there was another woman who was . . . *with* him when there was an attempt on his life. I know for a fact she had nothing to do with it." Teary sadness replaced the fear in her eyes. "But he had her executed."

"Okay," I said crisply. "I won't send you away. Come with me, and while I change you will tell me what you know about the Unseelie High King."

She wilted in relief and then curtsied again. "Whatever you wish, Your Majesty. I'm forever in your debt."

My page led the way, walking with quick, irritated swiftness, and took us to my quarters. There, he left us to fetch clothes for Eunice. I left the door to my dressing room partway open so I could talk to the woman.

"Now," I said as I began peeling off my clothes. "I want to know everything you know about Finvarra, Eldon, Periclase, and anyone else who's an enemy of the Seelie."

"Oh my," she said in a fretful tone. "I'm not sure I have much to offer."

"That's okay," I said, trying to be patient. "Just tell me whatever comes to mind."

I heard her take a deep breath. "Well, for one thing I don't think the Fae sorcerer Eldon is truly on the side of the Unseelie. I don't think he wants to be helping the Unseelie High King and his buddies at all."

I blinked and froze with one leg in a fresh pair of pants.

"Why do you think that?" I asked carefully.

"Well, because he said so."

I stuck my other leg into my pants, pulled them up, and leaned around the corner. I crooked my index finger at her. "Why don't you come in here and tell me more?"

Chapter 5

EUNICE'S BROWS ARCHED, and she sat there for a second, seemingly uncertain about my invitation.

"Your Majesty?" she asked.

"Yes, come on in and have a seat on the ottoman," I said.

She gathered her sheet around her and did as I instructed, perching on the edge of a huge round, upholstered monstrosity that sat in the center of the dressing room.

She opened her mouth to speak, but I heard the door chime followed by the sound of the latch releasing.

"Yoo-hoo, Your Majesty!" hollered Claudine, my loud and possibly hard-of-hearing attendant. "It's just me, come with clothes for your, ah, guest."

I went out and met her, taking the stack of garments.

She curtsied. "So very happy to be in Your Majesty's service!" She leaned to one side to look around me, obviously trying to get a look at Eunice. I shifted to block her view. "And is there anything else I can do for you or your girl on this fine—"

"No, this is all we need," I interrupted. "Your services are much appreciated."

She cocked her head at my abruptness, but to my relief, she turned to go. I locked the door after her, went back into the dressing room, and handed Eunice the stack of clothes. I turned around to give her some privacy.

"Continue, please," I said. "How do you know Eldon is not truly with Finvarra?"

There was the sound of rustling fabric. "Once when I was leaving King Finvarra's quarters late at night, I decided to take a shortcut back to my own room."

"Where was this?" I cut in.

"Oh, well, the Undine realm, Your Majesty," she said. "King Finvarra lived there for a spell."

I had, in fact, first met Finvarra in the Undine kingdom. Jasper and I had gone there to confront the banished Unseelie High King, and that was when we'd learned of his alliance with the Tuatha De Danann. That was many weeks ago.

"So you've been with Finvarra for some time, then," I said.

"Yes, oh yes," she said. "Nearly half a year now."

My brows shot up. "Please continue with your story."

"Yes. So. I was taking a shortcut. There was a dark courtyard. I didn't know Eldon and his friend were there until I was halfway across, as the Fae sorcerer used his gloaming magic to conceal them."

"But you could hear them?"

"I have very exceptional hearing on occasion, Your Majesty," she said.

I scoured my knowledge of Fae races for one that had such an attribute but came up empty.

"What race are you?" I asked. It wasn't a rude question in Faerie. Bloodlines were important and often a point of pride to Fae.

She made a short humming noise and then cleared her throat. "My mother was a halfling. Half human and Daoine Sidhe. My father was also a halfling, his Fae blood a mix of which I do not know."

I didn't comment, not wanting to embarrass her, but it was exceedingly rare for two halflings to have offspring. Halflings were nearly always infertile.

"When I heard voices, I froze," she continued. "I recognized Eldon, but not the other one. I was sure I'd be caught any second, but I was also too terrified to move. I shouldn't have stayed there, but I did, and they kept talking."

Eldon should have sensed an eavesdropper. Or more likely, he would have woven magic that prevented anyone from hearing his private conversation. Yet somehow, Eunice had heard it. Perhaps it was a magical talent of hers. Those with little Fae blood usually had weak magic, or no magic at all from the Fae races of their parents, but sometimes they had unusual talents.

There was an insistent knock at my door.

"Your Majesty," called the voice of my male page. "I must escort you to an audience with Queen Vida and King Moreau."

I cursed under my breath. My conversation with Eunice would have to wait.

I turned to find she'd dressed in the simple brown gown and matching ballet flats that had been brought for her.

"Come with me," I said, and went to get the door.

She followed me.

"This is Eunice," I said to the page. "She needs a room and a meal. Can I trust you to take care of it?"

He bowed. "Of course, Your Majesty. I'll escort you to your meeting room and then take care of your guest." He turned to Eunice. "Please accompany us."

On the way to Vida and Moreau, I wanted badly to ask Eunice to finish her story, but not knowing everything she might reveal, I didn't want to take the chance of someone overhearing.

"I ask that you keep all of your information to yourself until we speak again," I said quietly to her.

"Oh, my, absolutely, Your Majesty," she said. She took a breath as if to say more, but hesitated.

"Is there something you need?"

She pressed her lips together, and then her gaze met mine. "I do not want to seem impertinent, but I must admit I don't recognize you among the Queens I know of. May I ask . . . what realm do you rule?"

I chuckled. "You may. And you don't recognize me because I only very recently acquired the throne of a brand new kingdom. I'm the Queen of the Carraig Sidhe, formerly known as New Gargoyles."

Surprise flashed abruptly across her features as if she'd been hit with a splash of water. "Oh. Oh!" She glanced at the sword I carried on my back, and a new realization dawned. "You're Petra Maguire, Champion of the Summer Court."

I nodded. "I am that as well."

We'd reached my destination, my page waiting with his hand on the knob of a simple white-painted door.

"Eunice," I said. "I need you to keep to yourself everything you're observing here. No gossip and no outgoing messages. Can I trust you?"

She clasped her hands in front of her. "I owe you my life," she said, her violet eyes misting. "I will serve you loyally for the rest of my days to repay you, Queen Petra."

My brows rose slightly at her outpouring of sincerity. I awkwardly patted her shoulder. "I'm not sure that's necessary, but I do appreciate your discretion."

The page cleared his throat impatiently. I stepped past Eunice, and he opened the door for me. Inside, I found a small but luxuriously appointed sitting room with pretty white divans supported by carved wooden legs, a tall stained-glass pane with a comfortable-looking window seat under it, shelves filled with volumes of hard cover books, and a dark fireplace. Moreau and Vida both stood at the coffee and tea cart, helping themselves to steaming cups of liquid. There were also baskets of light fare—pastries and fruit.

My stomach growled noisily as I approached, and Vida and Moreau stopped their quiet conversation and turned my way. I pressed my palm into my midsection, trying to quiet the rumbling.

Vida, Queen of the Sylphs, wore one of her signature velvet gowns—a deep red-wine color, this time—with matching lipstick. Everything about her was curvy, from her long curling eyelashes to the roundness of her shoulders, to the hourglass shape of her torso. Like most of her kind, she gave off an undeniable sultriness. But she was also whip-smart and one of the most highly educated women in Faerie.

King Moreau was all wolfish sex appeal, with his ruggedly handsome face, dark stubble around his angular jaw line, broad shoulders, and quick, gleaming smile. As ruler of the Dobhar Sidhe, the canine shifter kingdom, he and his wife were the alphas of their people who organized themselves according to the rules of the pack. Moreau and Idara had ruled for a decade and a half, besting every challenger the pack had thrown at them. Moreau was quick to grin and had a lively energy about him, but he was vicious when challenged. No one held the Dobhar alpha spot for that long without being a serious badass, and I'd heard his wife was every bit as tough as he was.

Vida and Moreau were the only two rulers who'd offered to aid me in my quest to oust Periclase, Eldon, and Finvarra from the stone fortress. I wasn't offended that the others had declined. Every Seelie kingdom had committed some or most of their military to the fight here at the Summerlands. That meant their own realms were largely unprotected. The bottom line was, no one really had soldiers to spare these days.

"Queen Petra." Moreau greeted me with a magnanimous sweep of his hand. "It's excellent to see you again." His expression sobered, his dark brows pulling down over his eyes. "Though I heard Finvarra escaped."

I shook my head. "We were so close, but Finvarra shifted and got away under the cover of Eldon's gloaming magic."

Vida hummed her disappointment low in her throat. "Pity. It would have been quite a victory to knock off that Unseelie bastard. But we all knew it was a shot in the dark."

"Still," I said. "It weighs heavily on Jasper. On all of us."

Moreau pursed his lips, inhaling slowly through his nose. "Well, in any case, we must move on."

"Yes," I said, going to pour myself a cup of coffee. I set the porcelain cup on its saucer and dosed the dark liquid with two generous spoonfuls of sugar and a splash of cream. My mouth nearly watered as I brought the rim to my lips for a sip. "I want you both to know how deeply I appreciate your generous offers. I won't forget your generosity."

Moreau and Vida exchanged a look. It was just a brief flick of eyes, but my stomach tightened.

The Sylph queen set her cup on its saucer. "You understand as well as we do these are very uncertain times. Not only are we fighting to maintain Seelie rule of Faerie, there is the Tuatha's threat."

"Uncertain times, indeed," I said, eyeing her warily.

"As such," she said, "we all want to do everything we can to protect the future of our realms."

I nodded. Something was coming. If I were speaking to anyone but a king and queen, I would have demanded they come out with whatever it was they wanted. But days of such casual conversation were behind me.

"Moreau and I would ask something in return for our support in your efforts to reclaim your stronghold," Vida continued.

"Yes?" I prompted.

"We want the protection of the Carraig Sidhe when the Tuatha descend on Faerie."

I looked from one to the other and then shook my head. "I don't understand. You each have militaries at least ten times the size of the New Garg—ah, Carraig fighting force. Your kingdoms aren't the largest of the Seelie realms, but neither are they insignificant. What possible protection could I offer either of you?"

Moreau and Vida shared another look and seemed to silently determine between them that it was the Dobhar king's turn to speak.

He gave me a smile, flashing teeth that seemed impossibly white against his tanned face and dark stubble. "I can understand why it might seem an odd request. But we believe your people aren't just important in keeping Seelie control of the Summerlands. We believe you are the key to defeating the Tuatha."

I tipped my head at an angle and peered at him. "Why?"

"King Oberon mentioned his oracle before, the one who told him you must not lose the stone fortress to the Unseelie. Well, we have our own seers," Vida said. She interlaced her fingers and held her arms loosely in front of her. "They have advised us to align ourselves with you and your people."

I pinched the bridge of my nose and then lowered my eyelids and moved my thumb and forefinger wider to rub my eyes for a moment. I tried to think through how agreeing to their request might bite me in the ass later but couldn't come up with anything. What did I really have to lose? And more importantly, did I really have a choice? I needed every advantage at my disposal, every bit of strength I could round up, to have any chance of taking back the fortress.

I opened my eyes, grabbed a croissant, and ripped off a big bite with my teeth. "If I go along, what specifically am I agreeing to?" I asked, chewing. Gods, I was starving. "I mean, we're all Seelie. We're all on the same side anyway, and we'll be fighting together, right?"

"In theory," Vida said, but her doubt was clear. "But even if we all have the same larger goal, each kingdom is going to be vying for advantage. Deals will be struck. There likely will be some backstabbing and betrayals."

I gave a low, disgusted growl. "And *that* is exactly why the Tuatha want to wipe us out and start over." I waved my croissant and a few crumbs flew onto the coffee service setup. "All this political bullshit. Doesn't anyone understand we don't have that luxury anymore?"

As soon as I said it, I heard Jasper's voice in my head, his passionate speeches about how we all needed to rise above the usual Faerie ways. He understood it. He'd been saying it all along. Oberon had even come around to recognize the importance of uniting everyone and finding better ways. But it had taken sky iron torture to get the High King to see it, and it seemed as though very few others were picking up the message.

Moreau's face hardened, his green eyes icy. "Some of us do realize that the political bullshit, as you call it, isn't going to save us. But most politicians will keep on being politicians until their dying breaths. To some extent, I even include Vida and myself in that category. We've been at this so long we don't really know any other way."

"So, what, you both want a promise that I won't turn on you? That we'll be allies no matter what happens?" I tried to curb in my irritation, but impatience still leaked through in my voice.

"Yes, essentially," Vida said.

I blew out a slow breath through clenched teeth and slanted my gaze off to the side. This was one of the reasons I'd left Faerie to try to make a life on the Earthly side of the hedge. The irony was, the political bullshit was almost as thick over there. On the other side, I could largely avoid it, or at least ignore it. But here in Faerie? I was a frigging *queen* of a *realm*.

I faced them. "Okay. I'll agree to an alliance with you."

Moreau's face relaxed with relief, and Vida gave me a thin, close-lipped smile. Neither of them seemed the least bit smug about getting their way, though. And honestly, their seriousness scared me a bit because it meant they truly believed their survival depended on their alignment with the Carraig Sidhe. And I had no idea exactly what that meant for my people in the days ahead.

They'd already had paperwork drawn up, so we moved over to the dark wood secretary desk near the door and spent a few minutes signing documents and sealing them with magic.

Moreau lifted his coffee cup. "To a beneficial and fruitful alliance." He inclined his head to me and then took a sip.

"Hear, hear," Vida chimed in.

I managed a slight smile, but I wasn't in the mood to toast or celebrate. I couldn't shake the feeling that they were taking advantage of me, though I didn't believe either of them had deeply malicious intent. It was more the sense that they knew they could manipulate me because I was such a green ruler. I wished Maxen were there. He would have known exactly how to negotiate Moreau and Vida's proposal.

The thought of Maxen brought me back to what I had to do next: force the Unseelie out of the fortress and attempt to lead the new kingdom. My insides tightened as the reality of it hit me all over again, and I couldn't help thinking of my father and wishing he could be at my side as I tried to take back the fortress.

Chapter 6

I DIDN'T MAKE it far from my meeting with Queen Vida and King Moreau before a castle page caught up to me. This one was a young woman with green-tinged blonde hair and the leggy build of a Kelpie seahorse shifter.

She gave a hasty curtsy. "Your Majesty. Melusine sent me to fetch you, if you will please follow me."

I raised a hand, indicating she should lead the way. The thought of seeing the Fae witch gave me a tiny pinch of relief, but I didn't allow it to take root. I wasn't sure what she had in store, and it was best not to get my hopes up.

My page escorted me into a corridor of apartments and stopped at an unmarked door and pressed the button for the bell. A tinkling chime sounded within, and a moment later Melusine opened the door.

I tried not to stare around at her quarters as I followed her inside, but I couldn't help curiosity. The décor was vaguely gothic, like Melusine's own appearance. Lots of ornate metal work, rich fabrics, and a spindly iron chandelier hanging from the ceiling of the formal front room. I also wanted to be sure one of her giant hairy pet spiders didn't sneak up on me.

She went to the coffee table in the middle of the front sitting room and lifted a thick metal object.

"I've devised a little something for you," she said, giving me a tiny but wicked grin.

My eyes widened as she approached me. The thing she held appeared to be a wide metal cuff, possibly brass, that she'd unclasped.

"Your arm," she demanded.

I lifted my left arm. As I'd guessed, it was indeed a cuff. She snapped it closed around my forearm well away from the creases of my wrist. It was a very snug fit, with barely enough space for tendons and muscles to move when I flexed my hand back and forth. Magic tingled against my skin and began to spread in a warm rush over me. Then the sensation faded.

"What does it do?" I asked, lifting my arm to examine the cuff more closely. I couldn't even see the seam where she'd fitted it together.

"It will block Eldon's magic."

My gaze whipped up to her orange eyes. "All of it?"

She cackled. "Yes." Bringing her hands under her chin in a prayer position, she gave a few little claps. "Oh, won't he be infuriated?" She was positively glowing with glee.

I couldn't help grinning, and I gave her a bow and a flourish of one hand. "Your power is remarkable."

"Of course it is."

I straightened and looked her in the eye. "You seem to relish battling him. How well do you and the Fae sorcerer know each other?"

Her brows lifted at the boldness of my question, but she didn't seem upset by it. She turned and wandered over to a settee with cream cushions and delicately carved wood details, where she sat and spread out the folds of her layered skirt.

"Oh, not so very well," she said. A hint of a smile touched her lips. "But we've crossed paths a few times over the years."

I gave her a sly look. "Would you like to know him better? He is, after all, your male counterpart. And he's a *very* handsome man."

I didn't actually think he was particularly attractive, but he had a certain intrigue about him. I seemed to have struck a chord with Melusine, though, and she tittered and waved a hand through the air, looking demurely off to one side.

"Maybe you should come with me," I said. "Convince him to abandon the Unseelie and join us. I bet you could. I could tell he was captivated by you."

She turned back to me and bit her lower lip for a moment, as if considering it. It would give me a huge advantage to have her in the fortress with me, even if only for a small amount of time.

But she shook her head. "The High King has ordered me to stay here. With new enemy forces soon to descend on the Summerlands, he wants me here to make sure all of my energy goes into maintaining the ward around the castle."

I felt my face fall, but I nodded. "Then that's what you'll have to do."

She leaned forward a little, and her expression became intense. "Might you take a message to Eldon from me?" she whispered.

I pulled back a little, surprised, and stumbled a bit over my words. "I—he tortured my father, Melusine. If I see him, I'm—well, I'm going to kill him."

She paused, seeming to stare off into the distance. "Hm. Well. Take the message anyway."

I frowned but didn't want to waste time arguing. I'd take a message, but I wasn't promising to deliver it.

I expected her to give me a verbal message to pass along to the Fae sorcerer, but she jumped up and went over to the little writing desk in the corner. She pulled a notecard from a stack, plucked up a pen, and dashed off a few sentences. Then she sealed it with wax and magic.

When she handed it to me, her pale cheeks were flushed. I was absolutely dying of curiosity, but she'd become agitated. She grabbed my shoulder, spinning me around and pushing me toward the door.

"Off with you," she said.

Her shoving was a little much, but I did need to get going.

"I'm deeply indebted to you for this." I held up my forearm, encircled with the brass cuff.

She halted abruptly. "Oh! I almost forgot. It'll only fend off his magic for a limited time."

I lifted one brow. "That seems like an important detail."

She flicked a hand impatiently. "I can only force so much magic into one charm. You'll feel it weakening, so you'll know when it's about to expire."

"Got it," I said. "Anything else I should know about the charm?"

"Nope." She shoved me out of her quarters. "Try not to die!"

The door slammed shut. I wasn't sure whether to laugh or curse at Melusine under my breath. At least there was someone in Faerie with social skills rougher than mine.

I tucked her note into a pouch on my belt, feeling odd about carrying it, seeing as how I didn't plan to let Eldon live if we happened to cross paths, but taking comfort in the solid heft of the charm the Fae witch had made for me.

The next few hours passed in a blur as I readied myself to leave. Oberon sent a messenger with a special portal jewel that would take a large number of us through a doorway and into the stone fortress all at once. The glimmering orb was nearly the size of my fist, and it arrived nestled in a velvet-lined box. I couldn't imagine its value. Oberon had made it clear that he couldn't support my efforts with official decrees or the aid of Summerlands soldiers, but he was trying to help in other ways, and I was grateful.

A page came to let me know that Moreau and Vida's soldiers had arrived and were ready to go. When I reached the yard where they were waiting, my heart deflated a little. Each ruler had promised a battalion, and I belatedly realized I should have asked for hard numbers. Turned out they only provided me with a dozen fighters apiece. But they all looked sharp and fit, and I could tell at a glance that Vida and Moreau had sent me some of their top fighters even if they were few in number. They snapped to attention in neat rows when they caught sight of me.

"At ease, soldiers," I barked.

Moving as one, they widened their stances by half a foot. I walked their ruler-straight lines, inspecting them.

Vida's people rested their hands on the weapons they wore at their hips. Sylphs wielded unique swords that looked impossibly thin and lightweight. I'd seen one once and knew that inside those sheathes the slim blades were carved to look like long feathers. The double-edged swords were incredibly sharp.

As beings affiliated with the air element, the Sylphs' entire fighting style was based on blinding agility, lightness on their feet, and fast, vicious strikes. If a skilled Sylph warrior caught you on your heels, she could slash you five times before you even drew your weapon. It was deceptively deadly, as their blades were sometimes poisoned. Even if they weren't, Sylph soldiers were trained to cut so precisely they'd make an enemy bleed out before he even realized he was mortally injured.

The Sylphs ran the gamut in terms of body type, some rounder like their queen and others more gangly. Each of them had the same impossibly long, curling eyelashes.

King Moreau's people, in contrast, were all animal ferocity. They carried no weapons, as nothing they could wield was as effective as their canine form. They were trained to attack in small packs, and their jaws were strong enough to rip off limbs.

"King Periclase is our enemy in the stone fortress," I said. "His military currently occupies there. We must force him to withdraw. The Fae sorcerer Eldon will be there. Let me deal with him."

There were some shifting eyes at the mention of Eldon.

"The foot soldiers Periclase has in the fortress aren't his best," I continued. "His top fighters are protecting his kingdom or fighting outside the walls of this castle. He's already subdued my people, so right now he's feeling in control. Once we're inside, split into smaller groups and make your way through the fortress. This isn't a time for mercy. Periclase will not show you any. A swift and brutal attack is our best strategy. Mow down the Duergar as you have the opportunity."

Vida and Moreau's people had already been briefed on the layout of the fortress, including the area where we'd be entering. I'd chosen a spot near the jail. I wanted to free Maxen and any other important New Gargs right away. I also wanted to be able to arm my people, and I was guessing that the weapons the Duergar had rounded up were locked in the fortress jail.

I palmed the box containing the deluxe-sized portal jewel, opened the lid, and took out the sphere. Palming it like a baseball, I faced the soldiers. Vida's people took up one of their whooping battle cries. The Dobhar were shedding their clothes, already growling in anticipation. Their bodies began contorting and disfiguring, each of them disappearing in a cloud of smoky magic momentarily, and then emerging in their canine forms—dogs as big as grizzly bears, with teeth as long as my fingers.

I shifted the orb to my left hand and drew Aurora with my right. Looking up, I tossed the jewel and whispered the words that would take us through the netherwhere.

The orb exploded with shockingly bright light, and then the dark chill of the void claimed us.

I didn't know if my people would see me as an enemy for killing Marisol and taking her place on the Carraig throne or a savior for trying to reclaim the fortress. I was about to find out.

Chapter 7

THE SYLPH SOLDIERS, Dobhar dogs, and I all emerged simultaneously in the hallway outside the stone fortress jail, thanks to the portal jewel. Vida's swordspeople made quick work of the half dozen or so Duergar we surprised in the immediate vicinity, some of whom had been blown backward by our abrupt arrival. But others had seen us from a distance and were already running to alert their captains.

The Dobhar and Sylph broke into groups of three and began spreading out.

I whirled around and punched my heel into the double doors of the fortress jail, blasting them open with surprising force, actually bending hinges. Magic flowed from my blood to my skin, forming armor. A couple of Duergar were on duty in the jail but had clearly been messing around on the job. One of them still had his feet propped up, and he was looking at me with the shock of a man suddenly awakened from a nap.

The other was slightly more on top of things. He reached for his short sword, charging me. I batted his arm hard with Aurora and then rammed the end of my blade through his diaphragm.

Scooping up the fallen short sword, I lunged at the door and shoved the blade through the door handles, creating a makeshift lock. I turned just in time to strike the other guy's oncoming sword. Metal clanged, and Aurora shone with yellow-orange light, flaring brighter as I pushed magic into the blade.

The soldier was still sleep-slow, and my connection with Aurora quickened my reflexes. When he swung again, I easily ducked under his arm, came up behind him, and ran him through with a forceful stab angled up under his ribcage. He fell forward, and I jerked my sword free. For a moment, I just stared. I'd just pierced clear through armor. Adrenaline and Aurora's power combined with my magic and seemed to give me additional strength.

Shouting and banging at the door snapped me out of my daze. I turned and ran to the reception desk, frantically searching for the controls of the jail cell doors. A tablet lay off to one side, but I found its charge had died. Controls, controls . . . Or keys. Keys would work. I scooped up a heavy ring with a mess of long, intricate keys hanging from it.

The door leading back to the hallway that ran along the cells was unlocked. I made a tsking noise. Sloppy. But the Duergar carelessness was my good fortune.

I skidded to a stop in front of the first cell but then thought better of my choice and continued on. I needed to get Maxen out first, and he'd be held toward the back in one of the warded cells.

"Maxen?" I hollered when I reached the end of the row. "Maxen! It's Petra!"

"In here," came his muffled voice from my right.

I swiveled to that door and began jamming keys in one by one. The third try freed the lock. Maxen stood in the dark box of a room, pale, rumpled, and thin. I knew he'd been sneaking in and out of his cell, unbeknownst to Periclase, but had been unable to do anything about the occupation of the fortress on his own. He blinked at me, his lips parted.

"I've got Dobhar dogs and Sylph swords with me," I said hurriedly, turning back the way I'd come.

Maxen followed me back to the start of the row of cells. I unlocked that door and found Shane McNab inside. He was one of the youngest officers in the Carraig battle ranks.

Shane pulled back, shock etched on his face. "Petra?"

"Yeah," I said. I tossed him the set of keys, and he bobbled them but managed to hang on. "As I was telling Maxen, I've got about two dozen Dobhar and Sylph soldiers with me. They're working through the fortress from here. Shane, unlock the rest of the cells, would you?"

He was staring at me with conflicting emotions flickering over his face, clearly unsure how he should treat me. I didn't really blame him. I'd killed his monarch.

Shane turned his gaze to Maxen, apparently not willing to take orders from a traitor.

"Do it," Maxen said. "And it's not Petra. It's Your Majesty."

Shane's mouth fell open. "What?"

"By Oberon's order, we're now the Carraig Sidhe and Petra is our queen. You might as well spread the news. We need to get the Duergar out of here."

I briefly closed my eyes as relief flooded through me. I should have trusted Maxen to do what was best for our people, but I hadn't been absolutely sure about how he would greet me. This was a start. I could work with this.

"Where did Periclase stick the weapons?" I asked.

Maxen pointed back down the hallway. "One of the warded cells."

"Get them," I said to Shane. "Arm everyone in here, and then go out and eliminate those Duergar bastards."

Shane's nostrils flared, his free hand tightening into a fist. He gave me a curt nod. "Your Majesty."

He turned and began unlocking the cells. I grabbed Maxen's arm and towed him into the reception area. There, I swiped the short sword still clutched in the hand of the man I'd stabbed through the back. I tossed it handle-first at Maxen, and he caught it with one hand.

"Where to now?" Maxen asked. Stone armor rippled over his skin as he swung the sword a few times, testing its balance and heft.

"Wherever Eldon is. I think we can best the Duergar soldiers, but the Fae sorcerer is the real pain in my ass. Fortunately, I have something that blocks his magic." I held up my hand, showing Maxen the brass charm locked around my forearm. "But its use is limited, so we'll need to work fast. Any idea where he'd be?"

"He tends to keep to the west royal wing." Maxen's blue eyes narrowed, and he tipped his head at the door I'd barred. "Let's do it."

I reached for the short sword, ready to yank it out, but paused and turned back to him. "I appreciate what you did back there." My gaze flicked to the door that led to the cells.

He nodded, his jaw muscles flexing.

I slid the sword from the door handles and reached back to stick the weapon in my scabbard. If I came across any Carraigs, I could at least arm one of them with the spare.

Maxen and I burst out into the hallway. Duergar guards had descended upon the area, as our arrival there had attracted a lot of attention. He pivoted right and I turned left, and we started swinging.

We needed to make our way left and up two floors. The west royal wing Maxen had mentioned was actually where his own quarters were. There was space for more people, but Marisol only had one child and no other living relatives. It was more or less Maxen's wing. No wonder he looked pissy when he told me where Eldon liked to hang out.

One small pack of three Dobhar had remained in the vicinity, their snarls cutting through the noise of battle and their wild musk hanging in the air. The mangled throats of several soldiers on the ground were the work of the dogs. The Dobhar, Maxen, and I finished off the rest of the Duergar nearby.

"This way," I said to the three Dobhar. I tried not to look too hard at the blood staining the fur around their mouths.

Maxen and I took off to the left, and the big dogs loped after us, snapping their jaws and growling in anticipation of the next fight. Maxen pointed his sword at a flight of stairs up ahead.

We reached the next floor before we ran into more Duergar. Two of them turned and fled when they saw the canine shifters, and we made short work of the other four who stayed to fight. One of the Dobhar took off to chase down the soldiers who'd run.

I'd turned, ready to sprint to the next flight of stairs, when a deafening whoosh of magic rushed through the corridor. The air around me darkened as if night had suddenly descended.

The gloaming. Eldon had arrived.

I couldn't see the dogs, but the Dobhar howled in frustration.

"Maxen?"

I turned to look for him just as the band on my arm began to tingle. It grew extremely hot, and then light as bright as the summer sun burst outward from it. There was a low cry and then a crash. I threw my other forearm across my eyes. When I peered around, the gloaming had burned away around me. Melusine's magic had also cut a path through the dark mist between me and the Fae sorcerer.

Even better, it appeared to have punched him backward. He was sitting against the far wall, his legs splayed out in front of him and his eyes stunned. That was the look of a man who'd just had his bell rung.

Brandishing Aurora, I strode swiftly toward him. He would recover in a moment, and my charm wouldn't keep me safe from his power forever.

I stood over him, and he peered up at me.

"Try that again," I growled.

He squinted at me and then raised his hand and made quick gestures with his fingers. Shadows streamed from his fingers. When they got within about six inches of me, my charm erupted again. I squeezed my eyes closed against the painful brightness as Melusine's magic erupted from the cuff. Along with the light had come an explosion. When I cracked my eyelids open, I found a hole low on the wall where Eldon had been sitting a moment before.

I went up and peered through it, waving my hand through the dust. Through the opening, I saw the bottoms of the Fae sorcerer's boots. My charm had shot him clear through the wall and he lay on the floor of a sitting room. I climbed through the hole.

"Had enough?" I asked.

He sat up. Blood was leaking from a cut at his temple. It dripped from one corner of his mouth, too. His eyes on me, he turned his head and spat to the side. His long white hair was a mess of tangles and sheetrock chunks.

The charm was vibrating and cooling off. I was pretty sure its power was about to run out. But Eldon didn't need to know that.

I went down on one knee next to him, my eyes level with his. Last time we'd been in the same room, he'd momentarily lost control of me when I'd convulsed and suddenly found myself transported into the body of an ancient warrior and to a place I didn't recognize. When I'd returned to my senses, Eldon had the same look on his face he had right now.

"I know you're not really interested in fighting for Finvarra and the Unseelie," I said, my voice soft. "We could use someone like you on our side. But you hurt my father, and unfortunately for you, that means I need to kill you."

His eyes tightened, but he didn't say anything.

I thought of Melusine's note, the one I was supposed to deliver to Eldon. Too bad. Acting as a messenger between Old Ones wasn't my job. I had a chance to end the Fae sorcerer, and I was going to take it because I'd sworn to myself that I would.

"I didn't kill your father," he said.

"Maybe you didn't deal a death blow, but you tortured him."

I lifted Aurora and pointed the sword at his neck. I braced my feet to run him through.

"Wait! I didn't torture Oliver Maguire," he said, his voice pitched high with fear. "And he's not dead."

"Bullshit," I spat.

"He's fine. The man you saw wasn't him. It was an illusion."

I flicked the end of Aurora upward, nicking his Adam's apple before he could jerk back out of the way.

"Then where is he?" I thundered, my voice cracking with a terrible mix of all the hope, fear, grief, and guilt I'd been holding back.

"Periclase has him. Oliver Maguire is alive and not seriously hurt."

My heart bobbed in my chest. It had to be true. Fae couldn't lie outright to each other.

I moved the tip of my sword down to the center of his chest. "Interesting. I'll look into that. But I can't let you go back to the Unseelie."

"I don't want to, I swear," Eldon said. "Let me go, and I'll help you. I'll help the Seelie."

I regarded him for a long moment.

Knowing that my father was alive, I wanted nothing more than to go through the nearest doorway, charge into the Duergar palace with sword blazing, and bust Oliver and Nicole out. But that was the old Petra, the one who could live by her sword with hardly a thought to anything else. Such freedom was no longer mine.

"Save my father and sister, and come to our side," I said. I noticed the end of my sword trembling, and I tightened my fist. "Give me a binding oath to guarantee you will free Oliver Maguire and my twin sister Nicole and that you will abandon the Unseelie and join our side, and I'll let you go."

He nodded. His entire body shuddered, with what I assumed was relief. Perhaps also defeat. He quickly spoke the words, and magic shivered through the air between us. I realized he had no power of his own left at the moment. Melusine's charm had blasted it right out of him. It was temporary, I was sure, but so was the protection of my cuff. I needed to get this over with.

"There is another thing you should know, now that we are on the same side," Eldon said. "Your destiny is irrevocably tied to Jasper Glasgow's. You must be there with him if he attempts to kill Finvarra again. If you're not, Jasper won't survive it. His mission must be yours, too."

I remembered Jasper lying dead on the grass of the Summerlands after a stray blow of magic had hit him. It had been a lucky shot from Eldon that wasn't intended for Jasper at all but aimed at Melusine. Yet it had nearly killed Jasper. I couldn't explain it, but in my heart, I knew Eldon was right. I had to be there with Jasper when he went after Finvarra again. Otherwise, Jasper would die.

I reached into a pocket and pulled out Melusine's note. When I tossed it onto his thigh, he flinched.

"That's for you," I said. I flicked Aurora at him. "Now go, before I change my mind."

He rose, brushed himself off, and walked past me through the hole in the wall. He had to duck to get through. I followed him out.

"Let him pass," I called to Maxen. To the Dobhar, I said, "Escort him to a doorway, and make sure no harm comes to him."

Maxen looked at me agape, his blue eyes incredulous.

"We have an arrangement," was all I said in explanation.

My head spun. I pitched to one side and stuck out an arm to catch myself on the wall. Everything was reeling.

"Petra?" Maxen's blue-eyed concern appeared in my field of vision.

I could barely breathe. "Oliver's alive. He's okay, but he's still in the Duergar kingdom. Eldon promised to free Oliver and Nicole."

Maxen's hands came up to cover his face for several seconds, and when he finally dropped them, his eyes were watery with relief and gratitude.

"Thank the gods," he whispered. He looked off down the hall and swallowed a few times, clearly trying to compose himself.

"Oliver will take care of her," I said.

He just nodded.

"Eldon also promised to abandon the Unseelie," I said.

Maxen looked at me with surprise. "That's great news."

I pushed away from the wall and took a long, steadying breath. "We need to finish clearing the fortress. Now it's just a matter of getting rid of the Duergar soldiers. Periclase won't come back here with Eldon out of the picture. He won't risk himself."

Just then, Shane appeared around a corner. He was running, leading a group of New Garg soldiers. They skidded to a halt and stared at the hole in the wall. Shane looked at Maxen expectantly, but instead of speaking, Maxen turned to me.

"Eldon is gone," I said. I lifted my chin and surveyed the haggard-looking men and women who'd followed Shane. They were peering at me as Shane had, with uncertainty, some with deep hostility. I pretended I didn't see the anger. I'd have to deal with it later, though. "Let's get the rest of the Duergar assholes out of here and take our fortress back."

Shane gave me a quick salute. "Yes, Your Majesty."

In spite of the way he addressed me, I could see apprehension in his eyes. I hadn't completely won him over yet.

He turned to the soldiers and began giving instructions. I let him take charge, as he was better suited to be giving orders to the fighters.

Maxen gestured to the right with his borrowed short sword. "Let's make sure the rest of this floor is clear," he said to me.

I gave him a grim smile, and we set off side-by-side.

For the next few hours, hunting down and eliminating every Duergar left in the fortress was our sole mission. I got lost in the physicality of the fight, letting thoughts of Oliver fade to the background. Swinging

Aurora, focusing on the kills, and exhausting my muscles was a welcome escape.

But after the Duergar were gone and we'd cleaned up the mess and only Carraig Sidhe remained in the fortress, the real challenge would begin. I would have to win over my people.

Chapter 8

ONCE THE DUERGAR soldiers had been eliminated, there was a lull in the fortress as everyone seemed to draw a collective breath, assess casualties, and take stock of the state of the place.

But the moment of peace didn't last long.

Queen Vida's swordspeople were about to depart. I was standing in the foyer of the fortress, speaking to one of the Sylph women, when I saw a knot of Carraig approaching out of the corner of my eye.

Raleigh, who'd been head of Marisol's security and was the only New Garg larger than my father, led the group.

My gut tightened as I sensed a challenge coming. I quickly ended my conversation with the Sylph and went to meet Raleigh.

Maxen was by the counter connected to the room where incoming messages were sorted and held for their recipients. He was attempting to sift through what'd been missed during his imprisonment, looking for anything vital that was intended for him. He noticed Raleigh's group striding in, too, but Maxen stayed where he was. I preferred it that way. I had to prove myself on my own. Not that Maxen would have come to my defense necessarily. He seemed to have accepted that I was Queen, but we hadn't really gone much beyond that.

Raleigh pulled up in front of me and took a wide stance. He, apparently, was not ready to accept me as his monarch. There was no bow. No dip of the head. None of the usual deferential things Fae were supposed to do when approaching their ruler.

Beyond his massive shoulders, about two dozen Carraig stopped too, and stood glaring at me. All were armed. A couple even had their swords drawn and held them loosely at their sides.

With his eyes locked on mine, Raleigh reached back and drew his own broadsword from his back scabbard. He took a menacing step toward me and lifted the sword, pointing it straight at my chest. Four feet of space separated the end of his blade from my sternum. I didn't flinch or reach for my weapon.

"I publicly denounce you as a traitor," he said, his deep voice ringing out. "You are charged with the treasonous murder of Marisol Lothlorien. The punishment for treason is death."

He really did want me dead. I could see it in his eyes. I'd killed the woman he'd served for a lifetime, and there was no room in his mind for any outcome except my execution.

His people drew their weapons and fanned out in a semicircle.

Maxen came up quietly behind me, stopping just beyond my left shoulder. "You don't have the authority to make that charge, Raleigh," he said, stating it simply as fact. "My mother is gone, but her absence doesn't leave you in charge. By the High King Oberon's decree, Petra Maguire is your queen. But you already knew that. Now you've drawn your sword against your queen. She could have you executed for this transgression."

Raleigh's eyes flicked to Maxen. The big man's fingers shifted on his sword's handle. He'd clearly been amped up for a fight and wasn't sure how to react to the little speech. He hated me, but he still had love for Maxen, and Maxen's words were making Raleigh hesitate.

I quickly weighed my options. I could kill Raleigh. He was huge and strong as an ox, but he was more bodyguard than swordsman. I was faster, and my skills far exceeded his. He hadn't even formed stone armor. I could run him through with Aurora before he drew enough magic to flood it over his skin.

I wanted to be merciful. But I couldn't be stupid.

In the space between breaths, I drew Aurora, pushed magic into the sword, and lunged. The colors of dawn flared, and then a bellowing scream filled the foyer. Raleigh fell to his knees, hunching over as he cradled one arm. Blood gushed down his knees and onto the floor, blending with the spray of crimson that had already splattered the tiles when I dealt my blow.

I'd cut off his sword arm just below the elbow.

His people stood there, stunned. Most of them stared at the severed arm, the hand still loosely holding Raleigh's sword, that lay oozing blood.

There was a strangled cry, and one of the New Gargs charged me. In two quick moves, I batted his blade to the side and cracked Aurora across his knuckles. He dropped his sword. I stabbed him through the shoulder. It wasn't a mortal wound.

My chest heaving, I whirled Aurora and looked around at the rest of them, meeting each of their eyes.

"Anyone else?" I asked, my voice cold steel.

Hearing Raleigh's cries, a crowd had gathered at the mouth of the foyer. The room was silent except for the big man's grunts of pain and outrage.

Some of his people dropped their weapons, the metal clanging and clattering on the tiles, and held up their hands in surrender.

"The proper etiquette would be to drop to one knee," came Maxen's flat voice from behind me.

I knew he was unarmed, and yet he'd stood there just feet away from me while two dozen of our people had threatened me with swords. Ballsy. But then, he wasn't the one they wanted to kill.

Most of the crowd that'd come with Raleigh followed Maxen's suggestion, kneeling and dropping their heads, some of them begging forgiveness. But four of them remained standing, though they did sheath their weapons.

Adrenaline still coursed through me, but I surveyed them coolly as I slid Aurora into the scabbard on my back.

I wanted to tell them that I didn't ask for this. I never wanted to kill Marisol. But she'd sent an assassin after me, leaving me little choice. I didn't want to be Queen. I didn't want to be standing there next to an arm I'd severed with my own sword as I tried to defend a throne I had no desire to occupy.

But I couldn't say any of it. They weren't words a monarch had the right to utter in public.

Instead, I raised my chin and surveyed the crowd. Except for Raleigh's moans, it was so quiet I could hear my own heart beating in my ears.

"Maybe some of you hadn't yet heard," I said, my voice carrying through the large room. "But the High King Oberon granted us kingdomhood. We are now the Carraig Sidhe. I am the queen of this realm, by the High King's decree."

I let my gaze slowly sweep across the people gathered.

"I do not seek your permission to take the throne. It is already mine. If any Carraig Sidhe draws a weapon in my presence without permission again, that person will be punished to the full extent our law allows. Your job now is to get our home in order. Go do it. That's an order from your queen."

I hated that I sounded like such a hardass. The entire speech made me cringe inside. But it worked. Everyone began to move away. A couple of Raleigh's people came forward to help him to his feet. He was breathing raggedly, his eyes pinched closed.

"Well done," Maxen said softly as we watched them depart. "You should have had him and all his followers executed, though."

I shook my head. "There's been enough death and bloodshed for one day."

I didn't say it, but I couldn't have rounded up all of them anyway. Not singlehandedly. There were too many, and I didn't have a security force of my own. Perhaps I could have tried to order others to do it for me, but I couldn't yet trust who would or wouldn't follow my command.

Suddenly, I was acutely aware of being in a building occupied by hundreds of armed Carraig Sidhe. If some of them decided to, they could gang up on me and kill me.

"Queen Petra?"

I nearly jumped out of my skin when I realized I hadn't heard someone approach me and Maxen. *Stupid.*

Turning, I came face to face with Emmaline's violet gaze. She'd served as my squire when I'd been named Champion. She was still a student fighter in training with dreams of someday wielding a spellblade like Mort, the broadsword I'd lost in the Giants' Causeway. She'd been a loyal friend, before. Now, she looked troubled. At least she wasn't threatening me, her sword stowed away in her own back scabbard, an almost identical model to mine, I absently noticed.

"Emmaline." My tone was wary.

She crossed one ankle behind the other and dipped into a low, slow curtsy. When she straightened, she leveled her chin.

"I want to offer you my services, Your Majesty," she said, loud enough for anyone within twenty feet to hear.

I pressed my lips into a hard line to still a slight tremble.

"You do?" was all I could manage.

She nodded solemnly. "I do."

"That is a risky thing for a person to do these days. You may have noticed I'm not winning any popularity contests around here."

Her face took on a look of teenage defiance. "I don't care about the risks. I want to serve you."

I cocked my head. "And what do your parents say about this?" I asked quietly.

"I'm eighteen, Queen Petra. I can make my own decisions." She also lowered her voice.

I inhaled slowly through my nose, as if considering her proposition, when really I was trying to quell the emotions threatening to rise up. No one, not Maxen, not any of my former classmates, not my old teachers, *no one* had offered me their loyalty the way Emmaline had just done. And we both knew she did it at the risk of her own life. Maeve help me if anyone harmed a hair on her head.

I gave a tight smile of approval. "Your offer of service is appreciated. Are there others who might be of your same mind?" I asked, my words soft. I had to be cautious.

She skirted a glance around and gave me the slightest of nods. We needed privacy for this conversation. But I also needed to stay visible. It wouldn't do for me to retreat into quarters somewhere, even for important business.

"Later," I said. "After we've gotten things cleaned up a bit."

All of us Carraig Sidhe began the process of clearing the wreckage and scrubbing away the blood. I worked along with the others, conferring with Maxen occasionally to make sure we were doing what we could to keep the fortress secure. Shane had taken charge of those duties, along with a couple dozen others who pitched in to help. Though he gave me the deference due to a monarch, he seemed more comfortable speaking with Maxen and taking orders from him. I hated the awkwardness that seemed to have sprung up between me and people I'd known my whole life.

Smells of cooking meat and roasting vegetables began wafting through the corridors, indicating the kitchens were back up and running. The prospect of a hot meal seemed to lift everyone's spirits, and there were more and more quiet conversations springing up around us.

As late evening came on, I knew I had to stop and eat, or I'd risk falling on my face from lack of calories. I chewed my bottom lip. Could I trust the food that came from the kitchens? Or would my detractors try to poison me?

Maxen caught my eye. "Dine with me in my quarters," he said loudly. "I will have food sent there."

I wasn't sure how he'd read my mind, but I was grateful. Regardless of how the Carraig felt about me, it was safe to assume their love for Maxen was almost universal. It always had been, and it was well-deserved. He'd been a servant of the New Gargs practically since he was born, but in contrast with his mother, he'd never displayed even a hint of a need for power. He was one of the more affable New Gargs in the fortress, with an easy smile and a deeply likeable disposition. Not only that, he was an extremely skilled diplomat. No one would try to assassinate him. If anything, my enemies would hope to eliminate me and put him on the throne.

I found Emmaline nearby and told her to join us. Twenty minutes later, Maxen, Emmaline, and I sat in the dining room of Maxen's quarters. The hole where I'd blasted Eldon through the wall had already been plastered over and had boards nailed across the inside. We were a few rooms away from the damage.

Two linen-covered food carts had arrived, and the three of us had steaming plates of food in front of us. But none of us had started eating.

"Maxen—" I started.

He held out a palm. "I need to explain something to you."

He lowered his hand. I waited while he looked at a spot on the floor, seeming to collect himself.

"I can give you privacy, if you'd prefer," Emmaline said, starting to get up.

"No, stay," Maxen said. Emmaline sat. He lifted his gaze to meet mine, and his sapphire blue eyes looked so pained I thought my heart might crack. "You killed my mother. I hated her for trying to kill Nicole and my unborn child, but still. She was my mother, and she was my

78

only family. Now that she's gone, I care about two things: my future family and my people. I will support you publicly as Queen because I don't want the New Gargs—the Carraig Sidhe—to implode. The last thing we need is a civil war. I can honor the part of my mother that I loved, the work she did that I believed in, by doing my best to hold us together. But that's all I can offer you right now."

I let a few seconds of silence pass before I spoke.

"Do you want the throne?" I asked.

"It doesn't matter. Oberon made you Queen."

"I know, but if he hadn't . . ."

His jaw muscles worked for a moment. "I always believed I would be my mother's successor." His voice was low and ragged, and he seemed tormented.

It wasn't really an answer, but I backed off. Perhaps he was right. Maybe his desire didn't matter.

He gestured to our cooling plates. "Let's eat. Then we'll talk about building support for the throne."

It wasn't lost on me that he said "for the throne," not "for you." He also hadn't counted Marisol's attempt on my life as a reason he hated his mother—he'd only spoken of Nicole and their unborn child. I chewed mechanically, barely tasting the food, feeling the awful weight of Maxen's resentment settling across my shoulders. Our relationship would never be the same, it seemed. Could I blame him? No, not really. But it still hurt with a pain so poignant I couldn't take a full breath.

I sat there, quietly eating and mulling things over, and my sadness and guilt began to loosen a little, giving away to something else. I looked up at Maxen, and I realized something. There were words I couldn't say in public, but I could say them to him. And I needed to. He needed to acknowledge a few things.

"Nicole is alive because of me," I said.

He slowly lowered his fork to his plate, swallowed, and looked up at me. His eyes were pinched, and he looked ready to lash out. I started talking again before he could.

"Your mother sent an assassin after me, and I escaped only by the grace of the gods," I said, my tone becoming heated. I didn't try to temper it. "If I hadn't, Nicole would be dead right now. Your unborn child would be dead right now. I didn't want to kill Marisol, but even before Periclase used Eldon to force me to do it, I knew it had to be done. She never, ever would have let us live. All Marisol Lothlorien cared about was becoming Queen of the New Gargoyle kingdom, and she truly believed Nicole and I had to die in order for that to happen. She didn't give two shits about your happiness either, Maxen. She was ready to murder the love of your life, murder her grandchild, in the name of her obsession. Nicole wasn't what she wanted for you, for the future heir of the New Garg throne. So, yeah. Your mother is gone, and it really is too bad it had to come to that. But *she* is the one who set all of this in motion."

By the time I paused for a breath, I'd raised my voice loud enough that the second of silence seemed to ring out in the room. I'd placed my hands on the table palms-down, pressing hard to try to still their shaking.

I forced my voice back to a reasonable volume. "You tell me now, Maxen Lothlorien, who would you rather have living? Marisol or Nicole and your child? Because there was never any way you were going to get both, and you know it. Your mother ensured that."

My chest was heaving with ragged breaths. Maxen just sat there staring bloody murder at me.

I raised my hands and slammed them down on the linen tablecloth. "Answer me!" I yelled as the dishes and flatware rattled back to their places.

His lips were pressed together and quivering with anger, agitated red splotches blooming on his cheeks. For a long moment, I thought he might reach across the table and punch me in the face. But instead he looked down at his lap, closed his eyes, and took a long inhale through his parted lips.

"Nicole and my child," he whispered. "And I realized I could have lost them as well."

I moved my hands to my thighs, pushing them forward and back across the fabric of my pants, and tried to focus on calming my racing pulse.

"You know what else I didn't want?" I asked. "The godsdamned throne. I didn't want to have to cut off a man's hand in the name of a crown I never wanted in the first place."

"I know."

We locked gazes, and I felt a shift between us, an acknowledgement. It wasn't friendship, and it certainly wasn't warmth, but it brought a small measure of relief.

"Good," I said quietly.

I looked over at Emmaline. She'd pulled back in her chair, as if leaning out of the way of the volley of words between me and Maxen, her violet eyes wide and unblinking.

"I'm sorry you had to be here for that," I said to her.

She looked at me, blinked a couple of times, and then drew a quiet breath. Her lower lip trembled the slightest bit before she was able to control it. "I'm sorry both of you have had to bear so much pain."

That caught me off guard. Maxen, too, apparently, as I saw his eyes before he quickly slanted his gaze down at an angle, trying to hide his emotions.

"It's been a painful time in the fortress in general," I said. "I think it's time we started making things better for all Carraig, to the extent we can."

It wasn't phrased as a question, but I waited for Maxen's slight nod before continuing.

"To that end, who else might the throne be able to count on?" I asked Emmaline.

"I think I've almost got Shane convinced he should follow you," she said. Her composed expression was a bit too forced.

My eyes narrowed slightly as something pinged in my memory. Oh, yes. Emmaline had a bit of a crush on Shane, who was one of her instructors in addition to being an officer in the battle ranks.

I arched a brow at her. "Soo . . . you and Shane, huh?"

"What? No, no. I mean, uh, that's not—all I mean is that he'd be a good ally, and I think he's almost on your side."

A tiny smile touched my lips, and I saw the amusement in Maxen's eyes, too.

"Okay, who else?" I asked.

"Most everyone in my class is with you, Petr—ah, Your Majesty," Emmaline said. "They were big admirers of yours before all this."

Great. A bunch of kids and maybe a young officer on my side.

I nodded. "All right. What about the students' parents? Or anyone else?" I shot Maxen a pleading look. He'd claimed to want to strengthen the position of the throne in the name of stabilizing things in our baby kingdom. Now would be a good time to speak up.

"Wait," Emmaline said, leaning forward. "If we can get Shane, that's key. Really key."

I tilted my head. "How so?"

Her tongue flicked over her lower lip, and she skirted a glance at Maxen before meeting my gaze again. "Because. Those guys who were with Raleigh? Several of them were high-ranking officers. I'm assuming, that, uh—" Again she cast a look at Maxen.

"It's okay," he said. "You can say it."

"Well, if you imprison those people, you're basically taking the old guard out of the battle ranks' officer corp," she said.

My brows shot up. Why hadn't I thought of this? I pointed at her.

"Ah. Good thinking. If they're stripped of their positions, that leaves Shane as one of the only officers."

"Yeah." Emmaline was nodding. "And if you promote some of the younger men and women, you can pick and choose the ones who support you."

I winced. "That seems phony, like—I don't know, not nepotism, exactly, but . . ." I trailed off.

"It's not," Maxen said. "It's politics. It's what a smart leader has to do. What good would it be to have a military led by dissenters? It would just further destabilize the realm."

The realm. I was in charge of a realm.

"So, you agree with what Emmaline's saying?"

"No question. All of your appointees need to be supporters. No one would expect you to do any different because it would be dangerous, stupid even. You can't put anyone who's disgruntled in a position of power."

I reached for my water tumbler. "Well, when you put it that way . . ." I took a slow drink, considering, and then set my cup down. "My biggest problem is finding enough supporters."

Maxen tipped his head in agreement. "That's your initial challenge, but once you have enough good people instated and day-to-day affairs of the fortress start running smoothly again, a majority will accept you as their ruler."

"It's that minority I'm going to have to figure out how to deal with."

"Yep."

"Any ideas?" I asked him.

"First, let's figure out who we can get on board. The sooner we have positions filled, the sooner things will start to settle."

I chewed my bottom lip for a moment, suddenly thinking of the battles being waged elsewhere. "Oberon grant us time enough to do that," I said soberly.

"Let's sleep on it and reconvene first thing," Maxen said. He looked at Emmaline. "You, too. We need to start a list of potential supporters."

We spoke for a few more minutes about the work ahead of us. Then I walked Emmaline to the apartment where she still lived with her parents. Then I went alone to my old, tiny apartment. I wasn't about to take over Marisol's quarters, even if it would have sent the right message to do so.

I barred the entrance to my quarters using an old practice sword wedged in between the edge of the door and the frame, went into my bedroom and locked that door, and lay down with Aurora beside me on the bed.

Staring into the dark, I considered all that had transpired and tried to work out how best to proceed with the royal appointments, the military, the dissenters, and about a dozen other equally grave areas that would need immediate attention.

The fact was, I couldn't be sure we'd even have the chance to get our little kingdom in order. The Summerlands was burning. Finvarra was still out there with the Stone of Fal. And the Tuatha were biding their time.

But I had to make at least some progress toward the Carraig Sidhe kingdom on its feet. My people needed me more than ever. I just hoped I could somehow summon the wisdom and strength I'd need to do right by them. At the same time, Eldon's words rang in my ears. Jasper was going to need me, too, when the time came to go after Finvarra again.

How was I going to manage it all?

Chapter 9

EARLY THE NEXT morning, Emmaline arrived at my door. She was dressed in the battle gear of the junior ranks, the students who weren't full-fledged soldiers but had been through many years of training and prep for a life in the Order's military if that was what they chose to pursue.

I looked her up and down. "Hoping for a fight?"

She gave me a fleeting but withering teenage glare before snapping her expression into something more suitable in the presence of her monarch.

"I'm hoping to *avoid* a fight, Your Majesty," she said crisply. "As your armed escort, I felt like I needed to be wearing something, well, official."

I didn't want to make her feel bad, but if I got into trouble in the corridors of the fortress, she wasn't going to be able to save me. Not against the likes of the men who'd come to threaten me with Raleigh leading them. I was just about to suggest we tone down the armed-guard idea when there was a rustle of many footfalls to the right. I leaned out of my doorway to see who was coming, ready to pull magic and form armor.

My brows shot up. It was a troop of young men and women around Emmaline's age, also wearing full junior battle gear.

"Ah, here's the rest of your security detail," Emmaline said, raising her hand in a half-salute, half-wave at the approaching group. "We'll be accompanying you to your meeting with Lord Lothlorien."

I blinked at her, my mind spinning. How was it going to look if I marched through the fortress surrounded by a bunch of armed kids from the Order's academy?

I quickly decided I didn't really care. They were supporters, and I had to start somewhere. Besides, I couldn't imagine anyone would actually attack them. These teenagers were the future of the Carraig Sidhe, and like all races in Faerie, we treasured our children.

The group, about thirty of them, strode in neat lines. They came to a crisp halt when Emmaline raised her fist.

She turned to me. "Please go ahead, Your Majesty. We will back you up."

I swept a gaze over the junior fighters. They all wore fierce expressions, their brows pulled low. I gave them a little dip of my chin, an acknowledgement of what they were doing and the statement they were making. I turned away before a slight smile could twitch at my lips. Leave it to New Garg kids to prove themselves to be badasses. I almost wished I were their age again. I'd have joined up with them in a heartbeat—especially if it'd pissed off Oliver.

As we began to pull away from my quarters, heads were poking out of apartment doorways. We'd drawn some attention, it seemed. Most who spotted me curtsied or bowed. But some quickly pulled back inside and shut their doors.

Emmaline walked beside me, and the rest followed us in two parallel lines. Her eyes roved left and right, vigilant, and her hand rested lightly on her belt, right behind the sheath that held a long dagger. She wore her broadsword on her back, as did all the junior fighters behind us.

"Hey," I mumbled to her without moving my lips. It'd just occurred to me that I'd neglected one little detail. "I don't know where Maxen wanted to meet."

"One of his pages told me where to go," she whispered. "The Opal Room on the first floor."

"Thank the gods. Otherwise, I'd just have to march you all over the fortress, trying to look as if I knew what I was doing, until I figured out where the hell he was."

She let out a soft snort-laugh, but quickly recovered her focus.

We trooped through the fortress. People stared. We let them, and we reached the appointed meeting room without a challenge. The double doors to the Opal Room stood open, and Maxen was already there, scanning the tablet he held in one hand and eating an apple with the other. Two pages stood off to the side, awaiting orders. For a split second, I could almost imagine it was any old day in the stone fortress. Marisol was somewhere else, and Maxen was just reviewing his itinerary for the day.

But of course it wasn't just any old day, and Marisol would never grace the fortress hallways again. A shiver spiraled up my spine.

He looked up when I walked into the room, set down his tablet on the table he stood next to, and bowed. His pages also bent at the waist, waiting until Maxen straightened before they did.

I glanced back to see Emmaline had stopped just outside the room. Her troops appeared to be arranging themselves on either side of the doors. She gave me a tiny nod and then turned on her heel in a sharp, well-practiced movement, positioning herself just beyond the doorway, facing the corridor and standing at attention with her spine straight and her chin lifted. I heard the unmistakable sound of many blades sliding from sheaths, which meant the troops were planning to stand out there with their swords drawn. My security detail wasn't messing around.

Maxen had been peering past me, taking it all in. We locked eyes, and his brow wrinkled with surprise.

"I know," I said, my voice low as my words were only meant for his ears. "She showed up at my apartment with them this morning."

"Impressive," was all he said. He beckoned at me to join him at the conference table.

His two pages went to the doorway and exited, pulling the heavy double doors closed behind them.

He pushed his tablet in front of me so I could see what was on the screen. "These are the positions you personally need to fill with your appointees."

He was obviously ready to get down to business, and I was fine with that. Our emotional exchange the previous night had been difficult, and we needed a truce.

I scrolled down the list on the screen. The titles included things like Head of Security, Royal Chef, Battle Master and Military Commander, First Attendant to the Queen, Prison Warden, a handful of Ambassadors to various kingdoms, and several other positions.

I lifted my eyes to his and shook my head. "I'm not even sure where to start."

Just as I'd started to speak, the doors had opened. Maxen and I both swiveled our gazes that way.

My lips parted as I sucked in a tiny gasp. I rose as two people strode in.

"You can start by greeting your father."

It was Oliver. Behind him followed Nicole. Maxen jumped to his feet so abruptly his chair toppled backward. He rushed past me to Nicole and embraced her, lifting her off her feet and spinning her around. But I couldn't tear my attention away from Oliver.

He'd been roughed up—there was fresh-looking pale flesh around his wrists and some slashes of newly-healed skin across his face. But both eyes were intact. Eldon had told the truth. Oliver hadn't been seriously harmed.

I hated that I hadn't been the one to break him out of the Duergar palace, but that wasn't a thing for a queen to do.

He stopped about five feet away from me. For a moment, we booth stood stock-still, our unblinking gazes locked. Then he pulled in his lips and bit down. I drew a shuddering inhale as I realized his eyes were misting.

"Father," I whispered. I took a step toward him, ready to throw my arms around his neck.

He held up a hand to stop me and then bent at the waist in an exceptionally graceful bow for such a large man. "Your Majesty."

As soon as he straightened, I flew at him. His huge arms wrapped around my midsection, squeezing until my ribs cracked and I couldn't pull in a breath. I didn't care. He could crush me if he wanted to. I'd heal.

"It is really you, isn't it?" I whispered.

"Of course," he said gruffly.

I knew it was. The way he smelled, the way he'd looked at me. There were things that couldn't be faked.

I wasn't sure how long we remained that way, but it was Nicole's tinkling laugh that brought me back to my senses. Oliver released me, and I saw that my twin and Maxen were still lost in each other, both of them teary and smiling. He curled an arm around her, drawing her close again and kissing the top of her head.

His gaze shifted to me, and he took Nicole's hand and led her toward me and Oliver. She let go of Maxen and took a couple of running steps to me, throwing her arms around my neck with another gleeful squeal. I squeezed her back. Over her shoulder, I watched Maxen offer his hand to my father. As they shook hands, Maxen murmured his gratitude for bringing Nicole safely back to the fortress.

But Maxen quickly backed off, and when I saw Oliver's face, I understood why. My father's expression had gone icy, and when the stone man looked like that, you instinctively wanted to put some distance between yourself and him.

At first, I thought Oliver was angry. But the emotions clouding his eyes were more complicated than simple anger. That was there, yes, but there was also sorrow, regret, and distrust.

The high of having my father and twin back in the fortress tempered as I realized the complexity existing between the four of us who stood in that room. Oliver had served Maxen's mother with unrelenting loyalty for decades, and most likely shared her bed on occasion. Then Marisol had tried to kill me and Nicole. I'd ended Marisol's life, but my sister carried Maxen's child. It was soap-opera worthy, except this wasn't bad TV. This was my life, and these were people I cared about.

"Is there someone who can take Nicole to the infirmary?" Oliver asked. "She says she feels fine, but after her ordeal with the Duergar, I'd like to have her checked out."

I blinked, my eyes misting all over again. Oliver knew Nicole and I weren't his blood daughters, but he was watching out for her as if it was his grandchild she carried.

I cleared my throat, silently chiding myself for being so damn weepy lately. "Emmaline will send some of her people with Nicole," I said. I shifted my gaze to Maxen. "If that sounds okay?"

Nicole waved her hands as if trying to flag us down on the side of a highway. "Um, hello? I feel fine. Better than fine. I don't need to see any doctors."

Maxen took both of her hands. "I'm sure you are fine, but would you go anyway? Just to be a hundred percent certain."

Her face softened, and a sweet smile touched her lips. "You know I can't refuse."

He smiled broadly, folded her into an embrace, and then pressed his lips to hers.

Maxen and I walked Nicole to the door, where I spoke quietly to Emmaline. She chose half a dozen of her troops to escort my twin.

I thought it was overkill—Nicole needed directions to the medical wing more than she needed actual protection—but it was probably better to be cautious.

Once the door closed again, Oliver turned to me. "How many attempts on your life since you took the throne?"

"None that were successful," I said, lifting my chin defiantly.

He grimaced at my smartass response.

"Raleigh and about thirty others threatened me with an accusation of treason last night." I lowered my eyelids partway and folded my arms. "He's now minus his sword hand."

Oliver's scarred face tightened, and he ran a hand over his cropped hair.

"I was there with her, and she did well," Maxen said quietly. "She showed her authority while diffusing the situation, and no one died."

"Well, they should have," Oliver barked.

Maxen raised a shoulder and let it drop. "I agree. I told her so."

I lifted my hands in the air. "I couldn't have taken on that many on my own. And I couldn't have forced them all into cells single-handedly, either."

My father didn't respond, but we both knew I was right. He gestured at the tablet on the table. "Where are you with establishing your court?"

My court. I resisted the urge to gulp.

"We were just about to start going down the list of appointments Petra needs to make," Maxen said.

Oliver cut a searing look at him. "*Queen* Petra," he said sharply.

I placed my hand on my father's arm. "You don't need to do that. He's given me his full support in public."

"And his mother tried to murder you," Oliver said harshly. "How do you know he didn't know about it?"

My eyes flicked to the closed door. "Because Marisol wanted to have Nicole killed, too. Maxen never would have—"

"I'm not talking about Nicole," Oliver cut in. "Maybe Marisol only told him about the assassin coming for you. Maybe he knew she wanted to kill you, but he didn't know she wanted to kill Nicole. Did you think of that?"

My lips parted. Well, no. I hadn't thought of that, and I felt stupid for having overlooked it. My eyes slipped over to Maxen.

"Maxen? Did you know your mother was planning to have me killed?" I held my breath as the question hung in the air.

"No. Of course not."

I exhaled. He couldn't lie.

"And after Marisol sent Jaquard to kill Petra, did you know about the attempt on her life?" Oliver asked.

"I knew only after he'd failed," Maxen said, steadily holding my father's gaze. His blue eyes shifted to me.

Cool relief spread through me, but Oliver grimaced. He didn't seem satisfied.

"But you'd discovered Nicole was Petra's twin," my father said quietly. "And you knew of your mother's prophecy, the one that said twin New Garg girls would have to die for her to become Queen of the New Gargs, as she so desperately wanted. You're not an idiot. You had to have put two and two together."

Something struck me like a bolt from the sky. I'd always thought Marisol's prophecy was that a pair of twins had to die in order for the stone bloods to get a kingdom. But I realized now, by the way my father had phrased it, that Marisol hadn't been completely truthful when she spoke about the prophecy in public. Dead twin girls weren't the requirement for kingdomhood. They were the requirement for a kingdom that had *Marisol* on the throne. She'd manipulated the New Gargs even more than I'd imagined.

A pained look pulled at Maxen's handsome features. "I didn't believe my mother would have the two of them murdered. Maybe it was naïve of me, but I honestly didn't."

Part of me wanted to know how Maxen had reacted after he'd found out Marisol tried to have me killed, but I didn't want to have that discussion in front of Oliver.

"We need to be satisfied with that," I said to my father. "I've got so much to do, and I need Maxen's help. We all know I can't do it without him. And like I said, he supports me publicly for the sake of our people."

Oliver's jaw muscles bunched, but finally he nodded and then went and sat at the table. Apparently, my father planned to attend our little meeting.

I went back to my chair, and Maxen joined us. And then, as if the prior conversation hadn't even happened, we started talking about possible candidates for the various positions in the Carraig court. It felt good to focus on something, and even better to make some progress, even if we didn't get very far.

When we got to the position of Head of Security, I turned to Oliver. "Would you take that post?" I asked. "There's no one better suited, and you're well-respected."

For a moment, his brow wrinkled, and I thought he'd refuse, but then he said, "Of course I will."

My gratitude was quickly followed by the worry that my actions might have negatively affected the way the Carraig viewed Oliver. But really, anyone who disrespected Oliver did so at their own risk. And as far as I knew, he'd lived a life of service that was beyond reproach. That had to count for something.

Oliver was actually quite helpful in suggesting people who might be willing to serve in my court, and I was surprised at the number of candidates he came up with. Perhaps Marisol had not been as universally admired as I'd thought. Oberon's words came back to me, his advice to seek out those who might not be shedding tears over the loss of Marisol Lothlorien.

We worked until lunch and decided to take an hour break and then reconvene. Oliver stood but didn't make a move to exit. Instead, he shot me a look of significance and waited for Maxen to leave.

"You still don't trust him, do you?" I asked.

My father shook his head. "Not completely. I witnessed for years just how firmly he was pressed under his mother's thumb."

I folded my arms, slanting a troubled look down at the floor. I had seen how controlling Marisol was, and I supposed I'd occasionally thought it might be good for Maxen to be more his own man. And perhaps, very deep down, there was a small part of him that was relieved to be out from under that pressure. Maybe not yet, but eventually.

"But he couldn't lie to us," I said. "He said he didn't know Marisol was going to try to kill me."

Oliver shook his head. "He clearly didn't know about the direct order, but he'd discovered that Nicole was your twin and he knew of the prophecy. So even if he didn't *know*, he still knew."

I sighed, suddenly tired. "Maybe. But like I said, I need him."

"It'd be better if you didn't."

I held up my hands in surrender. "Maybe. But we've got an uphill battle ahead of us, and we need Maxen. For now, can you just play nice?"

Oliver gave me a crazy-eyed smile that could chill the blood of battle-hardened soldiers. "Sure," he said, a growl edging his voice. "I'll play nice as long as he behaves himself, Your Majesty."

I shot him a playfully withering look, but my stomach was contracting into a tight ball. It wasn't going to make my life any easier to have such palpable tension between Maxen and my father. It was bad enough that Maxen and I were still strained with each other.

"So, Nicole must have told you?" I asked, eager to change the subject.

"She did," he said, and his expression relented a little. "Things between the two of them certainly . . . progressed. Didn't they?"

I gave a short laugh. "Yeah. I kind of suspected they were serious, but gods, she's *pregnant*."

"At least she seems happy to stay in Faerie."

"True."

We'd started strolling toward the door. My stomach was growling, and we had limited time to grab food and return to our official work.

"How are you?" I asked quietly, my eyes slipping down to the freshly-healed skin around his wrists. Only iron would have left marks that lingered for so long on a New Garg.

I expected him to immediately brush off my concern, but instead he gave a long sigh. "I'm alive and relatively unharmed," he said.

We'd entered the corridor, and Emmaline fell into step behind me and Oliver. I peeked over my shoulder. Behind her, the troops quickly sheathed their broadswords, formed two lines, and jogged to catch up before they fell into a military march.

Oliver's eyes flicked to the side, but he didn't turn to look. The corner of his mouth twitched with what passed for amusement from the stone man. We automatically began tracing a route to Oliver's quarters.

"What did they do to you? Did they try to demand information, or . . . ?" I trailed off. I wanted to know, and yet I dreaded the details.

"They kept me restrained, and that Fae sorcerer came into my cell with Finvarra early on. They spent quite some time weaving magic around me and sending it through me." He grimaced at the memory. "It wasn't painful, but it was intensely uncomfortable. Eldon seemed to saturate me with his magic, somehow."

"What was Finvarra doing?"

He squinted as if trying to picture the Unseelie High King. "He mostly stood there with his eyes closed. He formed a concentration of magic between his palms." Oliver lifted his hands out as if he held an invisible beach ball. "The magic Eldon put into me eventually streamed out my mouth, ears, and eyes and into Finvarra's orb."

I frowned. "Perhaps they were creating a servitor of your likeness, and that was the man they brought before me."

Oliver cut a swift look at me. "Brought before you?"

I stared straight ahead and nodded. "They had a man who looked like you, but who'd been tortured. His eye—" I swallowed convulsively. "His eye had been gouged out. He was in bad shape. He looked, moved, and sounded just like you. He even tried to warn me not to enter into any oaths with the Unseelie."

I pulled my lips in and clamped down on them with my teeth, still trying to convince myself that the image in my mind's eye wasn't really Oliver.

"You didn't, did you? Agree to any binding promises?"

"I thought they were going to kill you if I didn't go along with them," I whispered. "But no, I didn't make promises to Finvarra or Periclase."

We were silent for several long moments.

"Father, I—I made a choice," I started haltingly, my chest aching at the memory of the decision I'd made. "I chose to defy Periclase, even though he threatened me with your—your death."

He watched me, his face pained.

I swallowed hard. "It killed me, but I made a decision that I fully believed meant he would murder you." My eyes began to brim. Being in public was the only thing keeping me from completely breaking down. I kept my voice low. "It was awful, the worst thing I've ever had to do, but I can't deny that I believed it was the right thing to do at the time. Can you . . . can you forgive me for doing such a thing?"

"There's nothing to forgive," he said quickly, almost speaking over me. "It was the right decision. It's what I would have told you to do, if I could have. It's what a *queen* would do."

I took a quiet, shaking breath in and pulled myself together.

"You must have been in a cell for . . . days," I said, my voice still watery.

"It was a while."

"How'd Eldon get you out?" I asked.

"He just showed up at my cell with Nicole, removed my shackles, and took us to a doorway."

"No one tried to stop you?"

"I don't think anyone saw us. He used some kind of obfuscation magic. Seemed like a combination of his gloaming and some other optical illusion, though I wasn't on the viewing side of it, so I couldn't be sure."

I was a tiny bit disappointed. I was hoping Eldon had been forced to openly defy Periclase.

"Where did he go?" I asked.

My father shrugged. "I didn't ask what his plans were."

We'd reached Oliver's apartment. He pressed his hand to the door. The magic mechanism in it recognized him and the door unlatched and swung inward a few inches.

Emmaline's people lined up along either side of the doorway as they had outside the meeting room.

Once inside with the door closed, Oliver pointed his thumb over his shoulder and arched a brow at me. "Nice baby battalion you've got out there."

I flapped my hands and shushed him. "Don't let them hear you say things like that. They're taking their job very seriously. And they're taking a stand in a very public way. They deserve our respect."

"I suppose they do," he conceded.

He went to the phone mounted on the wall—there was no wireless service of any kind in Faerie—and called the kitchen to place an order for sandwiches to be delivered.

Oliver's quarters were spare and not exactly set up for guests. The only chair in the small living room, an old recliner, was his seat by default. I removed my scabbard, laid it on the floor, and sat cross-legged beside it.

My father crossed one ankle over the other knee, propped his elbows on the armrests, and steepled his fingers.

"You need to make a statement, literally and figuratively," he said. "Something to establish yourself, to make yourself visible as Queen."

"You have something in mind?"

He leaned back and shook his head. "It's not the thing itself that's important. It's the swiftness with which it happens. You need to go public as Queen immediately." His intense eyes met mine. "You need to do it today."

I knew he was right, but my stomach flipped at the prospect of it. I didn't know how to be Queen of the Carraig, how to make the people see me as their leader. But I was going to have to figure it out fast.

Chapter 10

MY FATHER AND I ate our sandwiches hastily, digging in as soon as they arrived. I was halfway through mine before I froze mid-chew at the sudden thought that occurred to me. What if my roast beef on rye had been poisoned? Oh well, too late. And if I died, at least I wouldn't have to deal with trying to rally the Carraig around me. I inhaled the rest of my food. And all too soon, we were leaving the peace and privacy of Oliver's quarters.

We went back to the Opal Room, where Maxen was already waiting.

"Nicole is home resting," he said. "The medics said everything is fine with the pregnancy, and she's in perfect health."

My brows twitched up and then down. Home? Ah, of course. When we'd been in the fortress before, Nicole had shared my apartment. Apparently she'd relocated to Maxen's quarters. It made sense that her home base was with him, but I supposed I still wasn't completely used to the idea of them as a couple.

The three of us sat down at the conference table.

I opened my mouth to speak, but Oliver beat me to it.

"Petra needs a formal event, a sort of coming out as the monarch of the Carraig," he said.

Maxen tilted his head. "You're right. And the sooner, the better."

Oliver leaned back and crossed his arms, nodding.

"We're thinking something should happen before the day's end," I said.

Slanting a gaze upward, Maxen pursed his lips. "Yes. A coronation ceremony."

I tried not to visibly cringe. But he was right. That was exactly the type of formality that needed to take place in our new kingdom.

"You're the expert on courtly protocol, Maxen," I said. "How does a coronation usually go?"

"Normally we'd want to invite foreign dignitaries to attend and make a week-long celebration of it," he said. "But given the short notice and the state of things in Faerie, we'll have to skip the pageantry. Pity, as it's a good opportunity to establish yourself with other rulers."

I shrugged a shoulder. "Eh, I've already crossed paths with a handful of them. Even made a couple of friends, I think."

"That's right," Maxen said. "You met with several in the Summerlands."

"Maybe we could host a party at a later date," I suggested, knowing full well it might never happen, given what we were facing with the Unseelie and at some point the Tuatha De Danann.

"Sure," Maxen said, and I could tell he was thinking the same thing. "For now, you should start notifying your appointees and working on getting their formal acceptances so we can get those jobs filled. Actually, let's back up a little. The coronation is your first big step. Getting your court and staff set and in order while establishing authority and keeping the peace is your next step. And after that, your focus must be taking action to help your subjects and the kingdom as a whole thrive."

I pressed the heel of one hand against my temple. I was starting to get a headache.

"But first things first," Maxen said. "I'll work on the coronation ceremony."

He stood, looking down at his tablet and swiping across the screen. I rose, too. I needed to ask him something, but it was a question I'd been dreading. He turned as if to go.

"Uh, Maxen?"

He lowered the tablet and looked up at me.

"Where should I establish myself for . . . you know, work?"

His eyes hardened, but only slightly. If he suggested I take over his mother's office suite, I was going to have to refuse. There had to be somewhere else.

Maxen shifted his gaze to Oliver. "Would you show her to the offices of the Head Administrator?" To me, he said, "It's a good layout. We can have it redecorated to your liking."

He didn't wait for a response but absorbed himself in the tasks on his tablet and left.

"What happened to the head administrator?" I asked my father.

"She's Raleigh's wife."

"Oh." I'd known that, but somehow hadn't made the connection.

Oliver, along with Emmaline and a dozen of her troops, escorted me to Raleigh's wife's former office suite. It had a small reception room with a desk, which led into a well-appointed sitting room with a fireplace, and beyond a large office furnished in oak. A skinny door revealed an attached private bathroom. Thank the gods, there wasn't much in the way of personal items. And not five minutes after I arrived, three pages showed up, sent by Maxen, to clear out the desk and possessions of the former occupant. Ten minutes later, they were gone.

Another page, a young woman of maybe seventeen with a build too thin for a full-blooded Carraig, arrived with a tablet. "This is yours to keep, Your Majesty," she said. "I was told to stay here. I'll be your runner, should you wish to summon anyone. I'll await your orders at the reception desk. Just lift that phone and press the large button at the top to ring me." She pointed to the hardwired phone on the edge of the desk.

I nodded, eyed the phone, and thumbed the power button on the device she'd handed me.

"I'll be in my office putting together a plan for security," Oliver said. He slipped out along with the page and closed the door behind them.

I stood for a moment, alone in the inner office. Behind me, there was a glass-paned door that led out to a small courtyard with a hawthorn tree and a stone bench. Planter boxes were filled with brightly colored flowers. Birds flitted around in the warm Faerie sunshine, and for a moment I was tempted to go out and sit. But I couldn't afford such a luxury.

The tablet booted up, and I plugged it into the cord that connected to a port. With a little notification ping, a document icon popped up. I opened it and found it was Maxen's list of positions and possible candidates. I scanned the list, trying to decide where to start. I only had one formally filled—Oliver as Head of Security—and about a bazillion left to go. At least, that was what it felt like.

For a fleeting moment, I allowed myself to think of Jasper—his golden eyes, the warmth of his hands, and the touch of his lips. I knew he had important work to do, but for a few selfish seconds, I wished I could look forward to seeing him. But I had no idea when we'd cross paths again.

With a stifled sigh, I faced the list on the tablet. I decided to start with Head Administrator, which was an important and broad-reaching position. Maxen had suggested Amalie, a distant relative of his on his father's side. I didn't really know much more than her face and name and that she, like Maxen, had been trained as a diplomat. He'd seemed confident she'd be willing to serve. I lifted the phone and asked my page to summon Amalie.

While I was waiting, I scanned the rest of the list, mentally trying to rank them in order of difficulty. Two appointments popped up, one with a tailor. The other was with Maxen. A moment later one more appeared, and my heart did a hard thump. It was a fortress-wide meeting, summoning all subjects to the auditorium at eight o'clock that night. The coronation.

I didn't have much time to ponder it because Amalie showed up a few seconds later. With raven hair, large eyes, and great curves, she was strikingly pretty, though she didn't look a thing like Maxen.

"Your Majesty," she said, spreading the skirt of her simple A-line dress with her fingertips as she sank into a lovely curtsy.

"Please rise and join me," I said. I indicated the seat across from me. "Your promptness is appreciated."

I watched her, trying to gauge how she felt about me on the throne, as she sat, placed her hands in her lap, and looked at me with a pleasant expression. I stifled a sigh. This was probably her practiced diplomat-at-rest face.

"You're related to Maxen," I said.

Her brows twitched the tiniest bit, as if she was expecting me to say more. When I didn't, she nodded. "Yes. We are distant cousins."

"How do you feel about the death of Marisol Lothlorien?"

Her mouth opened and then closed. She swallowed. "I was quite shocked by the whole sequence of events, from the assassination attempt on your life to the . . . death of Lady Lothlorien." Her eyes tightened, and I saw the faint pain there before she composed herself.

"It's okay to be sad," I said. "It's okay to miss her. I did not want her to die. I had a great deal of respect for her, until she tried to kill me."

Amalie blinked and nodded.

"What I need to know is, can you serve me with complete loyalty?" I asked, gazing steadily into her pretty, wide eyes.

"Yes," she said without hesitation. "I'm of the same mind as Maxen, in that I want to serve our new kingdom. It's vital that we get through these early days smoothly."

Understatement of the year.

"But you're not thrilled about me as your queen?"

"I would have thought that, in the absence of Lady Lothlorien, Maxen would rule."

A polite way of saying she wasn't stoked by the idea of the crown on my head.

"I'm sure you're not the only one," I said wryly.

She pulled herself up a little taller. "If I may speak frankly . . ."

"Please do."

"You wouldn't have been my first choice for the throne," she said. "But I think I see why King Oberon insisted on you. And if the High King sees a ruler in you, I'm more than willing to assume those qualities are there. It's just a matter of you demonstrating them, Your Majesty."

I tilted my head. Had she just said she expected me to prove myself? Faint irritation prickled through me, but it quickly dissipated. She was being honest, and I needed straightforward people around me. I suspected every Carraig subject was waiting for me to prove myself, too, so I couldn't fault her for the sentiment.

"Do you have the skills and knowledge to carry out the duties of Head Administrator for the Carraig Sidhe?" I asked.

"Absolutely," she said.

I was fairly certain she'd been aiming for something much more in her career than the domestic position I was offering her. "But this wouldn't be your first choice, would it?"

"Well . . . no. My more recent training was in diplomacy, and I was being groomed for foreign relations."

"If you can help get things running inside the fortress, I would like to see you transition to a diplomatic role," I said.

Assuming Faerie would be in a state where we actually had a *need* for ambassadors.

She gave me a careful smile. "I would appreciate that."

"And I appreciate your willingness to serve," I said. "Welcome aboard."

I stood, and she rose, too. I extended my hand across the desk. She looked a little surprised but accepted my offer of a handshake.

After Amalie left, I flopped back, looked up at the ceiling, and let out a whooshing breath. Damn, but it took a lot of energy to be so formal.

I pushed myself forward and looked at the list. Two down. I scanned for more low-hanging fruit on the list. Ah, Royal Chef. That would be an easy ask—I planned to see if the current Chef would continue in his position—though of course there was no guarantee he'd agree.

I rang my page to fetch the man, who arrived in his white uniform and smelling of onions and fresh herbs. A man a bit younger than Oliver, he seemed a bit stunned to be sitting in my office. But he appeared to have no problem with me, and his greatest agitation was being pulled unexpectedly away from his kitchen. Our conversation was short and with a positive outcome. I dismissed him five minutes after he arrived.

Before I could summon another victim, the phone on my desk rang. I picked it up.

"Yes?"

"Your Majesty, it's time for your fitting," said the voice of the page, Jaci, who'd taken the temporary role of my receptionist.

"Oh." I'd lost track of time, and an appointment had crept up on me.

"Your stylist is here to do final measurements."

"Ah. Okay. Please send her—him?—in."

"Her name is Vera," Jaci said in a low voice, as if trying not to be awkward in front of the stylist.

I was already smiling when Vera swept in. She'd helped me get ready for a little voyage into the Duergar realm a few months back, and though she and I couldn't have been more different, I'd enjoyed her.

"Your Majesty," she addressed me, bending into a deep curtsy.

"Vera," I said. "I'm happy to see you."

"I'm pleased to see you as well, Queen Petra," she said, and as far as I could tell, she sincerely meant it.

She'd come in wheeling a covered garment cart. She lifted the sheet and brought out a dress. It was a creamy-white gown that appeared to be sewn and embellished with bronze thread. The neckline was a halter style, and it had a narrow A-line skirt. It was unfussy yet incredibly elegant.

"I knew you wouldn't want frills," she said. "But obviously I wanted something regal for your coronation."

I nodded, took the dress, and went into the bathroom to change into it. When I emerged, she'd placed a little square riser on the floor. She had me step up onto it, and then she moved around me, making little adjustments and sticking pins into the fabric here and there. There was a narrow mirror on a stand, so I could see how the gown looked. She'd selected a perfect shade of white for my skin tone, and the bronze details accentuated the tawny yellow in my eyes.

"It's really quite lovely," I said.

"Oh, this is nothing," she said around a pin she held in her teeth. "Wait 'til you see the robe that goes over it. And the crown, of course."

She finished with the pins and went back to the cart. Pulling up a garment bag, she revealed a robe that must have been made completely out of the bronze-colored threads. It was edged with white-flecked brown fur. The upper part that draped from my neck to my elbows was positively encrusted with opals. The design was repeated around the bottom hem.

When Vera settled it around my shoulders, I swore it weighed fifty pounds. She slipped a bronze rope belt around my waist and cinched it.

I stared at my reflection. Even with my simple braid, no makeup, and no crown, I couldn't argue that she had indeed succeeded in making me look regal.

"Once again, I'm in awe of your skill," I said. "Especially on such short notice."

She leaned in, speaking across the back of her hand as if telling me a secret. "I had these pieces started even before there was any mention of a coronation ceremony."

I gave a short laugh. "Still, that only gave you, what, a couple days' head start? It's positively gorgeous."

She beamed at the compliment.

"We'll do a final fitting right before the ceremony this evening."

She helped me out of the cape, and I changed out of the dress in the bathroom and tried not to think about facing the entire population of Carraig Sidhe.

"Your contribution is deeply appreciated," I said.

She gave me a little bow as she left with her covered garment cart.

I didn't have time to meet with any more candidates before my appointment with Maxen, so I asked my page to figure out where Oliver was. I wanted a moment alone with my father before the ceremony. While I waited, I stared at the list of positions that were still vacant and tried to ignore the uneasiness I felt about finding suitable people to fulfill all of those duties. Not just suitable people, but Carraig who didn't have strong objections to calling me Queen.

I'd had a few victories, of course, and some who'd stepped up—like Emmaline and her student army—were a welcome surprise. But the little time I'd spent in the corridors of the fortress left me with the distinct sense that the majority were not with me. Sure, most of them bowed and curtsied, but I could see it in the hardness in their eyes: most didn't want me in charge. I suspected there existed two groups within the population of my dissidents: those like Raleigh who saw me as a traitorous usurper and still felt loyal to Marisol Lothlorien, and those who could perhaps swallow the loss of Marisol but wanted Maxen to wear the crown.

My phone rang, and I grabbed it while the ring was still sounding.

"Oliver Maguire is here for you," my page said.

"Please send him in."

My father entered and bowed.

I snorted and waved a hand. "You don't need to do that."

He straightened. "Maybe not when we're alone, but I need to follow protocol whenever there are eyes on us. Better to practice."

Angling the chair across from me so there was room for his long legs, he settled into the seat, interlaced his fingers, and brought his palms to the back of his head, elbows splayed out. It was a casual posture on the surface, but his sharp-eyed gaze said there was nothing relaxed about this man.

"How did things go today?" he asked.

"They went well, all things considered. We filled a couple of posts."

I picked up a pen and rolled it between my fingers, and Oliver watched my hands for a moment.

"I'm waiting for the but," he said. "Things went well, but . . ."

I drew a long, measured breath through my nose. "I have a bad feeling about tonight. They're not happy about this out there." My eyes flitted to the closed door and then back to Oliver. "If I had to guess, I'd say there are very, very few New Gargs who think I have any business at all taking the throne. Emmaline and the youngsters like the idea of being rebels, of supporting a strong fighter but an underdog. But the rest? A handful of them are politely tolerating me. And that's about the best I can say about my so-called support."

He nodded slowly. "I'd say that's about right."

I tossed the pen down and flipped my hands over in a palms-up gesture of frustration and helplessness. "So what the hell do I do?"

"Like Maxen said. Stay alive through the coronation, assert your authority to keep the peace, get your administration established, make sure everyone's needs are met, and figure out how to make the kingdom grow. The best you can. In that order."

I grunted and gave him a long-suffering look. "I was hoping for, oh I don't know, some specifics."

He unclasped his hands from behind his head and shifted his weight forward, leaning toward me. "It's my honest estimation that if you can do those things, everyone will accept you. Eventually."

"I guess for the moment I'll just have to focus on getting through tonight, then," I said. "How are things looking for security?"

His face tightened ever so slightly, and my heart dropped about a foot in my chest. Whatever he was going to say next, I was pretty sure it wasn't going to be great news.

"I'm challenged finding trustworthy people," he said.

"Are you being too stringent in your selection process?" That would be like Oliver. He didn't take any crap from people in general, and faced with the task of protecting his own daughter, well . . . I could imagine he might be a bit too rigid about who he deemed worthy.

"No," he said bluntly. "I've loosened my expectations considerably."

I leaned forward, my eyes wide with alarm. "You haven't found *anyone?*"

"I've recruited two for sure."

I didn't know what to say for a moment. "I didn't want to attend the ceremony with Aurora on my back, but I think I should."

"Probably wise," he agreed, which just made my stomach knot itself tighter. He rested his elbows on his knees and peered at me intently. "You're right to be worried, Petra. I don't want you to become sick with paranoia, but I think it's a good idea to stay on your toes tonight. Make sure Maxen is near you. Use your baby battalion. Put them along the front of the stage. If someone comes at you personally, strike first. You have the skill. And of course I will do everything I can to back you up and prevent a shitstorm in the first place."

I closed my eyes, pushed my fingers against my eyelids, and then pulled my hands down my face.

"Okay," I said, digging for some resolve. "Guess I'll be taking the throne with my sword drawn. Only figuratively . . . I hope."

My tablet pinged with a calendar alert, and two seconds later my phone rang. "Crap, that's probably Maxen."

I answered, and my page affirmed my guess.

Oliver rose, gave me a nod of encouragement, and departed. Maxen stepped into my office as soon as my father was gone.

"We don't have a lot of time, so I hope you'll allow me to dispense with pleasantries," Maxen said.

"No, please don't make me skip the pleasantries," I moaned, going for a little joke.

He didn't even look up, let alone crack a smile. Okay, then.

He pushed one of the two tablets he'd brought across my desk. "This is a diagram of where everyone will be positioned."

Maxen outlined what would happen at the ceremony. The most significant thing about it was that Maxen himself would place the crown on my head. Otherwise the whole thing was pretty bare-bones.

"I don't think there would be much tolerance for pageantry," he said, his voice tight.

My heart thumped uneasily. "I'm sure you're right," I said quietly. I waited for his eyes to meet mine. "I'm going to be wearing Aurora."

His brow creased. "I encourage you not to."

"I've already decided," I said. "I don't want to, but given the general attitude toward me at the moment, I can't stand up there unarmed with the entire population of the fortress in the same room with me."

His jaw tightened, but he didn't try to talk me out of it.

I couldn't help thinking back to when Maxen had prepared me for the opening ceremony of the Battle of Champions. So much had happened since then.

We talked through more logistics, and before I knew it, our hour was past. It was time to start getting ready.

Emmaline and her troops escorted me to my quarters, and Vera and a couple of stylists showed up a few minutes later. The next two hours passed in a flurry of fabric, last-minute tailoring adjustments, hair styling, and makeup application.

I slung my scabbard over the lovely opal-studded robe, and to her credit, Vera didn't even wince at the eyesore I'd added to her ensemble. She helped me into the heels I'd have to endure for the ceremony and then rose and stepped back.

She curtsied solemnly. "You're ready for the coronation, Your Majesty."

My pulse kicked up. The moment had come. I was going to officially take the throne of the Carraig Sidhe kingdom.

Chapter 11

MAXEN DIRECTED THE movements and logistics that took place before the ceremony, for which I was grateful. I knew I could leave that part completely in his hands, and he'd make the right decisions.

The corridors of the fortress had been eerily quiet as I'd made my way with my entourage to the backstage area of the auditorium. The ceremony wasn't set to start for another twenty minutes, but obviously everyone was eager to claim a seat.

Oliver, dressed in his battle ranks uniform with a tailored coat thrown over the ensemble, never strayed more than five feet away from me. Nicole hovered nearby, too.

I suddenly realized that we should have had a kingdom seal designed and ready for this event. The Carraig Sidhe needed official colors, emblems, livery, banners . . . small details, perhaps, but things that would nevertheless help unify our small realm. Then again, maybe such touches wouldn't have made much difference, given the unrest in the small realm.

Gods, we really were *small*. By far the tiniest kingdom in Faerie, both in population and territory. We couldn't do much about increasing the population, not quickly, anyway, but we'd have to look into carving out more area for the kingdom. As an official kingdom, we had the right to expand.

My mind was trying to spin out with the long list of things yet to be done. I inhaled sharply, bringing in my focus. All of that would have to wait. Tonight, I needed to do my damnedest to make sure the fortress didn't riot as Maxen attempted to place the crown on my head.

Emmaline remained with me backstage, but save for half a dozen student soldiers, the rest of her young battalion filed out. On Oliver's suggestion, Maxen was sending them to line the floor along the front of the stage.

I edged over to Maxen, who was consulting one of his tablets. I leaned in and kept my voice low. "What's the mood out there?"

He looked up, his sapphire-blue eyes distracted. "The tension is palpable."

At least he wasn't going to blow smoke up my ass. My gaze skirted over to Oliver. He had his people, few as they were, out there, watching for threats.

"Super," I muttered.

"I'm making some last-minute changes to my speech," he said. "I'm going to shorten it. I also set up a reception immediately to follow. I'm hoping the prospect of food and drink might be some small placation." His tone clearly said he had doubts about how effective that would be.

My insides pulled tighter. I subtly pressed my hands against the sides of my thighs, trying to wick off the sweat slicking my palms. I wasn't even half this edgy when I'd faced the arena for the Battle of Champions. Perhaps it was because I knew I would only have to face one foe there. Out in the fortress, there could be hundreds of enemies waiting to take me down.

"Five minutes until go," Maxen said.

I nodded.

He directed the handful of people who would be on stage to their marks. A few minutes later, the curtains at the front edge of the stage swept aside, and everyone backstage except for me, Oliver, Maxen, and Maxen's handful of assistants and pages filed out.

The stage was set up with a dais that supported a throne of sorts. The raised platform was covered with shimmering white fabric. I'd recognized the chair as the one Marisol usually had set up at the head of the largest table in banquet rooms when she'd hosted official functions. The dark wood had been hastily sanded and repainted the same bronze as the details on my clothing. Standing backstage, I caught a chemical whiff of the barely dry paint.

The crown was propped on a little display stand to one side of the podium Maxen would stand behind to say a few words. I'd asked him if I should speak, and he said it would be better if I didn't. He said it was a time to establish me as the figurehead of the kingdom, for the Carraig to see me as a ruler. He was afraid that, given the circumstances, any kind of speech would be seen as me attempting to ingratiate myself to my subjects.

I figured the decision also had something to do with the fact that my public speaking skills were shit.

"It's time," Maxen said. A page took his tablets and scurried off to the side.

I leveled my chin, blew out a long breath, and waited for the curtain at the back of the stage to lift. Flanked by Maxen and my father, I walked slowly down the carpet runner that created a path along the right side of the dais. When the three of us reached the throne, we paused.

For a split second, you could have heard a pin drop in the auditorium. Then the entire room shifted and rose to their feet in a rustle of fabric and shuffling shoes. I let out a small breath. I'd been half expecting that no one would stand, that the entire population would sit on their hands and stare at me like children who'd been forced into their dress clothes and marched to some distant relative's wedding. Or, perhaps, funeral.

Maxen waited while I placed my hand in Oliver's and he helped me up the short step onto the dais. I sat on the chair that smelled of paint fumes and faced the completely packed auditorium. The audience took their seats. Oliver stepped up to stand beside me, while Maxen continued on to the podium and the sparkling crown.

Resisting the urge to squint into the glaring stage lights, I tried to spot faces I recognized. Or faces that looked like they wanted my head on a spike. I could make out the rows and rows of people, but all other details were lost in shadow. As I squared my shoulders and folded my hands in my lap, cold sweat rolled down my spine.

Maxen began to speak about a new era for the New Gargoyles, making history, and other platitudes, but I only partially registered his words. My gaze skipped over the crowd. The mood of the room was grim with a side of anticipation. I could feel it in the stillness, the frigid silence. Oliver shifted his weight beside me. He sensed it, too.

With the short speech done, Maxen reached for the crown. It was so quiet, his footfalls across the stage seemed to echo in the huge space. He approached me, holding the crown in both hands. His lips were parted, and he seemed slightly breathless.

Stopping just short of the dais, he bowed. Then he stepped up and came to stand directly in front of me. I leaned forward and dipped my chin slightly, and he lifted the crown and settled it on my head.

Just as he was taking his hands away, I spotted movement beyond his elbow.

"Shit," I muttered. A few bulky figures were making their way from the seats toward the stage. They were coming fast.

Quick glances left and right showed more approaching from either side.

Oliver drew his sword. The crowd was beginning to react, the murmurs of voices growing. A few cried out in alarm. Some rose to try to escape.

Emmaline shouted a quick command, and the student soldiers all drew their weapons. Stone armor flowed over their skin.

I stood but didn't reach for Aurora. Instead, I raised my arms.

"Stop!" I thundered, trying to be heard above the noise. "Stop now, or you sentence yourself to death. I command you!"

The young soldiers moved to intercept the would-be attackers, and my heart clutched. Please, gods, don't let them kill the kids. The first couple of dissenters reached the area in front of the stage. They wielded clubs, using them to knock aside Emmaline's soldiers' swords, though a few of the students managed to get some slashes in, and one of the men screamed and clutched at the side of his neck.

I pulled magic and formed stone armor. Chaos began to erupt in the auditorium as others decided to join in the attack on the stage and more seemed to want to flee.

Oliver moved in front of the dais and crouched in a ready stance, turning his wrist to swing his huge broadsword.

Pulling the crown off my head, I tossed it back on the throne and kicked off my shoes. With an anguished growl, I drew Aurora and stood behind my father. The attackers were trying to avoid hurting Emmaline's troops, but the kids were defending the stage with full force, and the violence was escalating. I had to do something before the situation completely unraveled.

Oliver lunged forward and swung at the first attacker to make it past Emmaline's people. The young man with wild green eyes was no match for my father.

"Make them drop back!" I shouted at Emmaline.

She gave the command, and all of the students retreated up to the stage.

I wanted to scream at the idiots flying at us. They could object to me all they wanted. But they were putting innocent people in danger. And they were forcing my hand. I would have to order the execution of anyone who raised a weapon against me. I'd already given fair warning, and now I'd have to follow through.

Anger, despair, and frustration flowed through me in the background. But I couldn't afford to give my emotions full attention. Oliver had worked over the next attacker to break through, forcing the man back and off the stage's edge. My father didn't want to kill anyone, but we both knew any attackers who survived and got caught would face the ultimate punishment.

My entire body was vibrating. My sword arm shook so hard, I gripped Aurora with both hands to try to steady the trembling. At first I thought it was my pent-up anger, but something was happening in the auditorium.

It felt like a tremor, but the ground wasn't shaking.

Oliver whipped around. "Do you feel that?" he shouted at me, his eyes round.

"Yeah," I said, shifting my gaze beyond my father.

The chaos and commotion seemed to slow. Everyone else was noticing it. What the hell was going on?

Suddenly a shockwave punched through the auditorium. I didn't know how else to describe the invisible force that launched me clear off the floor.

The back of my head hit the edge of the throne's seat, and white light flooded my vision. The light shimmered and then dissipated, and a familiar sensation swept through me. I was in the body of that ancient warrior woman, the one I'd inhabited when I'd killed Marisol. But unlike last time, I was only there for a brief moment, just long enough to recognize it.

I gasped as if I'd breached the surface of the water after being held under. Blinking rapidly, I wildly swiveled my gaze. I was back in the auditorium. The fighting had stopped. Everyone else was looking around, their faces as dazed as I felt.

"What in the name of the gods . . . ?" Oliver trailed off. He squinted back at me, then turned to look out at the auditorium seats. "Petra, I think we're under attack."

I frowned, not understanding. Of course we were under attack. We'd been trying to hold our ground for the past several minutes.

"There!" Oliver pointed with his sword and then took a running leap off the edge of the stage. He shoved people out of the way as he tried to make his way up one of the aisles.

The house lights flickered. Then every bulb in the place lit up, probably flipped on by one of Maxen's people. I looked through slitted eyelids, trying to see what had caught my father's attention.

There, at the top of the stairs, stood Finvarra. He held something bright, faceted, and pulsing in one hand. White curls of smoke flowed off it like mist from dry ice. The other arm was at his side, and it was missing a hand and the lower part of his forearm. That was my doing.

With a strangled cry, I hiked up my dress with one hand and tried to charge forward with Aurora held aloft. Hands grabbed me from behind.

"No, Petra!" It was Maxen.

I let go of the fabric to try to peel his fingers away.

"It's Finvarra with the Stone of Fal," I said, but I wasn't sure if Maxen heard me. The auditorium was erupting in shouts as people began to recognize the banished Unseelie High King. I whipped around to face Maxen. "We need to capture him! If we can hold him and get Jasper here, we'll—"

Maxen squinted at me as if I were mad, and then another shockwave hit. Same as before, it sent me into that other place, that other body. Then I returned, this time still on my feet.

My vision cleared just in time to see Finvarra tuck the misting Stone of Fal under his shortened arm and whip his good hand up to toss a small, sparkling object into the air. A blinding flash burst outward.

I knew it was too late, but I hurled myself off the stage anyway, struggling to move with the heavy robe on and the skirt of my dress twisting around my legs.

The light faded, and Finvarra was gone. He'd used a portal jewel to spirit himself away. Just as he'd tossed the small orb, I'd seen his face. It was tight and red with fury.

I stopped at the base of the stage, still staring at the place where he'd been. Oliver had made it about three quarters of the way up the aisle. Now, he turned to race back down to me.

Everyone gazed around, stunned, and for the moment the insurgents appeared to have forgotten they were trying to kill me.

Oliver grabbed my arm and started hustling me toward the exit to the side of the stage.

I didn't try to fight him. "What just happened? Did you see?"

"He tried to use the Stone of Fal on us," Maxen said. "He attempted to activate it."

I twisted to look over my shoulder at him. He'd snatched Nicole and was right behind us. "Are we . . .?" My blood chilled as it all began to sink in.

Maxen's face was screwed up in a look of concentration. "Do you feel any loyalty to Finvarra?" he asked.

"*Hell* no," I spat.

Nicole made a horrified face.

"I don't either," my father said. "If that was truly the Stone of Fal, it must have misfired."

Oliver pushed me ahead of him through the door. The four of us began running, my bare feet slapping the tiles. He pulled me around a corner and sped up, half-carrying, half-dragging me with him.

"Where are we going?" I panted.

"My apartment," he said. "It's the safest place in the fortress for you right now."

He was right, but that was going to have to change. I needed secure quarters of my own. It wouldn't do for the queen to hide out in her daddy's place.

I winced as images flashed through my mind. "Did you feel as though you went somewhere else?"

Maxen slid a look at me, and I knew the answer, though it took him a few seconds to respond. "It was . . . an odd hallucination."

Oliver gave me a grim, pursed-lip glance.

"Yeah, I felt like I was a character in a scene." Nicole passed a hand down the side of her face, as if reassuring herself that she was in her own body.

I blew out a noisy hiss of a breath through clenched teeth.

I looked at Oliver. "I think you're right. The Stone didn't work on us," I said. "He tried it twice, and it didn't work."

No one had the breath to respond. None of us had any further answers, anyway.

We'd reached Oliver's quarters. He passed his hand over the door, and it unlocked for him. He pushed me inside, rougher than necessary, but I could tell his adrenaline was still pumping full force.

I gulped air. "I need to get a message to Oberon," I said.

"I'll do it," Maxen said.

My father gave me a hard look. "Don't leave here until I come for you. Don't open the door for anyone."

Maxen and Oliver slipped out, and I went and bolted the door and then turned to my sister. She'd wrapped her arms around herself, and her eyes had gone glassy.

"Are you okay?" I asked.

She nodded, but she looked pale.

I took her elbow and guided her to Oliver's chair. "Here, sit down. I'll get you some water."

As I filled a glass at the kitchenette sink, my thoughts tumbled and my stomach churned. I took the water to Nicole.

"What's the Stone you were talking about?" she asked.

"The Stone of Fal," I said.

I pulled off the heavy coronation robe, and having nowhere else to put it, I draped it over the kitchenette's small peninsula counter. I happened to glance down at my bare arm and noticed the fine hairs on my skin were standing on end and moving back and forth in waves. There was another sensation, too, this one through my entire body. A tiny electric current seemed to be sweeping through me in a rhythm, keeping time with my arm hair.

I turned to Nicole, who was sitting on the edge of the recliner with parted lips and splotched cheeks.

"Do you feel that?" I brushed my hand down my arm.

She slanted a look up at the ceiling and squinted. "I do feel something. A little shiver. Maybe it's the delayed effect of the Stone. Maybe it takes time to work." Her gaze sharpened on me, her face fearful.

"I don't think so," I said. "Finvarra wouldn't have left in a pissy huff if it'd worked. He'd have stuck around to see us grovel."

I went over to her and gently pressed her shoulder back, encouraging her to relax into the chair. "Drink some water and try to take slow breaths. I don't want you to get any more upset."

She sipped from the glass and scooted deeper into the recliner. "Thank you, Petra. I mean, ugh! Damnit."

A faint smile tugged at my lips. "It's okay. Just don't say those words to—"

"Anyone who might exact an oath from me," she supplied. "I know, I know. I just forget the rules sometimes when I'm stressed."

She absently dropped one hand to her belly, which at this early point in her pregnancy was still ballet-dancer flat.

I was just beginning to wonder how long we'd have to sit there waiting when I heard someone approach the door. I drew Aurora, even though only Oliver could access these quarters. I didn't trust anything anymore.

"It's me, Petra," came my father's voice just before the door unlatched.

He slipped inside and shut the door behind him. In one hand he held my discarded crown. He lifted the jeweled bronze circlet. "Emmaline saved it and gave it to me."

I didn't really want the crown, but he extended his arm, offering it. I reluctantly claimed it.

"Are her people all okay?" I asked.

"No deaths," he said. He gestured impatiently to the crown. "You might as well put that on. It's the safest place for it."

It was the last thing I wanted to do, but I settled it on top of my head anyway. "Is there still fighting?"

He shook his head. "The situation's been diffused. Maxen reached Oberon. He's summoned you to go to him right away and give your account of what happened here with Finvarra and the Stone. We've got a clear path to a doorway."

"How many of the attackers were caught?" I asked, my voice low.

His mouth hardened. "Only a handful captured. The rest of them escaped the fortress through doorways. They're probably hiding out in other realms. We'll have to put a price on their heads, of course, as soon as we know for sure which ones got away."

I didn't want to think about having to enforce the law on my would-be assassins. It would have to be dealt with, but for the moment I had to answer the High King's summons.

"I don't know the sigils to get into any Summerlands doorways," I said.

Oliver pulled a folded piece of paper from in inner pocket of the ceremonial overcoat he still wore. "Yes, you do."

I lifted my hand to take the note but then dropped my arm. "It seems a very bad time to leave the fortress," I said, shaking my head gravely. "My first duty is here, to the Carraig."

Oliver looked like he wanted to agree but said, "Petra, when the Seelie High King summons you, you have to go."

I closed my eyes briefly. "You're right. I'll get back here as quickly as I can." Turning to my sister, I put on what I hoped looked like an encouraging smile. "Rest. You're safe here, and I'm sure Maxen will come for you soon."

"Be careful, Petra," she said. "Hurry back."

I nodded and sheathed Aurora.

Oliver placed his hand on the door handle. "Ready?"

I took the folded note with the sigils. "Let's go."

He pushed the door open, and as soon as I stepped into the hallway, Emmaline and her troops, plus a few full-fledged Carraig soldiers, surrounded me. Oliver led the way as the group hurried me through the corridors to a courtyard. It was the same one I'd charged through, not knowing if my father was alive or dead, to escape the Duergar when Periclase had taken the fortress.

My guards took me right up to the arch. I unfolded the piece of paper and studied the sigils for a second, memorizing them. Then I began drawing the shapes in the air and murmuring the words that would take me into the netherwhere.

Suddenly aware of the soft grass under my feet, I remembered I wasn't wearing any shoes. Too late. I stepped forward, and the chill embrace of the void claimed me.

Chapter 12

THE NETHERWHERE SPILLED me out beneath a giant maple tree just beyond the drawbridge of the Summerlands castle. The green expanse behind me was riddled with dark craters, evidence of the continued Unseelie attack. I didn't linger to survey the damage.

Using both hands, I reached for the hem of my skirt, hiked it up to my knees, and sprinted for the stronghold. Someone saw me coming, and the bridge began to lower rapidly. It crashed down, and I scampered across, punching through the thick bubble of the protective magical ward.

Inside, a uniformed page in the livery of Oberon and Titania's realm was running into the foyer where I stood.

He skidded to a halt and bowed hastily. "Your Majesty," he said. "I was sent to bring you to Oberon right away." Before turning to lead me to the High King, his eyes flicked down to my bare feet and registered quickly-restrained surprise.

I let my skirts fall back into their intended shape and tried not to think about the soft slap of my feet on the flagstones. I probably presented an interesting sight, my dress and hair mussed from the fight, and my crown on as if I were playing Queen. Usually rulers reserved their crowns for wearing at formal events. Not that I really cared about idle gossip, but I could just imagine people whispering about how the new Carraig queen ran around with the Champion's sword on her back, her crown on her wild hair, and no shoes.

The page took me straight to Oberon's study, where the High King was pacing the carpet in front of his desk. He was the only one in the room.

I made a quick curtsy. "Your Majesty."

"Finvarra used the Stone in the fortress," Oberon said, dispensing with all niceties.

"Yes, he appeared during my coronation," I said. I swallowed, trying to catch my breath after my dash into the castle. "I believe he tried to use it twice."

Oberon held up a hand and looked past me. "Hold on, I want him to hear what you have to say."

I twisted to see a slim man with long white hair entering the office.

My brows lifted. "Eldon?" I turned back around to look at Oberon.

The High King nodded once. "We have a new ally."

I narrowed my eyes at the Fae sorcerer as he approached us. He skirted a look at me, his expression unreadable. Stopping a few feet away, he bent in a quick bow. He was here, which meant he'd abandoned the Unseelie as he'd promised, but I wasn't sure I trusted him.

"Your majesties," he said.

"Now, tell us exactly what happened," Oberon said to me.

"Of course, Your Highness," I said. "Finvarra appeared in the auditorium of the fortress during my coronation ceremony. He had an object that must have been the Stone of Fal, and he appeared to try to invoke its power."

Oberon stopped me, asking me to describe the Stone. I gave him as thorough a description as I could recall.

My gaze found Eldon as I continued. "Something happened when he tried to use it. I went to . . . another place. I inhabited the body of a female warrior, in a place and time that felt, well, old. Ancient, even. Others had similar experiences. In fact, I believe it's possible every

Carraig went to that place, too."

Eldon turned to Oberon. "I believe it's the god blood, Your Majesty," he said in his thick brogue. "The Fomoire, is my guess."

A bell went off in my head. The Fomoire were the predecessors to the Tuatha De Danann. Actually, the Fomoire were the gods who were predecessors to the Tuatha's predecessors. In the legends, the Nemedians, seafaring gods, had eradicated the Fomoire. Then the Tuatha had come along to do the same to the Nemedians. These were stories, or they had been, until I'd learned that the Tuatha weren't just myths. They were very real.

Oberon's forehead creased. "Describe exactly how it felt," he said to me.

I explained the shockwaves, the feeling of disappearing from my surroundings and then coming back. "And I believe Finvarra tried again. Same result. He looked extremely angry by the time he left. He used a portal jewel to escape before we could get to him."

The High King's eyes gleamed, and his lips parted as his breath came quicker. "Do you realize what this means?"

"Finvarra has used two of his three chances with the Stone," Eldon said. "And the Stone seems not to work on the Carraig."

I inhaled a sharp breath.

The Fae sorcerer continued, "And further, it seemed to have activated the god blood in the whole population of Carraig and others with stone blood."

I shook my head. "What does that mean? It felt like a body-switching hallucination, and one that we can't control. What good does that do us?"

Oberon's tongue darted out to moisten his lips. "It means the ancient blood runs through your people. It means you have the power of gods. If you can learn to use it, you can fight—"

"The Tuatha De Danann as equals." I finished his sentence in a whisper. "Or something close, anyway."

The High King and Eldon stared at me.

"But I don't know anything about it. I have no idea how to use it," I said. "If it's true, I don't know that it actually carries any power at all."

"It does," Eldon said, his voice low. He cut a sharp look at the High King before locking his intense gaze on me. "The Fomoire didn't die. I heard whispers of this eons ago, that they disappeared underground to slumber, waiting for the time when they could awaken their power and take their revenge. Patiently abiding until the time came for them to take revenge on the usurpers who took their land. To emerge and reclaim their place as the gods of the realm. The god race who defeated the Fomoire is now gone, but the Tuatha took their place."

Shivers cascaded up my spine, over my scalp, and down my arms.

The door opened again, and I glanced at it, still trying to process what Eldon had said. When Jasper appeared in the doorway, all I could do was gape for a second or two. He gave me a broad smile, and I pulled my lips in between my teeth and clamped down to hold in the little squeal of happiness that wanted to leak out. Warmth spread through me.

"Glasgow here reported a strange phenomenon around the time Finvarra would have been making his appearance in the fortress," Oberon said.

"Yes," I said. "He has some stone blood, even though he is—was—a Duergar subject."

My eyes followed Jasper as he joined us. I wanted to run to him. I pressed my hands to my sides, my fingers itching to reach for him and tangle in his hair. I still hadn't completely gotten over seeing him dead on the lawn outside the castle. I was forever in Melusine's debt for bringing him back.

"Aye, Your Highness," Jasper said, his Old World accent a much milder, softer version of Eldon's. "I felt myself leave my body. I stood on a hilly green holding an unfamiliar sword, facing people I'd never seen before. The armor I wore was in a very, very old style. Primitive, almost."

"The descriptions match," Eldon said. "From the reports, it sounds as if it may have affected all those with enough stone blood to form armor."

"We need to discover what this so-called god blood can do," Oberon said. "And we need to do it quickly."

Something suddenly occurred to me. "Your Majesty, Marisol Lothlorien spoke of more New Gargs. She said there were more of us in hiding, waiting to be brought back into the fold. To be honest, I wasn't sure it was true. But if it is, that means there could be even more of us who can invoke the power of the Fomoire."

Oberon clapped his hands together sharply a couple of times and let out a low laugh. I drew back a little, his sudden joy taking me by surprise. "Petra Maguire. Do you have any other lovely surprises for me?" The gleam had returned to his eyes, and I realized that it had probably been a very long time since the High King had felt he might have the upper hand against Finvarra and the looming threat of the Tuatha.

"Uh, nothing more that I can think of at the moment, Your Highness," I said.

But the handsome High King's grin was infectious, and I felt a small tugging at the corners of my mouth.

"Well, I suppose that's understandable, and I shouldn't be so greedy," Oberon said. He wagged a finger at me. "But you are now my lucky charm."

I glanced at Jasper and Eldon. Jasper's golden eyes glinted with amusement and pride. But Eldon's face was guarded. He peered at Oberon with tight lines bracketing the corners of his mouth, distrust that wasn't quite disguised. That cooled my mood. Was there some bad blood between these two men? Or was there something more I should be wary of?

"I know you must return to your own realm and attend to things there," Oberon said to me. "You're free to depart, if you wish. I'll be in touch again soon as we learn more about this untapped power and how we will use it."

Not waiting for Jasper and me to bow and curtsy, Oberon turned to Eldon and placed his hand on the Fae sorcerer's shoulder, drawing him toward the far side of the room. They began talking about scholars and libraries, presumably trying to come up with resources who might help them understand the power of the Fomoire that supposedly flowed through those with stone blood.

Something prickled at the back of my mind, leaving me slightly unsettled. Maybe it was the nearly fanatical glint in Oberon's eyes when we spoke of the potential power of the god blood.

My unease dissolved as I walked toward the study door at Jasper's side.

"I figured you were treasure hunting in the far reaches of Faerie, looking for the Chalice of Dagda," I said to him.

He tipped his face toward me, his golden gaze flickering to my crown and then fixing on my eyes. "I've been searching, but so far only to run into dead ends," he said. "Nice hat, by the way."

I reached up to firm the crown down on my hair. "I left in a hurry. Finvarra interrupted my coronation." And various attempts on my life.

We exited the study, and Jasper took us down the hall to a door. He held it open for me. I knew I couldn't stay long but couldn't resist stealing a minute or two with him before I faced my failed assassins in the fortress. When I realized he'd taken me to a small resting room with a vanity, a chaise lounge chair, and relaxing music, I turned to him in confusion. He flipped the lock on the door and then with cat-like swiftness had me pressed up against the tile wall with my wrists pinned over my head. Aurora's scabbard dug into my back. But I didn't care.

Jasper covered my mouth with his. My lips parted, inviting, and the tip of his tongue swept over mine. A hum of pleasure vibrated low in my throat as the kiss deepened.

He pulled back, his tri-colored eyes filling my field of vision. "Congratulations, Your Majesty, on officially taking the throne," he said, growling the words in a way that made me want to grab the front of his shirt and rip it open.

"Considering a significant portion of my subjects didn't want to see me live to the end of the ceremony, I'm not sure that's the appropriate sentiment," I said, the heat of my attraction to Jasper chilling as I recalled the events in the auditorium. The coronation had been the first step in the plan to fully take on the role of queen and begin gathering support for my reign. It'd survived it, but I wasn't sure I'd really count it a success.

He stepped back and curled his hands around mine, peering down at me with concern etching lines across his forehead and around his eyes.

I shook my head. "Don't worry, I'm handling it. It's just going to take a while to sort things out in the Carraig Sidhe kingdom."

He reached up to smooth a strand of hair behind my ear. "I wish there was something I could do to help."

I allowed myself a small smile. "That would be nice. But you have more important work to do."

He puffed his cheeks as he blew out a frustrated breath and mussed his sandy hair. "I'm nearly at my wits' end. Every lead has been a dud."

"What about Morven?"

"Morven?"

"Yeah, the Ghillie Dubh who knows just about everything about everything?"

"Oh, I knew who Morven is," Jasper said. He frowned. "I just don't trust him."

I shifted my weight.

His gaze sharpened on me. "You've used his, ah, services?"

I nodded a bit reluctantly. "On more than one occasion. It's not fun, but I've always found it was worth it. Saved my ass at least once."

He pressed his lips into a line of displeasure. "I'll go to him. If ever there was a time, it's now."

I couldn't disagree. I'd used Morven's services for far lesser needs than what Jasper sought.

Someone rapped on the door, and we both jumped guiltily.

"Occupied," Jasper called out, giving his voice a gruff edge.

Our eyes met, and I sighed. "Can't we just stay in here a while?"

He arched a brow. "You want to hang about in the restroom?"

"I think we could figure out how to have a good time in here," I said, eyeing the wide, upholstered bench set up against the wall.

"I have no doubt," he said, heat growing in his eyes.

He bent in for one more kiss, and then all too soon we were back out in the hallway. He walked me to the castle's foyer, where there was a doorway I could use to return to the fortress.

"Please send word about how it goes with . . ." I glanced around at the bustling room and lowered my voice. "With the man who knows things."

"Aye. And be on guard, Petra. I can't lose you," he said simply, his eyes full of intense sincerity.

My insides melted a bit, but standing there in such a public place, all I could do was nod.

Jasper turned to go, and I was just about to face the arch in the stone wall when someone came running through the foyer.

"Your Majesty, Queen Petra," a woman called.

It took me a moment to recognize Eunice, Finvarra's companion who'd come with me to the Summerlands seeking refuge.

She stopped in front of me, breathless. "Oh, my, oh. Thank the gods I caught you." She spoke and curtsied at the same time. "Please, Queen Petra, I know I have no right to ask anything more of you, but oh my, I just must make a request."

"What is it?"

"Allow me to come back to the fortress with you," she said. She swallowed, her eyes pleading. "There is nothing for me here. It was sheer luck I was even able to escape my room to catch you. They don't trust me."

"You're not a Carraig Sidhe, Eunice," I said. "I'm sorry, I can't take you back to the fortress. We don't allow non-subjects to reside there."

"What if I could help you?"

I crossed my arms. "Help with what?"

Her voice dropped to a whisper. "The Unseelie High King. I know his habits."

My eyes narrowed, and I took in her desperation. "Did you extend your offer to King Oberon?"

"I tried, but he never deigned to allow me audience with him."

"Okay," I said. "You may come as my guest. I can't guarantee you permanent residence in my kingdom, though."

Maybe I was making a mistake in bringing a virtual stranger back with me, but I believed her. And if she could give us an edge with Finvarra, she was more than worth the room and board in the fortress.

Her head was bobbing in fast nods. "That's fine, Your Majesty, that's fine."

I nearly asked if she needed anything from her room before I remembered she'd arrived here naked, with only the sheet from Finvarra's bed.

"Then to the fortress we go," I said, turning to the doorway.

She heaved a grateful sigh and placed her hand lightly on my shoulder. I traced the sigils and said the words, and together we stepped forward. The solid stone wall dissolved, giving way to the netherwhere.

Chapter 13

AS I STEPPED with Eunice from the void and into the foyer of the stone fortress, it occurred to me that I had no idea what I would come back to. I hadn't been gone long—less than two hours—but enough time had passed for my enemies to stir up trouble if they'd caught wind of my absence. It also occurred to me that I needed to find more private, secure doorways through which to come and go. Surely Marisol had one or two tucked away in discreet places where she was able to slip in and out without attracting notice.

But with the situation as it was in the fortress, I really wasn't in the mood to hide or skulk around. If someone wanted to come at me, they weren't going to get a second chance.

"Oh! Oh, dear my," Eunice exclaimed beside me. "This place is just lovely. The granite, the tiles, and oh, so many gemstones."

The fortress foyer was indeed beautiful, but I barely saw the intricate patterns of inlaid semi-precious stones. I was immediately on alert, trying to take in the entire grand room at once, but without appearing worried about my own safety.

To a large extent, it looked like business as usual in the fortress. Clerks were sorting notes into cubbies in the mail room to one side of the foyer. Pages scurried around. Most notable to me was the pair of soldiers—one full-fledged member of the battle ranks and the other a youngster I recognized from Emmaline's troops—who rushed to me as soon as they noticed my presence. I tensed, but they simply came to stand by me, one on each side, as if it were planned. Oliver must have stationed patrol pairs around the fortress with orders to protect me when I appeared.

I gave my guards subtle nods.

"Where to, Your Highness?" asked the older one.

"I need someone in housing to find quarters for Eunice, here, a friend of the kingdom who will be staying with us for a while," I said. I could only hope that Amalie, the newly appointed Head Administrator, actually had someone to help her with housing.

The soldier flipped his fingers at a nearby page, beckoning the girl over. She curtsied to me, and he spoke a few quick words to her. She looked curiously at Eunice.

"Please follow me, madam," the page said.

Eunice glanced at me, her face tense, and I gave her an encouraging nod. "You're safe here. Make yourself comfortable and let this young lady know if there's anything you need right away. I'll call for you when I have a moment."

Out of the corner of my eye, I noticed a young man arrive at the far end of the foyer. He stopped short and peered at me with narrowed eyes and then wheeled around to go back the way he'd come.

The page and Eunice bobbed quick curtsies and then headed away.

As we'd been standing in the foyer, more and more people had taken notice of my return.

"Did you see that man who turned around and left when he saw me?" I asked my guards.

"Yes, Your Highness," the younger said.

"I'm guessing he's not one of my supporters?"

"You guess correctly, Your Majesty," the older solder said, his face hardening in a way that reminded me of Oliver. "I suggest we make our way out of the public's eye. Your new quarters have been prepared. We'll take you there."

"Good idea," I said.

As we moved through the hallways, more pairs of soldiers joined us. They didn't say anything, they just fell in step with us. By the time we'd reached a gilded door in one of the residential wings, I was surrounded by ten guards. I appreciated the protection, but it irked me that I even needed it. And more significantly, it made me look weak. What kind of ruler needed to be protected in her own home? My mouth twisted as I silently answered my own question: One who'd taken the throne against the wishes of her people.

Four of the guards accompanied me inside my new home and made a sweep through the rooms. I trailed behind them, trying to orient myself in the unfamiliar space. Ten minutes later, I was alone, though I presumed some of the soldiers had stationed themselves outside my door.

Placing my hands on my hips, I turned away from the front entrance and faced my living room. Digging into my memory of the fortress's layout, I recalled these quarters were in an area usually reserved for foreign dignitaries. As long as it wasn't Marisol's old apartment, I didn't really care where my new place was.

The furniture was opulent, but not brand new. Amalie, or whomever was helping her, probably hadn't a chance to actually move anything around in the short time there'd been to prepare these rooms.

I did a quick exploration and found a library, a small office, an entertainment room with a large darkened screen on the wall, a master suite with a ridiculously cavernous attached bathroom designed around a raised spa tub, a small formal dining room, two spare bedrooms, and a kitchenette.

I snorted and shook my head. Who needed this much space?

I couldn't help a little inhale of delight when I discovered another, less formal living room with French doors that opened into a private courtyard. It featured a little circular winding stream that fed into a pond with a tinkling waterfall at the far end. I heard the low hum of the pump that recirculated the water. A frog sprang from the tall grass and plopped into the water.

For a moment, I just stood there in the Faerie sunshine, taking in the chirp of birds, the soft breeze that subtly stirred the leaves of the miniature Japanese maples growing on either side of the waterfall.

The ring of a phone jarred me from the serene moment. Reluctantly, I went back inside and pulled the French doors closed. I found a phone on a side table and picked up the handpiece.

"Yes?"

"Your Highness, this is Amalie. I'm having your personal tablet delivered to your quarters, and also, Lord Lothlorien wants to meet with you immediately, if you're available."

My brows lifted in surprise. Not at what she'd said, but because she was the one calling me.

"Of course, tell him to come to my rooms as soon as he can," I said. "And Amalie?"

"Yes, Your Majesty?"

"I don't claim to be an expert on these things, but I'm guessing that fetching my lost items and attending to my schedule don't normally fall under the duties of the Head Administrator."

There was a pause.

"Well, they are my duties in the strictest literal sense," she said, clearly choosing her words carefully. "In that all pages, assistants, and similar support staff are officially under my department, so anyone managing your schedule would report directly to me."

I pinched the bridge of my nose and closed my eyes briefly. "Have you not been able to find anyone to work under you?"

"Oh, I have," she said. "I've got a handful of employees. It's just . . . I'm not completely sure who I may be able to rely on without worry. I can only question potential employees about their trustworthiness so much before seeming like a tyrant."

Stifling a sigh, I thought for a minute. "How about employing some of the younger Carraig?"

"Your Majesty?"

"You may have noticed that I have a contingent of young volunteer guards," I said. "To be blunt, they showed up at my door the first morning I returned here as Queen, and they were the only ones to so publicly demonstrate their support. I seem to have quite a fiercely loyal faction among the senior academy students. Perhaps some of them would be willing to help you. They also may have like-minded friends who would rather fulfill administrative duties than carry swords and wear armor."

"That's a fine idea, and I'll follow up on it right away," she said, her tone brightening.

A cheery chime rang through the quarters.

"That's the page or Maxen," I said. "I'll let you go."

I hung up and made my way to the front door. Peering through the peephole, I confirmed it was Maxen and let him in.

He held up a tablet and passed it to me. "Got this from a page headed this way."

I let out a short laugh. "I was just lecturing Amalie about not performing duties that her underlings should be doing."

He appeared to be in a somewhat buoyant mood, seemingly more at ease in my presence than he'd been in a long time. Perhaps having Nicole home had boosted his spirits enough that he could be less dour in my presence.

I crooked my finger at him. "You've got to see this."

I led him through the quarters and back out to the courtyard. I figured if it had lifted my spirits, it couldn't hurt to take him out there for our meeting.

A faint smile tugged at his lips as he took in the little outdoor scene.

"Quite lovely," he said.

We started to wander around the perimeter of the courtyard.

"I'm sure there are things you need to discuss," I said. "But I want to let you know about something I brought up with King Oberon."

He tilted a look at me.

I took a breath. "I mentioned the hidden New Gargs th—that Marisol spoke of months ago," I said, faltering a bit when I got to her name.

Maxen took it in stride, but he looked concerned. "How did that come up?"

I recounted the discussion with Eldon and the High King about the blood of the Fomoire awakening.

His blue eyes widened with surprise and wonder. "That's . . . well, it's almost hard to believe. But in some strange way it seems right."

We were silent for a few moments.

"Oberon was practically giddy," I said. "He seems to think this—we—will be his secret weapon against the Tuatha. The power of ancient god blood to fight the vengeful gods of today."

Maxen's concern deepened into two vertical lines between his brows, and he exhaled a long breath through his nose. "That's not surprising. After what the Tuatha did to him in the Giants' Causeway, I'm sure he's extremely eager to hit hard when they attack."

I blinked. "First of all, I wouldn't expect Oberon to just be thinking of himself. Isn't he more focused on the larger purpose of saving Faerie? After all, he's the High King of the entire realm."

Maxen slid a significant look at me, his mouth tightening. "Oh, sure he is. But it's also become intensely personal to him."

I frowned at the ground and then squinted up into the blue sky. Of course Maxen was right. I'd sensed something off about Oberon's behavior but brushed past it at the time. I could only blame my inexperience with kings and politics. But now it made sense. Oberon's eagerness was, of course, partly driven by his own agenda. Maybe largely driven by it. The realization didn't really change things, not in any profound ways, but my view of the entire situation had subtly shifted. It was a small shift, but not a meaningless one.

Maxen was still watching me. "There was a first of all. What's the second of all?" he prompted.

My lips parted. "Uh, I don't remember," I said sheepishly. "Too much going on in here, I guess." I tapped my temple. "I'm losing my edge. But back to the so-called hidden New Gargs. Was that true?"

He tucked his chin into his chest. "Yes, it's true."

"Where are they?" I asked, gaping at him. I realized I hadn't quite believed it, that there were more people of stone blood out there. When Marisol had spoken of them, it had felt more like a myth than a reality.

"Mostly in the Earthly realm."

I shook my head once. "Are they changelings? Do they even know they're Fae?"

"Most of them know."

"How many?"

We'd reached the little waterfall, and Maxen stopped to gaze at it. I stood beside him.

"I'm not sure, exactly," he said, staring at the moving water. "We'd only barely started the project of contacting them, before . . ."

Before I drove a sword through his mother, cutting that work short.

"It's going to be quite a job to locate them," he continued, saving me from having to respond. "And most of them are of my mother's generation. One of her prophecies told her long ago that the New Gargs needed to hide some of their numbers, that it was the only way to ensure the survival of our people."

I frowned. "But if there were enough of them, it really could have helped her bid for kingdomhood to have them join us here in Faerie. I always believed that was her top priority."

When Marisol had petitioned to have the Order raised to an official kingdom, one of the arguments against her was our small numbers.

"I guess you could say she had two top priorities," Maxen said. "One was a kingdom for the New Gargs. The other was the survival of our people. She had to balance both of them. I would guess there are maybe four hundred more stone bloods out there in the Earthly realm."

I wasn't sure what to say for a long moment.

"Those people," I said quietly. "They gave up everything based on Marisol's prophecy, going across the hedge to try to live as humans. Non-Fae. I can't imagine how difficult that must have been for them."

Sure, I'd run off from Faerie as soon as I graduated, but I hadn't left for *good*. I was still Fae, and I never had to pretend to be otherwise. As badly as I'd wanted to leave the fortress, I would have been devastated to be completely cut off from my homeland, though I might not have admitted it as a cocky eighteen-year-old mercenary.

"Most of them have been completely cut off from all news of Faerie this whole time," Maxen said.

My frown deepened. "Are they going to feel their sacrifice was all in vain? Now that Marisol is gone?"

"I don't know. They left many years ago, knowing it was a safeguard, that no one truly knew what the future held."

"Some of them may not even want to come back. By now they've got jobs, friends, probably some have families."

"If Finvarra's attempt to control us with the Stone affected those of New Garg blood like Jasper who weren't even in the fortress, it may have also happened to those on the other side of the hedge. I have a funny feeling most are feeling the tug of their homeland right now."

I wasn't sure if that made me feel better or worse.

"Then we definitely need to invite them to come back to Faerie," I said. I let out a quiet, heavy sigh.

"I will continue the work of finding them," Maxen said.

I nodded. "I imagine that Oberon's going to be calling upon us very soon to figure out what our god blood can do. When I left, he and Eldon were talking about consulting experts and scholarly works."

"Let's wait until he pushes us on that. We have enough to contend with here for the moment."

"Right," I said. I took a deep breath. I'd been avoiding a topic that I knew I couldn't dance around any longer. "On that note, what of my failed assassins?"

I braced myself as I looked at him, as if his response would come as a physical blow.

"Oliver is probably the better one to fill you in on that topic, but . . ." Maxen met my gaze, and his sapphire blue eyes were full of regret. "Some were caught. Several escaped through doorways to other realms before they could be apprehended."

I passed a hand over my eyes. "How many were caught?"

"Four."

"I'm going to have to execute them, aren't I?"

"You're Queen of this realm. The choice is yours."

"But?"

Maxen chewed his bottom lip for a second or two. "You were clear. You said that any subject who raised a weapon at you would be punished to the fullest extent. Going back on that would only weaken your position."

My stomach was trying to compact itself into a hard little point, and my rib cage seemed to constrict around my lungs.

"I don't want to kill my own subjects, Maxen," I whispered.

"I know, Petra." His face was drawn. "But they chose their actions. They knew the consequences if they were caught."

Misery crept through me, gripping me until I ached. I dropped my head and squeezed my eyes closed, wishing with everything I had that I could figure out another way.

Maxen's hand touched my upper arm, and I looked up. "This, figuring this out, will be the worst moment. This will be the lowest point of your reign. You simply have to find a way to get through it."

I nodded, but I honestly couldn't imagine how I'd do it.

Chapter 14

I CONSULTED MY father about the four traitors who'd been caught, and I broke down once briefly during the conversation, pleading for an answer, any alternate solution. He'd remained quiet, his hand on my shoulder, until I composed myself.

Ultimately, we decided the sentences needed to be carried out soon. He said he could have things arranged by the following evening. The four traitors would be executed by a poison that put the victim to sleep before killing. It was the most humane method we could come up with.

That night in my new quarters, I paced, utterly heartsick. I tried to find solace in the moonlight-bathed courtyard, listening to the trickle of water over the rocks of the waterfall, but it didn't soothe me.

I knew Oliver and Maxen would disagree with me, but I had to offer the traitors something other than death. I had to do it because I didn't want my first major act as Queen to be that of killing my own people. Not without some shred of mercy in it. In thinking about the hidden ones who'd willingly left Faerie, cutting themselves off from their homeland for decades, I realized there was a grave enough punishment that I could offer, one that would spare the traitors' lives but still take nearly everything from them. And I planned to give them the choice.

At two in the morning, I put on my coronation dress, still dirty from the ordeal of the day but the most regal thing I owned, and threw the heavy jeweled robe over it. I stepped out of my quarters to find a couple of surprised guards posted there.

"I'm going to the fortress jail," I said.

"I'll escort you," one of them said, a burly woman with cropped hair.

She went ahead, leading me through the quiet corridors down to the basement.

I went into the reception area of the fortress jail and found Nanette, an older woman with reading glasses on a thin chain around her neck, on duty.

"Nanette, how are you?" I asked.

She rose and curtsied. "Can't complain, Your Majesty."

She'd always been a woman of few words.

"I need to speak to the four prisoners awaiting execution," I said. "Can you safely gather them all together?"

"Let me get a deputy to help me," she said. She sat down, put on her glasses, and tapped on the tablet wired into a wall. "Patrick will be here in just a few moments, Your Majesty."

I nodded and went to sit in one of the hard plastic chairs. I imagined she'd had to rouse Patrick from sleep. To his credit, he arrived in less than ten minutes, panting lightly and with his hair a little messed, but dressed in uniform.

The two of them went into the corridor beyond the desk that led to the cells. I heard the clangs of heavy doors opening and closing.

Nanette and Patrick returned.

"Your Majesty," she said. "We've collected the prisoners in the first cell. We left the door open."

I rose and nodded. My guard followed me back.

"I'll speak to them alone," I said.

I went into the cell and pulled the door closed behind me.

Four Carraig slumped on the narrow bed, their hands restrained behind their backs. Two men and two women. One of the women looked several years younger than me, twenty-one or twenty-two, I guessed.

I stood before them with my chin raised, regarding each of them in turn.

"You've been informed that you'll be executed for the crime of attempting to murder your monarch?" I asked.

One of the men scowled. The other three prisoners nodded, and the young woman's face crumpled for a second as she fought to keep her composure.

"The executions will take place about eighteen hours from now. Death by poison."

I allowed several seconds of silence to pass. The young woman was crying, silent tears streaming down her face. I focused on my own breaths and maintaining a stony expression. Inside, I wanted to cry with her.

"I was stupid, Your Majesty," the sobbing young woman said, her breath hitching. "So stupid. I know it's too late, but I want you to know that I see the error of my choices. I listened to people I shouldn't have. I didn't think for myself. And now I know I must face my punishment."

By the time she finished speaking, she'd managed to control her voice. Her dark brown eyes met mine, and I could see she was sincere.

"And the rest of you?" I asked.

"I have a son, Your Majesty," said one of the men, the one who hadn't scowled. He had pale blue eyes and orange-blonde hair. He pressed his trembling lips together for a moment. "I thought I was being principled, but all I've done is make my boy an orphan."

He turned his head to the side, and a tear leaked down his cheek. I held my breath, willing my eyes to stay dry.

The other woman was perhaps a bit older than Oliver, muscled and jowly. She looked like she'd be a formidable foe in a swordfight.

"I live with my choice, Your Majesty," she said. Her voice was raspy and deep for a woman. "I regret it now, but it was mine to make, and I have to live with it."

I shifted my attention to the other man. He squinted up at me with dark eyes and then spat on the floor. Okay, then.

"I've come to offer you something," I said. "But it's not without a grave price."

It was quiet enough to hear water dripping somewhere.

"If you have sincere regret for attacking me, I will allow you to live. But you will be stripped of your magic and sent across the hedge to the Earthly realm, and you will never be able to return to Faerie."

"My regret couldn't be more deep or sincere," the young woman said.

The man with the son looked up at me with watery eyes. "I've never regretted anything more, Your Highness."

"I already said I regret my actions," the thick lady said.

The scowling man sneered. "I regret nothing, except that I failed to end your traitorous life. Marisol Lothlorien was the greatest New Garg to ever breathe the fair air of Faerie, and you murdered her, you worthless whore of a girl."

I blinked but didn't otherwise react.

"Three of you will be expelled from Faerie by this time tomorrow night," I said. I faced the angry man. "And you've clearly decided you will die for your crime."

I turned, opened the door, and exited the cell. With my guard trailing me, I left the jail and walked woodenly back to my quarters. Cold sweat dampened my underarms, and my legs felt unsteady. As soon as I was alone inside my apartment, I sagged against the wall.

I didn't feel disappointed or relieved. I just felt hollow. And I hoped with every shred of my being that Maxen was right, that this would be the lowest point of my reign.

I'd hoped the morning would bring some peace, but it didn't. I still had to face one execution and expel three Carraig from Faerie.

I went about making arrangements for the three prisoners who would be set free in the Earthly realm. It required a consultation with Maxen about the fortress coffers, as I had to hire a Druid monk on short notice to come and perform the rites that would cut the prisoners off from their magic, and it wasn't cheap.

I hadn't given much thought to the financial aspect of running a kingdom up to that point. In Faerie, money didn't hold the power it did in the Earthly realm. Barter was a more common method of exchange, and each kingdom carved out niches of goods for trade and struck deals with other realms for supplies they lacked.

The Stone Order was so small in territory, we had to import much of our food and nearly all of our supplies. Besides the fortress itself, our only other land holdings were a handful of mines in very secret locations. Having a great affinity for all types of stone, from lowly gravel to priceless precious gems, it was fitting that the Carraig realm fed its treasury by mining such materials.

The fortress had been riding on the existing agreements Marisol had put in place. But I would need someone to step in to manage that aspect of the kingdom, and soon. I had no clear sense of the extent of our dependence on any Unseelie realms for our supplies, but we would need to have backup plans in place if those agreements crumbled.

The Druid arrived late in the afternoon. I asked Amalie and Oliver to appoint people to oversee the process, as I had other things to attend to. I also had no desire to witness it firsthand. Returning to my office, I took up the list of still-vacant positions in my court. Trying to focus on that task instead of the impending execution, I called the page at the reception desk and asked her to track down Shane, the young commander in the battle ranks.

About twenty minutes later, he arrived. Only a couple of years out of the academy, he'd quickly established himself as an excellent teacher as well as a rising star in the military. We used to be on good terms, but since I'd returned as Queen, he'd been openly wary of me.

He bowed and sat in the chair across from me. I studied him for a moment. His quick, dark eyes had an exotic shape to them. He was a bit on the slim side for a Carraig, but he was all wiry muscle. Dark, straight hair just brushed the tops of his ears, his last military cut grown out enough to almost look shaggy. Shane was a handsome man, skilled, ambitious, and passionate about what he did. I could see why Emmaline crushed so hard on him. Plus, there was the titillating aspect of the teacher-student relationship. From the way she'd spoken of him recently, I got the sense that something might have developed between them. They were only three or four years apart.

I decided not to beat around the hedge. "How many officers are there who outrank you?" I asked.

"Seven, Your Highness," he said, clearly hesitant to speak of my detractors.

"And if you don't count Raleigh and his followers?"

"Two. Me and Kristen."

Kristen had graduated the same year as Shane.

"You outrank her, correct?" I asked.

"Yes, Your Majesty."

I placed my forearms on the desk and leaned forward. "I have a problem. I can't keep men like Raleigh and his followers in high-ranking posts in my military."

He tilted his head in acknowledgment.

"I'd like to offer you the position of Battle Master and Military Commander." He opened his mouth, but I held up a finger to stop him. "But I know you're not a hundred percent behind me. I'd like to talk about why."

His jaw worked for a second. "Don't get me wrong, Petr—Your Majesty. As a soldier, I admire you immensely. You're one of the fiercest fighters I know. You could kick my ass up and down the practice field." He blinked, obviously uncertain about speaking so casually.

"It's fine," I said. "Please, continue."

"I just don't understand why you were chosen for the crown. *You* should be leading the military. Not sitting on the throne."

I peered at him from under partly lowered lids. "I don't doubt you believe that, but it seems as if there's something else. Some other reason you don't trust me."

He shifted on his seat, and one knee began a quick bouncing rhythm. He looked at the floor.

"Just say it, Shane," I said quietly.

He looked up, his dark eyes piercing. "You left."

My brows lifted. "I left?"

"You graduated from the academy, and you ran out of here as fast as you could. That never sat right with me. While all of us were here fighting to carve out a spot for the New Gargs, you were in the Earthly realm, doing . . . whatever you were doing."

I leaned back. "Well, everything you say is accurate. I couldn't wait to get the hell out. I wanted freedom. I wanted to get away from my father. I was pretty damn immature at eighteen. Not that I'm trying to make excuses."

He nodded, but his mouth still formed a tight line. I waited.

"Don't you think others would have preferred to go, too?" he asked. His gaze lifted and roved around. "This place can be fricking *stifling*. All of us crammed into this building, living under a monarch obsessed with her own vision."

My eyes sharpened on him. "So you're not angry at me for killing her?"

He shook his head. "I understand you had to do it. She tried to have you and your sister murdered. I get that you had no choice, and I would've done the same."

"You don't think I deserve the throne because I abandoned the Order is what it comes down to."

He lifted a shoulder and let it drop. "Yes, I question your loyalty.

That's part of it. The other part is that you just seem . . . an odd choice, considering there are other options."

I nearly agreed with him, but Oberon's advice came back to me, and I straightened and squared my shoulders. I shouldn't be sitting there offering apologies. It wasn't as if I'd done *nothing* to serve the Order of late. And meekly eating shit in front of everyone who disapproved of me wasn't going to get me anywhere.

"Were you at the Battle of Champions?" I asked.

His eyes widened slightly at the abrupt change of topic. "Yes, Your Highness. Every New Garg was there."

"You remember how I ended up there?"

"You saved Nicole from the Duergar. It set off a shitstorm of hostility between us and them."

"Yes. And then I had to pay for my actions, for saving my sister, by entering a battle to the death. I won. And I secured a temporary peace for the Order, getting Periclase off our backs for a brief time. Remember that?"

He nodded. I casually reached for the scabbard holding Aurora that I'd placed on the floor, tipped against the desk beside me. Placing the sheath on the desk, I slowly drew the legendary blade. It wasn't to threaten. I laid the sword parallel to the scabbard.

"I also went into the stronghold of the Tuatha De Danann with Jasper Glasgow," I said, looking down at the swirling rosy colors of the metal. "The gods had taken Oberon there and had him shackled in sky iron. Jasper and I entered the Giants' Causeway and faced the gods to take our High King back."

I looked up at Shane. His eyes were riveted on Aurora. Any swordsman would be transfixed by the Champion's blade. I waited until his gaze met mine.

"I lost Mort under that mountain," I continued. "Oberon called Aurora to my hand. The trick only worked because I'm the Champion of the Summer Court, which ties me to this blade in ways I don't fully know. Jasper and I escaped with Oberon because I wielded Aurora. Then we had to outrace the Dullahan to get away."

Shane's eyes popped wide.

"None of this qualifies me to be the Carraig queen," I said. "But don't you think I've done a few things lately to show my love for my people?"

He looked back down at Aurora and swallowed. After a moment, he inhaled and met my gaze again.

"You're right, Your Majesty," he said. "I was in error for judging you the way I did. I have no doubts of your loyalty to the Carraig, of your commitment to us."

I gave him one crisp nod. "Good. As to the oddity of me as Queen, there's not much I can do about that. Maxen was the obvious choice. But Oberon chose me. So here we are."

"Yes, here we are," he said quietly. A few seconds of silence past. "If the offer still stands, I would be honored to accept the position of Battle Master and Military Commander in your court, Queen Petra."

I allowed myself a small smile. "I'm very glad to hear that. It's yours."

I stood and reached out, offering my hand, and he grasped it. Then he bowed, bending low from the waist. I waved him off, and he turned to go.

"Oh, Shane?" I said.

He stopped and turned, his hand on the doorknob.

"Don't toy with Emmaline."

His lips parted, and he blinked a couple of times. "I . . . wouldn't do that." Crimson splotches began blooming on his cheeks.

I arched a brow at him. "Good."

He shut the door behind him, and I collapsed in my chair, tipped my head back, and groaned at the ceiling. Why did everything have to be so *damn* intense?

I blew out a long breath and then pushed forward and reached for my tablet. Shane felt like a victory, an important one. But the day wasn't even close to over. There were still many positions to fill, and an execution to oversee that evening.

Chapter 15

BECAUSE THERE HAD never before been an execution in the Stone Order, Oliver, Maxen, and Amalie had scrambled to devise a setup for it. It was a grisly assignment, and I couldn't help a deep stab of guilt over pressing it upon them. But it had to be done.

The fortress was a former Earthly realm prison, with a room that had once been used for lethal-injection executions. Since Marisol had the prison transmuted into the Faerie realm and remodeled most of the original structure, the lethal injection room had been used for storage. Amalie had found workers to clear it out.

The execution room itself was the size of a small rectangular bedroom, with a window opposite the door. The window looked into a slightly deeper room. When the fortress had still been San Quentin State Prison, the larger room had been used as a viewing area for people attending the execution—usually the family members of the victim, a few press, and sometimes family of the criminal.

I learned all of this from Amalie, who seemed well-versed on the history of the fortress. She and the others had arranged this execution in a manner that imitated the lethal injections that used to take place when the fortress was an Earthly prison.

I would be in the viewing area for the execution of the man who'd wanted me dead. Carlton Kanab was his name. He was single, no children, and a bit of a loner, by all accounts. It was hard to imagine how anyone could manage to be much of a hermit in the fortress, but perhaps it was part of the explanation for how he'd ended up here, facing death because he'd hung his very existence on his belief that Marisol Lothlorien was the greatest of our people ever to have lived.

However we'd ended up here and regardless of how deeply and remorselessly Carlton Kanab hated me, my chest ached for what I had to do. I wished he'd repented, but he'd been given the choice and rejected my offer.

The Druid had come to strip the other three prisoners of their magic, and that process was still underway when I entered the viewing room for Kanab's execution. Druidic magic usually involved chanting—the more intricate the magic, the more chanting needed—so it could be hours yet before that was finished. It wasn't a simple process, and it was one that the subjects had to willingly submit to.

"Here, Your Majesty." Oliver indicated I was to sit in a high-backed chair on a small platform that was situated at the back of the viewing room. I'd insisted that I not sit in front. I had absolutely no desire to be staring right into the man's face when he died.

Maxen was the first attendee to come in after me. He bowed and then went to stand at my right while Oliver took the position to my left.

"It'll be over soon," Maxen said softly.

I nodded without meeting his gaze. Realizing I was pushing my palms backward and forward across my thighs in a nervous gesture, I stilled my hands by intertwining my fingers and holding them in my lap.

Deciding what to wear to the execution had been yet another macabre little task that I was eager to forget. I'd ended up in trousers and a dark shirt, feeling it wouldn't be right to put on some fancy dress as if I were attending a ball. I did, however, wear the crown. We'd opened attendance to anyone who wanted to come, up to the limit of the size of the room, and some of my dissenters—not those who'd tried to kill me, but who didn't want me on the throne—would be in the audience for the execution. I wanted them to remember who was in charge.

They began to arrive, and Oliver's people who were stationed just outside the door made sure none tried to enter with weapons of any kind.

Raleigh, the stump of one forearm heavily bandaged, was among the first to come in. He stopped to bow before me as etiquette dictated. Tension hung heavy and ugly in the air, but I speculated by the way his shoulders curled forward and his sunken, haunted eyes skirted off to the side he wouldn't be coming at me again. I imagined he was thinking about how this easily could have been his execution. If he weren't thinking about how he might be the one facing death, he was a very stubborn and stupid man indeed. I would have been well within my right to have Raleigh sentenced to death after what he'd tried to pull against me in the fortress foyer. But unless he was putting on an act, the loss of his sword hand appeared to have left him shamed and broken.

For me, Raleigh's presence was a vivid, gut-wrenching reminder of the difficult choices I'd faced. I could only hope that these punishments—Raleigh's missing hand, the permanent banishment of three Fae from their homeland, and Carlton Kanab's death—would be enough, and I wouldn't be forced to take any of these actions ever again.

I hoped, but I also had to remain realistic.

Another half dozen people filtered in and quietly took seats in the three rows of folding chairs set up between me and the viewing window. There was no conversation, only quiet, careful shifting, clearing of throats, and other subtle noises.

Belatedly, I wondered if we should have made more of a spectacle of the event, perhaps requiring all adult Carraig to attend. But that felt too tyrannical, even if it might have been effective in dissuading more attacks against me.

Maxen went to pull the door closed and turn down the lights. Half a minute later, the curtain on the other side of the viewing window was pulled aside, revealing three people in the execution room.

Carlton Kanab was strapped to a gurney. One of the fortress's lead medics was hunched over a stainless steel surgery tray. And next to the prisoner was Jaquard. A master swordsman and one of my former teachers, Jaquard was also my failed assassin. Marisol had sent him to kill me, but he'd found a loophole in her command and allowed me to escape. He and I hadn't spoken since I'd returned to the fortress to take the throne, but Oliver had informed me that Jaquard had been keeping a low profile, being very careful to avoid association with anyone who opposed me.

Apparently, Kanab had chosen Jaquard as the one person he was allowed to have as support at his execution. I wasn't entirely sure how to feel about my former teacher's presence on the other side of the glass. I decided to focus on how Jaquard showed me mercy and saved my life at the risk of his own and was now offering comfort to a man who was facing death.

The medic straightened and faced the viewing window holding a small vial filled with pinkish liquid in one hand. Then he turned to Kanab. To his credit, he opened his mouth and allowed the medic to pour in the poison without struggle or resistance. Carlton Kanab had balls. In spite of his actions, I couldn't help thinking it was a terrible shame we had to lose him.

It was over quickly. Kanab's body slackened, his head falling to one side, as if sleep had suddenly overtaken him. After about a minute, the medic felt for a pulse at the side of Kanab's neck. The medic stepped back and gave a slight nod. An unseen hand pulled the curtain back across the window.

Maxen raised the lights and opened the door, and the spectators filed past me, offering their bows and curtsies as they left. I sat rigidly, enduring it with as much stoicism as I could muster.

When the room was finally empty except for me, Maxen, and Oliver, I slumped. I thought I'd mentally prepared for what had just happened, but the full force of reality barreled into my chest, and I realized I'd been kidding myself. I squeezed my eyes closed for a second.

"Thank Oberon that's done," Maxen said, his voice low and ragged.

"Maxen, Nicole and I will join you in your quarters," Oliver said to me. "I'll bring my Gnome-made single-malt. We could all use a drink. Except Nicole, of course. She can have herbal tea."

My father wasn't a drinker. He also wasn't an offerer-of-comfort. He recognized how deeply the execution had affected me and was trying to help, but I couldn't stand the thought of trying to make conversation. I needed to be alone.

I shook my head. "I'm not good company right now."

Avoiding Oliver's and Maxen's eyes, I rose and swiftly walked from the viewing room. Guards trailed me as I strode to my quarters, but my father didn't try to follow me. With numb fingers, I let myself in.

A man was dead, but he probably hadn't even been one of the leaders in the uprising against me. Several of them had escaped through doorways before Oliver's meager security team had managed to apprehend them. It all felt so senseless in one respect. But I knew I'd had to follow through on the threat of execution. I'd managed it, but I'd hated it.

Walking through the dark rooms, I pulled the crown from my head. It slipped from my fingers and fell with a series of metallic pings on the tiled floor somewhere along the hallway leading to the second living room. I heard the jeweled crown roll to a stop.

In some corner of my mind, a thought tried to form about how I shouldn't treat such a valuable item so carelessly. But the admonition was crushed under the weight of my guilt and sorrow.

I pushed through the French doors and went out into the courtyard, where I began tracing the same path around the lovely grounds that Maxen and I had followed earlier. The darkness enveloped me as I walked and walked, wishing I could just dissolve into the refuge of the night as if stepping into the netherwhere.

A man hated me on the throne so much he had voluntarily chosen to die.

I turned the thought over and over, my mind trying to reason it out in ways that lifted some of the responsibility from me. Perhaps he'd been bitterly unhappy long before I took the crown. Maybe he'd been infatuated with Marisol—he certainly wouldn't have been the only stone blood to have harbored feelings for the exquisitely beautiful, obsessively driven leader. He might just have been one of those people who couldn't accept change.

But it didn't really matter why he'd done it. Carlton Kanab was dead because of me.

There were too many Carraig who didn't want me on the throne, and it was for good reason. I wasn't fit for the job. I knew it. Maxen knew it. Everyone knew it. I couldn't let this farce go on. I was a fighter, not a queen, and nothing in Faerie was going to make me into the queen the Carraig Sidhe needed. Oberon had forced me under the crown, but I would find a loophole. I'd give the Carraig what they wanted, what they deserved. I would create a position that made Maxen Lothlorien the de facto leader of the Carraig Sidhe, and I'd go back to what I did best: wielding a sword.

My tension eased a little after that, but I continued on my circular path as if the night air could cleanse me of all troubles.

I wasn't sure how long I paced around the dark courtyard, listening to the cheery little trickle of the waterfall, but at some point, the phone began to ring. I ignored it, but it insistently continued. Finally, I went inside and snatched up the receiver.

"Yes?"

"Petra, let me in." It was Oliver.

"What?"

"I was pounding on your door for ten minutes." His irritation came through in the snarly edge to his voice. "I had to leave to find a house phone to call you. Now that I know you're not dead, I'm coming back. You'll let me in."

He hung up.

I scowled at the phone and then dropped it back on its cradle. I wanted to be pissed, to tell him to leave me alone, but I was too damn exhausted. Letting out a long, weary breath, I passed my hand over my eyes and began trudging toward the front of the apartment. When I reached my fallen crown, I bent to retrieve it and left it in the kitchenette.

The sound of a heavy fist pounding wood echoed through the formal living room.

"I'm coming!" I hollered irritably.

When I opened the door, I found not only Oliver, but also Maxen and Nicole. They crowded inside before I could protest. Nicole gave me a quick hug.

True to his word, Oliver held a velvet bag that contained his bottle of Gnomish whiskey. I knew what the bag held because I'd found his stash back when I was still living at home. The bottle was nearly full back then, as my father rarely drank, and I'd slugged down about an ounce just to try it. It'd slid like smooth fire over my throat, but even as a dumb teenager, I realized it was good stuff. I'd never touched the bottle again, though, for fear he'd notice some was missing.

"I'll grab some glasses," I said, resigned to playing host.

I went back into the kitchenette and opened cupboards until I found neat rows of water glasses, wine goblets, champagne flutes, narrow highballs, and shorter lowballs. I grabbed three of the latter. I also grabbed the electric kettle, a box of herbal tea, and a mug for Nicole, and put everything on a tray.

In the living room, Oliver poured three shots. He, Maxen, and I each took a glass, raised them, and then knocked back the amber liquid. I cleared my throat and licked my lips. It was even better than I remembered.

Nicole busied herself making tea.

Oliver leaned back in his chair and crossed one ankle over the other knee.

The warmth of the Gnomish whiskey spread through me, loosening the ache in my chest by a fraction.

"What's the news from the Summerlands?" I asked Maxen, breaking the silence. The day had been so intensely personal, I needed to focus elsewhere, beyond the fortress.

He leaned forward and propped his elbows on his knees. "It's not good. Finvarra's nowhere to be found, but it hasn't affected the Unseelie assault. They've come up with some new weapon that seems to be slowly weakening Melusine's shield around the Summerlands castle."

I blew out a loud, irritated breath. "If only we could have caught the bastard when he was here in the fortress."

"Oberon thinks Finvarra is still helping to direct things from wherever he is. Periclase is the face of it, but Finvarra is probably still heavily involved in the decisions."

Nicole made a small hum of agreement and took a sip from her steaming mug. She was sitting on the sofa next to Maxen, nestled into the corner with pillows around her, shoes off and legs curled up.

I tilted my head and slanted a look at a corner of the ceiling.

"What are you thinking?" Maxen asked.

"We need to take Finvarra out before the Tuatha decide to show up." I was stating the obvious, but I also had the seed of an idea.

"Yeah? How?" he said.

"Do you remember Eunice?"

He gave me a blank look.

"The, uh, naked lady who came through the doorway with us to the Summerlands after we surprised Finvarra."

"Ah, yes. Of course."

"She's here in the fortress," I said. "Apparently they were keeping her under house arrest in the Summerlands, and she begged me to come back here, so I had Amalie set her up."

Maxen's dark blond brows rose slowly.

"We should talk to her. She spent several months as one of Finvarra's companions, going back to when he was hiding out with the—"

"The Undine." Maxen finished my sentence. He straightened. "Do you think Finvarra's gone back there? He and Queen Doineanne seemed to have an arrangement."

A crawling sensation worked up the center of my back at the sound of the Undine queen's name. She'd held me and Jasper captive for a short time, and she'd had obvious designs on Jasper, boldly propositioning him. Beyond that affront, she was cold, wild, and rather creepy with her too-round fishlike eyes.

I lifted a shoulder and let it drop. "Maybe. Or Periclase might be hiding him. Good old blood dad was doing his damnedest to ingratiate himself to Finvarra last time I had the displeasure of being in their presence." I squinted at Maxen. "Don't we have spies or something?"

He snorted a laugh. "We have contacts and allies, but Carraig aren't exactly built to be spies."

He had a point. As a race, we weren't known for grace and subtlety. Stone bloods preferred sword fights to intrigue and sneaking around.

"The woman, Eunice. You think she might legitimately be able to help?" Oliver asked, circling us back.

I shrugged. "She seems to think she has some useful knowledge about Finvarra, and she's very eager to help."

"Let's get her in here, then."

My brows rose a fraction, and I flicked a glance at Maxen.

I stood and went to one of the house phones and dialed the reception desk in my office, where I knew one of the three pages Amalie had assigned to me was on duty.

"Hello, Jaci," I said when a female voice answered. "I need a guest brought to my quarters."

"Of course, Your Highness."

I gave her Eunice's details. It was late enough that the woman might have retired to bed, but I was willing to take the chance. Things were worse in the Summerlands, and we needed to take down Finvarra.

Eunice arrived fifteen minutes later, and if she'd been sleeping, she did a good job of looking alert and put-together. She was an attractive woman, probably a bit older than I'd initially pegged her—maybe fifteen years my senior.

She looked around, her eyes snagging on my father. Her lips parted, and her cheeks pinked subtly. Oliver's expression didn't budge.

"Your Majesty." Eunice dropped into a deep curtsy.

"Apologies for the late hour," I said. "Please take a seat, Eunice."

She went to the chair opposite Oliver's and perched on the edge with her knees pressed tightly together, her hands folded in her lap. She peered at me expectantly.

"We'd like to know anything useful you can tell us about Finvarra. Anything that might help us discover where he is now."

Her eyelashes fluttered. "Oh, yes, of course. I'm happy to help, Your Highness. Ah, let's see. Well. He has a deep affinity for squid from the Kelpie realm. He adores linen sheets produced by the Sylphs, can barely sleep without them, the baby. Oh! And he favors Elvish wines. The dark, meaty reds, you know, the ones that pair well with—"

"But do you know where he *is*?" Oliver cut in impatiently. "His alliances. Friends. People who might be willing to hide him."

I shot him a hard look and gave a slight shake of my head.

"I believe I see where you're going, Eunice," I said gently. I was trying to think of what Maxen would do to try to draw out information he needed. "Whatever ruler has taken him in would consider it an honor to have the Unseelie High King as a guest and would want to please him. If we can discover where some of Finvarra's favorite things are being delivered, it could lead us to him."

She nodded vigorously. "Yes, Your Highness."

"And what of his potential allies?" I asked. "Did you ever overhear him speak of realms where he might feel safe?"

"You already know he's spent time with the Undine," she said.

"Yes, you'd mentioned you first met Finvarra when he was in Doineanne's realm."

She nestled further into the plush cushion, and her expression became shrewd. "Well, he's not there now."

I tilted my head. "Oh? Why not?"

A conspiratorial grin tugged at the corners of her lips. "He and the Undine queen had a falling out."

"Really," I drawled. Seeing she enjoyed gossiping, I leaned in and smiled encouragingly. "What happened?"

She looked down at the floor, a smirk still playing across her face. "She propositioned him. He refused her. That made Queen Doineanne positively livid." Her gaze lifted to me, and she covered her mouth with one hand, giggling behind it.

Oliver let out a noisy, annoyed exhalation through his nose. My father abhorred this type of chatter and rumormongering, but even he had to see that it was useful information. Fortunately, Eunice didn't seem to notice his disapproval.

"So Doineanne kicked him out?" I pressed.

"Pretty much, yes. And that's when we all moved to the Duergar realm at the invitation of King Periclase, your esteemed birth father." Her eyes sharpened on me.

I snorted. "Periclase is a horrible man. No need to speak of him with any deference in my presence."

Her lips formed a surprised little O. "I can't say I disagree with you there," she whispered and then looked around with paranoia, as if someone would jump out of the walls and punish her for not protesting my criticism of the Duergar king.

I imagined Eunice had spent most of her life as a companion to powerful men, or at least men who had more power than she did, and it was clear from my interactions with her that she wasn't the type to use her sexuality to try to gain control. She'd taken a different approach. For someone like Eunice, a harmonious and subservient demeanor was a matter of survival. I liked the thought of her coming to a point in her life where she could speak more freely.

"Do you think Periclase might be aiding Finvarra?" I asked. "Maybe that's where he returned."

She shook her head. "It wouldn't be my first guess. I imagine King Periclase would have offered, but I think the High King Finvarra would instead go some place a bit less obvious."

I nearly told her to stop calling Finvarra "King"—the title was self-proclaimed, as the man didn't even have a defined realm of his own—but held back. She couldn't help her habits of etiquette.

"One of the less civilized Unseelie kingdoms, perhaps?" Maxen suggested.

"That's my assumption, my lord," she said. Her brows drew together, and she tapped a finger against the corner of her mouth for a moment. "Not the Ogres. Not the Boggart realm. I'm sure he mentioned not being on good terms with either. I'd say Daoine Sidhe or possibly the Salamander kingdom."

I turned to Maxen. "I thought there was bad blood between Finvarra and his former tribe?"

Finvarra was Daoine, though he'd broken from the kingdom generations ago, abandoning his homeland to seek greater power.

I'd expected Maxen to be the most knowledgeable on Faerie history, but Eunice answered instead. "You're right. There was. But while King Finvarra was supposed to be banished from Faerie, he mended fences with his people. All in secret, of course, as King Oberon never would have allowed it."

I drew a slow breath and gave Eunice a nod. "You've been extremely helpful. That's all for tonight. Please let me know if you think of anything else that might aid us."

She gave me a pleased smile, peeked at Oliver, and then curtsied.

Once she'd departed, my father harrumphed and shifted around irritably in his chair.

I gave him an amused look. "She liked you. You could have been a little nicer to help grease the wheels."

He grunted and reached for the bottle of Gnomish single-malt and splashed a bit into his glass.

Nicole stifled a yawn against the back of her hand. "I think I need to turn in," she said. "I just can't seem to stay awake into the night these days."

Maxen turned to her, a soft smile on his face. "Let's get you home." To me, he said, "I'll see what I can do with Eunice's information."

I had a feeling he would be up late making inquiries.

Oliver also stood. "I should be off as well." He left the Gnomish whiskey on the table.

I rose and saw them out. I would speak to Maxen soon, to inform him of my decision to appoint him as the acting leader of the realm, a sort of prime minister to my crown, but I needed to quickly get some things in place first.

I stayed up late, scouring the archives and by-laws of the kingdom for information about establishing a new position in the realm. It was very late by the time I found what I needed, but I wrote up a document that I believed would suffice as a royal decree. It was designed to give essentially all decision-making power to Maxen and written as an order from his monarch, which he couldn't refuse. I felt a tiny stab of guilt at laying all of that on him, but it was the right thing to do. He would accept the responsibility, and it would ease tension in the fortress. I'd tried to do it Oberon's way, but it was obvious how disastrous his decision to put me on the throne had turned out to be.

I sent the documents off to Amalie for processing and then collapsed onto my bed.

I awoke to the ringing of my house phone.

"Your Highness, one Jasper Glasgow has arrived outside the fortress seeking audience with you," came Jaci's voice. "He says it's urgent."

My heart bumped at Jasper's name. "Please admit him to the fortress and send him directly to my quarters."

I straightened the creased clothes I'd slept in and quickly twisted my hair up into a loose bun.

My stomach tightened with the uncertainty of whether Jasper was bringing good news or bad. The way things were going in Faerie lately, I wasn't optimistic.

Chapter 16

WHEN I WENT to answer the door, I froze in surprise at who stood on the other side. Oliver bustled past me with a paper plate of freshly-baked pastries.

I closed the door and turned to follow his progress as he made his way through the front room.

"Got coffee on?" he asked over his shoulder. The smell of dough and frosting wafted past, and my mouth watered a little.

"Uh . . ." I trailed after him to the kitchenette. "What are you doing?"

He lifted the plate and then plopped it down on the counter. "I brought breakfast."

I cast a glance toward the front door. Jasper was going to arrive any second.

"I'm really okay," I said. "There's no need to check on me."

"It's just breakfast, Petra," he said with a gruff little growl to his voice that told me he was still worried about how I was handling the execution. He plugged in the coffee pot and began rummaging around in cupboards for grounds.

The doorbell chimed.

"That Maxen?" Oliver asked, setting a couple of mugs next to the pastries.

"No," I muttered and went to answer the bell.

Jasper stood there with a gleam in his eye and a little grin on his face.

His smile broadened as he stepped inside and kicked the door closed with his heel, his golden eyes doing a slow burn as they roved over me. With a rough-edged gesture, he snaked an arm around my waist and pulled me into him.

"Greetings, Your Highness," he whispered against my neck.

A wave of delicious heat stoked low in my middle, but thinking of Oliver only a couple of rooms away, I tried to disentangle from Jasper's embrace.

The sound of a throat clearing behind me told me I was too slow.

I stepped away from Jasper and straightened my shirt.

My father strode forward and stopped next to me, his face stony as he sized up Jasper.

"Jasper, this is my father, Oliver Maguire," I said quickly, trying to assume control of the awkwardness that was growing by the second. "Oliver, meet Jasper Glasgow."

Jasper stepped forward and extended his hand. "Well met. I'm glad to see you escaped the Duergar realm unharmed."

After a moment's hesitation—that split second somehow saying everything about Oliver's lack of approval—my father grasped Jasper's hand. The muscles in Oliver's arm bulged as he squeezed, likely much more firmly than was necessary.

Jasper's jaw tightened momentarily. But he managed a brief, genuine smile. Oliver nodded, apparently seeing something that satisfied him the tiniest bit. Enough for that moment, anyway.

"My page said your visit was urgent," I said to Jasper, speaking more formally to him than I had in a long time. Maybe ever.

I tried not to fidget as I felt Oliver observing us. I hadn't really mentioned to my father how . . . *involved* I'd become with Jasper Glasgow. Not that Oliver would have expected such a disclosure. He and I had never engaged in talk of our romantic involvements, and that'd been fine by me, especially considering my suspicion that he'd been involved with Marisol at some point—maybe multiple times—in the past. I'd lived most of my adult life outside Faerie, which gave me the freedom to date without worrying about my father's judgment. So this—having the man in my life in the same room with my serious-as-a-funeral father—was an entirely new experience. I wasn't loving it so far.

Jasper nodded and kept steady eye contact with me. "Aye. To cut to the heart of it, I took your advice and paid the Ghillie Dubh a visit." A grimace of annoyance flashed briefly over his handsome features. "Morven refused to deal with me. He asked for you."

"Maybe he just misses my sunny disposition," I joked. No one laughed. "Did he give any hint that he knew where the Chalice of Dagda was?"

"He did." The boisterousness of Jasper's greeting had faded, and his golden eyes had grown strained. "And I asked him if he knew Finvarra's whereabouts, and he swore he didn't."

"We're trying to develop a lead on that front," I said. "I'm hopeful Maxen will come up with something soon. But we need to jump on that information about the Chalice. I'll change, and we can go to the Aberdeen."

I turned to head to my bedroom, but Oliver caught my arm.

"You can't just waltz into the Duergar realm," he said. "Not now. It's too dangerous."

I peered up into my father's eyes. He looked every bit as worried as Jasper, but for slightly different reasons.

"I'll go in directly through the doorway in Morven's pub," I said. "And I'll keep a low profile. He'd never rat me out."

Oliver shook his head. "If Periclase catches wind you're in his realm, there's a good chance you won't make it back out."

Inside I was bristling, but I forced my expression and voice to soften. "I know it's a risk, but we desperately need help. Finvarra still has the

Stone of Fal. We've got to have something to counter it."

"No, you don't," Oliver argued, his face hardening even more. "Finvarra will likely wait until most of Faerie has gathered in one place to face the Tuatha, and then he'll use the Stone. But we don't know when that will be. The gods may wait a hundred years to attack."

I suspected his defiance was partly due to the fact that it was Jasper who was asking me to take the risk. But Oliver's point wasn't completely invalid. It also wasn't a good enough reason to put off the errand.

"No, we don't know," I said quietly. "It could be a hundred years, or it could be tomorrow. Either way, it would be unwise to assume we have the luxury of time."

Oliver's eyes narrowed, and I knew he took offense to my implication that he was being unwise in his advice. Perhaps if we'd been alone he would have continued arguing. But he let go of my arm and took a half step back.

"I'll go with you," he said.

I shook my head. "You're too recognizable. The two of us there together will attract too much—"

"I'm going," he barked, cutting me off.

I glared at him, annoyed as hell that he'd spoken to me that way, especially in front of Jasper. I brushed past Oliver and went to my bedroom, where I yanked off my clothes with irritated, sharp movements. I changed into slim-fitting olive cargo pants, a navy long-sleeved Henley, and tall boots. I swept my long brown hair back into a low ponytail. Last, I grabbed a dark gray cape-style cloak. I didn't normally wear such loose-fitting clothes, but Aurora on my back would give me away at a glance. So instead of my usual back scabbard, I transferred the sword to a belt sheath, which I could throw the cloak over to conceal.

I took a deep breath as my fleeting wish to spend the morning finalizing Maxen's new position as Carraig Sidhe head of state slipped away. Getting information on the location of the Chalice was more important than my desire to hand off my royal responsibilities.

When I returned to the formal living room, Jasper was alone.

"He went to change, too," he said. "He's going to meet us back here."

"Sorry about that," I grumbled. "Oliver can be a surly bastard."

"He's just watching out for you. You're the light of his life, Petra, that much is clear."

I snorted, but the center of my chest warmed a bit at Jasper's words.

I sidled up to him. "Too bad we only have a minute or two alone." I slipped my arms around his neck and planted my mouth on his.

"Aye, it's an absolute crying shame." He breathed when we finally had to come up for air.

There was a rap at the door, and I reluctantly let go of Jasper's neck. Nothing like the arrival of a grouchy father to kill the mood.

I patted Jasper's cheek. "Later, perhaps." I pulled away and turned to grasp the doorknob, but not before I saw the heat in his golden eyes.

Oliver stood waiting outside my quarters. He'd changed into garb common in the Duergar realm—loose linen trousers, a slim-fitting green button-down shirt, and a leather vest. A short-billed woolen cap covered his cropped hair that had distinctive stripes shaved into the sides.

"Come with me." He lowered his voice. "We'll make an inconspicuous exit out of the fortress."

Oliver wordlessly handed Jasper a long dark brown traveling cloak similar to mine.

As my father led us through the fortress, taking lesser-used hallways and staircases, I tried to shake off the drained feeling that pulled at me. The previous day had been long and difficult, leaving me weary even after a hard night's sleep.

Oliver took us into an office he had to unlock with his palm, indicating it was magically sealed and would only open for specific individuals. Through the back of the office was another room, what looked like a generic conference room. But it had an arch designed into the stonework mosaic on the far wall.

Ha! I knew there were secret doorways.

I stepped up to it and poised my finger in the air, ready to draw the sigils that would take us to the doorway in the Aberdeen Inn.

"Hope this place doesn't implode while we're gone," I muttered with a furtive backward glance. I reached back and pulled the deep hood of my cloak forward so my face would be hidden. Jasper did the same.

Oliver and Jasper each placed a hand on my shoulder, and I traced the sigils and whispered the words. Together, we stepped forward and into the abyss of the netherwhere.

We emerged in a roped-off corner of Morven's pub, the stale smell of fried food undercutting the stronger scent of hoppy ale with urine undertones wafting from the nearby hallway that led to the restrooms. Several Aberdeen patrons looked up to see who the new arrivals were. Fortunately for us, the lighting was terrible and particularly bad in the corner where we'd entered.

Morven—resembling a large, muscular Santa Claus with his bulging shoulders, white beard, and reddened cheeks and nose—was in his usual position behind the bar. His dark gaze darted our way as he topped off a frosty mug from one of the taps.

A shiver shimmied down my spine, leaving a wake of spreading goosebumps. Morven and I had always been on decent terms, but there was something deeply unsettling, almost predatory, about the way he looked at people. Especially at those who had very strong or unique magic.

He pushed the mug across the bar to the waiting hand of a man still in his Duergar guard uniform. Even though the man was facing away from me, I bowed my head, hiding my face in the shadow of my cloak's hood.

Morven flicked his fingers at me in a subtle wave but wisely didn't otherwise acknowledge me. He gave a tiny tilt of his head toward the stairway that led up to the loft that housed his living quarters. Head down, I quickly crossed the short distance to the steep, narrow staircase.

No one really knew how old Morven was, but he'd been running the Aberdeen Inn for as long as anyone could remember. There was a wide, shiny line in the wooden walls on either side of the stairs where his broad shoulders had brushed past countless times.

Oliver and Jasper both followed me up, though I knew Morven wouldn't allow them to stay during our transaction. I went to the straight-backed chair where I'd sat a handful of times before. Looking around at the dingy loft with its low peaked ceiling, I did my best to tamp down on the claustrophobia that was gathering into a little knot of nausea in the pit of my stomach.

My father was peering around with narrow-eyed suspicion. When Morven appeared at the top of the stairs, Oliver's chest puffed out a little. I wasn't sure if Morven had any fighting skills—probably not, considering he spent all of his time behind the bar of the Aberdeen—but if he did, he and Oliver might have been a good match. Both of them were muscled and massive.

"You must wait down there," Morven said in an accent that was certainly Old World, but from so far in the past the specific region was unidentifiable to my ear. He pointed a thick forefinger back down the stairs.

"It's okay," I said quietly to Jasper and Oliver.

They turned and left, both looking equally pissed about it. I resisted the urge to roll my eyes. I'd survived Morven several times on my own just fine.

The Ghillie Dubh came to the larger chair set up at a ninety-degree angle to mine, settling on one hip with one long leg awkwardly stretched out, as if he weren't accustomed to sitting on furniture. He eyed me silently for a few seconds.

"You possess . . . something new, Petra Maguire," he said in his gravelly voice.

I shivered again. "Yes. Some new ability has apparently been unlocked within me and the other stone bloods."

He nodded gravely. "I heard the rumors."

"I don't know what it is, exactly."

"That's okay," he said, his dark eyes gleaming with barely checked eagerness. He wanted some of it, whatever the supposed god power was that flowed through my veins.

Morven could have gotten some of the god-blood magic, if that's what it was, from Jasper, but for whatever reason, the innkeeper wanted it from me.

"You came here seeking the location of the Chalice of Dagda?" he asked.

"That's right."

I could have explained to him why we so desperately wanted the Chalice, but I figured Morven didn't really care. In spite of running a lively pub that was legendary throughout Faerie, he somehow seemed to remain apart from the affairs of the realm. People came in for a beer, or they came for information. The ones who wanted the former left only coin behind, but those who sought the latter left a bit of themselves—their magic—with Morven. He collected it in some way no one really understood. All I knew was that the process was extremely unpleasant.

"Well, I presume you remember how this works," he said with a smile that was almost jolly if it didn't give me a case of the creeps.

I nodded, acutely aware of the bucket next to my chair. I'd never puked after, but apparently most did.

His eyelids began to drift down, and I tried to loosen the tension that held me so rigid. But I couldn't kid myself. There was no relaxing when I knew what was coming.

"Wait," I blurted.

His eyes popped open. He didn't look happy I'd interrupted.

"The new power, it comes from the Fomoire, I've been told," I said. "Do you know anything of it?"

He peered at me, his face reddening even more than his natural coloring, and for a breath I thought he was angry. But he cocked his head.

"Aye, I may know something." He stared me down and seconds ticked by. "I'll give you that for free, Petra Maguire. I'll even give it to you before I do the taking, so you know I'm genuine."

My brows shot up, and my spine went rigid. Free? Morven never gave information for free. *Never.*

"Okay?" I said uncertainly, trying to think if there was a catch I was missing.

"The answers you seek lie within one of the caves," he said. "The fair-haired stone blood prince will know what I mean."

I squinted at him. Caves? And he had to mean Maxen. If Morven said Maxen would know, he would. Morven was always good to his word, and the information he gave was never wrong.

His lids fluttered and sagged again. A moment later, the air seemed to disappear from the room, and magic like brown smoke began to leak from his nose, parted lips, and ears. It crept toward me, and I grasped the armrests of my chair in a white-knuckled grip. In what seemed like excruciatingly slow fashion, the brown magic seeped into my body until every cell seemed to scream for relief.

It was a deep agony of a million pinpricks that was most intense in the center of my chest. I choked, tears springing to my eyes as it felt like my heart was being slowly pierced with a thousand tiny needles.

And then suddenly, the torture disappeared, leaving a horrible wave of nausea in its wake. I hunched and swallowed hard against the bile rising up my throat. I slapped my hand over my mouth as my stomach tried to reject what little food I'd had that day. When the gagging stopped, I lowered my hand, wiped away the tears that'd leaked from my lower lids, and took a shaking breath. Every muscle in my body trembled with weakness.

"And now you get what you paid for," Morven said, all twinkly-eyed. I kind of wanted to punch him. That'd been the worst "payment" I'd ever experienced. Morven spent the next two or three minutes describing the location of the Chalice.

I nodded, unable to open my mouth yet.

"There is additional information that I can give you," he said. "That I must give you."

My entire body tightened, but I tried not to show my alarm. Why was Morven in such a giving mood?

"What is it?"

"You must leave the quest for the Chalice for later."

"Why?"

"Because you and the Glasgow man must go after Finvarra. And you must do it right now. If you don't go now, you won't have another chance. Do you hear me? You must go *now*."

He leaned forward for emphasis, and the back of my head knocked against the chair as I drew back in alarm. A chill swept through me as I remembered Eldon's warning, that I had to accompany Jasper to kill Finvarra, or Jasper wouldn't come out of it alive.

"Do you understand?" Morven demanded, uncharacteristically irate.

I nodded. "I have to go with Jasper after Finvarra."

"Now!"

"Yes. Now. Immediately. We'll go as soon as we can."

He gave me a hard, unblinking stare. "Good."

Knowing I'd need a minute or two before I could stand, Morven rose and went toward the staircase. He always gave me some privacy to recover. At the top of the stairs, he stopped and turned to me. Pulling something from his pocket, he palmed whatever it was and then tossed it to me. It winked at me, reflecting the light of the bare bulb over the stairs. I caught it in one hand and peered down at the object. It was a coin—brass, maybe—and unlike anything I'd ever seen. It was about the size of an Earthly quarter, with a hole in the center.

"When the gods come, call me with that," Morven said.

I peered at him through the gloom of the loft. "How?" I croaked.

"Toss it in a body of water and speak my name," he said.

We locked eyes, and he gave me a nod.

"I will," I said. I tucked the coin into a pouch on my belt.

He left, and I remained in my chair for nearly ten minutes, deep-breathing with the sole focus of not vomiting, before I dared try to stand. My knees only wobbled a little as I descended the stairs. Dizziness forced me to keep a hand on the wall as I rejoined Jasper and my father.

"I'm fine," I said, before they could express any worry. Leaning into them, I lowered my voice to a whisper. "He told me where it is."

"Let's wait until we have more privacy," Oliver said. He began guiding me toward the roped-off corner with the doorway. "We should get out of here before anyone notices us."

"I agree." I pointed to a curled piece of paper with a broken wax seal in Jasper's hand. "Someone send you a message here?"

He shook his head. "It was delivered to Oliver. It's from Maxen."

I turned to my father. "You told Maxen where we went?"

"I did. No harm in it."

"What does the note say?" I asked, looking back and forth between them and trying to decipher the tension that hung around both men.

Jasper leaned down until his lips were next to my ear. "He believes he knows where Finvarra is," he whispered.

Chapter 17

MY BREATH CAUGHT in my throat, but I didn't have time to demand more information because Jasper and Oliver were pulling me through the Aberdeen's doorway.

Maxen was there in the secret doorway room of the fortress when we stepped from the void. He looked up when we appeared, and I guessed he'd been pacing in anticipation of our arrival.

"It went well at the Aberdeen?" he asked, his face tense.

I gave a curt nod. "We got what we were looking for. But if you know where Finvarra is, we need to go after him full force. The Chalice of Dagda will have to wait."

"Yes," Maxen said. His gaze shifted to Jasper. "You're up for the trip, I presume?"

"Aye," Jasper said, patting a sheath on his belt. "I've got a blade with Finvarra's name on it."

I'd nearly forgotten about Gae Buide, the lethal yellow knife Oberon had loaned to Jasper. It was a magical weapon that killed if a wound was inflicted with it, even just a nick. But it couldn't harm the wielder, as long as he kept a hand on it.

Adrenaline began to cut through the drain of paying Morven for his information. "Where is Finvarra?" I asked.

I was practically salivating at the prospect of an opportunity to draw my sword. It'd been too long since my last decent battle. It would do me good to fight a real enemy. Maybe it would help wash away some of the bitter taste of my recent struggles in the fortress.

"The Daoine realm," Maxen said.

Oliver's hands flexed into loose fists. "How sure are you?"

"I don't have eyes on him, but based on what his former companion told us, I would bet all I own that he's there." Maxen gave a short laugh. "We'll have to think of an appropriate way to reward Eunice."

"We will, if we get him," I said. "We need to gather a hunting party."

"Agreed," Maxen said. "Any ideas, besides Jasper?"

"I'm going," I said quickly. I shot a look at my father. "Don't try to talk me out of it. I'm not sitting here polishing the crown while others are out doing the real work."

Oliver's face tightened, but he didn't try to dissuade me. "I'll go."

If it were anything less important, I would have insisted he stay in the fortress, but we needed our best to go up against Finvarra.

"We need someone who knows the Daoine Sidhe realm very well," I said. "And if he or she can wield a sword or some other weapon, all the better."

"I propose two additions to our team," Jasper said.

We all turned to him with curiosity.

"Bryna Marcourt. And Drifte, one of my mentors. You met him." Jasper's eyes found mine.

"The raven shifter who took us into the cave?" I asked. Recalling the strange man with the solid jet-black eyes, I suppressed a shiver.

Jasper nodded. "He won't wield a sword or any other weapon, but we'll do well to take him along. He knows Daoine ways, and he knows the realm."

"He won't have a problem betraying the Daoine or being part of a mission to kill the Unseelie High King?" Maxen asked.

"Drifte is Daoine in blood only," Jasper said. "He answers to no king or queen."

"And you want to take *Bryna*? As in my half-sister?" I gave him a doubtful look.

An amused smile ghosted over Jasper's lips. "Aye, that very Bryna."

"For the love of the gods, why?"

"There's more to her than meets the eye," Jasper said. "She knows her way around most realms, and she's incredibly resourceful."

"We can't afford to have anyone along who needs protecting." I was trying not to sound whiny, but the thought of having Bryna along considerably dampened my eagerness for the mission.

"You don't need to worry about her," he said. "She was trained in knife wielding by a Sylph blademaster."

That shut me up for a second or two. I inclined my head in acquiescence. I trusted Jasper's judgment. "Okay. Drifte and Bryna are in, if they're willing."

Jasper turned to Maxen. "Where's the nearest door outside? I'll need to send messenger ravens to them immediately."

Maxen went and poked his head into the corridor, hailed a waiting page, and asked her to take Jasper where he needed to go.

"Do we know anything about Finvarra's specific location?" I asked, combing my memory for any facts I could dredge up about the kingdom.

The Daoine Sidhe realm was Unseelie-aligned and governed by a triumvirate. The three co-rulers typically represented the three major Daoine shifter categories—avian, marine, and reptilian. There were no mammalian Daoine shifters. Kelpies, seahorse shifters, were their own unique Seelie race apart from the Daoine.

"I believe we do," Maxen said. His sapphire blue eyes gleamed. "Rumor has it the ruling triad has planned a grand fete starting tonight that will last three days. They're not officially saying what the celebration is for, but they're bringing in beautiful female companions from other kingdoms. The featured menu item is squid from the Kelpie realm. And guess what the featured beverage for the event will be?"

"Elvish red wine," I said.

Maxen's mouth stretched in a little grin. "The Daoine court has reportedly ordered two hundred casks of it."

I tipped my head back and let out a short laugh. "Two *hundred*? That's nothing short of blatant. Nobody likes Elvish wine *that* much."

"I know," Maxen said. "Thank the gods for the hedonistic ways of the Unseelie, right?"

We shared a brief smile, but he quickly broke eye contact.

"Finvarra will be somewhere in Palace City, then," I said.

Each Daoine ruler and their respective families and courtiers occupied one of three palaces arranged in a triangle, collectively referred to as Palace City. It sat at the heart of the Daoine kingdom.

"I expect so," Maxen said.

I rubbed my hands together. "I need maps."

He picked up a tablet, swiped and tapped it with his fingertips, and the monitor on the wall directly ahead of me lit up. "Here's all we know about that region."

Maxen spoke in generalities about Palace City and the area immediately surrounding it. I stood back and studied the diagrams for a few minutes. Oliver was a few feet away doing the same.

"How close to Palace City can we come through?" I asked.

Maxen winced and shifted his weight. "That's a problem. The only doorway we're privy to is many miles from the palaces. And it's guarded round the clock. While the Stone Order never had any specific quarrel with the Daoine, the triumvirate never considered ours a valuable relationship and so didn't grant us access to more valuable doorways."

Shoot.

"What about concealing our identities?" I scrunched my mouth to one side, thinking. "We could see if Melusine would be willing to go and use her obfuscation magic to disguise us."

Maxen shook his head. "Oberon isn't going to let her go. At this point, he doesn't want her expending effort on anything except protecting his castle."

Jasper returned, and I turned to follow him with my eyes as he joined us. "How much notice would a small flock of Great Ravens attract in the Daoine realm?"

His eyes locked on the maps splashed across the wall. "They can be stealthy enough to make a quiet entrance." He turned his golden gaze to me. "Thinking transportation once we're there?"

"Not just that. We need to pop in undetected, and the only doorway we know sigils for is under guard."

"Shouldn't be a problem," Jasper said. "Drifte can help us avoid detection as well."

"So he's willing?" I asked.

"Aye."

That was fast. Jasper must have had some kind of direct line to the raven shifter.

Oliver crossed his arms and pushed his weight over to one hip. "Who exactly is this Drifte you keep speaking of?"

Jasper faced my father. "He's a raven shifter who's formed an arcane kinship with his animal form."

Oliver's eyes narrowed. "One of those creatures that's more animal than human?"

I started to take a step forward, sensing the conversation could begin to unravel. We didn't have time for arguments. But Jasper responded before I could.

"I suppose you could say that." Jasper's tone was mild, but he kept steady, direct eye contact with Oliver. "He has bonded deeply with his raven and feels most at home in that form. But I've known him half my life. He mentored me when I was becoming a Grand Raven Master. He saw the coming storm of the Tuatha's return earlier than most, and despite being more animal than human in the view of some, he cares deeply about Faerie."

I watched Oliver's expression closely while Jasper spoke. It darkened at first, but when Jasper revealed the bit about being a Grand Raven Master, my father's brows pitched in surprise and respect flickered in his deep-set eyes. A small measure of relief eased through my shoulders, but I knew better than to assume Oliver wouldn't be watching Drifte with suspicion.

"And Bryna?" I asked, trying to move things along.

"She'll be here within the hour," Jasper said.

I gave him a wry look. "Really? Did you fail to mention I'd be involved?"

Jasper's full lips twitched with suppressed amusement. "Nope. And she still agreed. Miraculous, isn't it?"

I snorted.

"We can expect Drifte soon as well."

Drawing a deep breath, I turned back to the maps on the wall. "Can you zoom into the palaces?" I asked Maxen.

The image shifted, and I took a few steps closer. "Any ideas about how we'll figure out Finvarra's exact location?"

"We'll have to do some scouting, I expect," Maxen said behind me.

Maxen, Oliver, Jasper, and I spent the next twenty minutes talking through different scenarios.

"I'm particularly concerned about how we'll get close enough to him," I said. "And then after, how we'll get out."

We pondered those problems in silence for a moment.

I tilted my head and slanted a look at Maxen. "What about Eunice?"

His brows knit together. "What are you thinking?"

"What if she asks for audience with Finvarra? She can truthfully say they had a falling out and she's there to speak with him. The implication will be that she wants to make amends." I paused, my mind whirling, and licked my lips. I knew she had no desire to return to Finvarra, and she couldn't lie outright. She'd have to speak around the truth. "Jasper could accompany her, posing as her chaperone. He'll have to be well-disguised, of course."

"I like it," Jasper said slowly.

Oliver made a soft grumbling sound of doubt in the back of his throat.

"She's eager to be of assistance," I said, ignoring my father. "And her skill set is distinctly different from any of ours."

Maxen's eyes widened. Jasper arched a brow.

"That's not what I mean," I said, planting my hands on my hips and casting withering looks at both of them. "She knows Finvarra well, and she understands how to navigate the people close to him. She's had to survive as little more than a slave in the company of powerful people. It requires a brand of finesse that deserves our respect."

"I worry that our party is growing too large," Oliver said.

Before I could respond, the latch on the door released. A lithe woman with long blond hair strode in.

Bryna stopped near Jasper, jutted a hip out, and planted her hand on it. "I heard the word 'party,' but this looks more like a wake."

I smothered a sigh in the back of my throat. "Hello, Bryna. I trust you know everyone here?"

She cast an unabashedly critical look around the group. Her eyes stopped at Oliver and she tilted her head. "You, I haven't formally met. You must be Petra's father."

She stepped up to my father, the top of her head barely reaching his chest, and thrust out her arm, offering to shake. After a moment's surprised hesitation, Oliver's huge paw engulfed her hand.

"Oliver Maguire," he said.

She nodded. "Bryna Marcourt."

I wasn't sure why, but seeing the two of them shake hands gave me a funny sensation in my middle. It felt like some sort of odd family reunion, except Bryna and I despised each other and she and Oliver weren't in any way related.

"We appreciate your help and your speed in getting here," Jasper said.

His eyes sparked warmly at her, and her sharp-edged expression softened under his attention. She inclined her head and then looked up and clapped her hands once.

"Okay, what's the plan?" she asked.

I turned to Jasper. "Should we wait for Drifte?"

He shook his head. "Let's lay down our strategy. If Drifte sees how we can refine our approach, he'll let us know."

I turned to my half-sister. "Here's what we have so far," I said, and gave her the rundown of how we planned to get into the Daoine realm and have Eunice get Jasper close to Finvarra.

After I finished, Bryna cocked her head and pushed out her bottom lip, considering. "Not too bad, but it's not good enough," she said finally. "Trying to get Eunice through the layers of people likely to be keeping the riffraff away from Finvarra is a stretch. She could get sent away at any point, and then what? Plus, it would waste way too much time. We need a shortcut."

"Okay. Any ideas?" I asked.

A slow, devious smile stretched the corners of Bryna's mouth, and her lids lowered partway. "Oh, yes," she said, drawing out the words.

I returned her grin, and for a moment forgot how much she grated my nerves. "Do tell," I said, lifting my palm in invitation.

Chapter 18

IT TURNED OUT my abrasive half-sister knew a hell of a lot about how to navigate the three castles of the Daoine Sidhes' Palace City. I tried to get her to tell me how she'd come by the expertise, but she'd just laughed loudly in my face. I managed not to punch her in the nose in response.

By the time Drifte arrived at the fortress, it was nearly midnight. While we'd waited, we fetched Eunice and explained our idea. She'd been more than eager to help. Maxen called for Vera, our top fashion and wardrobe expert, and she'd found suitable clothes for Eunice and Jasper. The outfits were simple and muted, clothes people with few means would wear. She'd also helped us with disguises. A short sandy-blonde bob wig and fake eyelashes long as a Sylph's transformed me into someone I didn't recognize when I looked in the mirror. For Jasper, she found a shaggy dark brown wig to go under a cap. Oliver grumbled about feeling ridiculous, but eventually accepted a wig with a dark ponytail at his nape. I wasn't sure it was enough. His stature and the carved features of his face still seemed too distinct to me.

We were waiting for Vera to find cloaks for all of us, and then we'd be ready to depart.

Drifte—with his long hair the blue-black of ravens' feathers, solid onyx eyes, and rustic garb—stood off to one side with Jasper. They conversed in low tones in a language I didn't recognize. Bryna, uncharacteristically quiet, was studying the images of Palace City that Maxen had pulled up to project on the wall.

Oliver stood next to me and kept casting furtive looks at Jasper and the raven shifter.

"He makes you uncomfortable," I said, my voice barely above a whisper.

"He's Unseelie," Oliver said. "How can we trust an Unseelie in these times?"

I frowned. "Are you talking about Jasper or Drifte?"

He grunted. "Maybe both."

"I'll tell you what Jasper told me." My gaze locked on Jasper as I spoke to my father. "This was before he and I became . . . involved. Just so you know that had nothing to do with it. This was also before Finvarra was known to be in Faerie, and it was back when there were only the bare whisperings of the possible return of the Tuatha De Danann. Jasper said he believed the only way through, the only way Faerie would survive, was if we could rise above the Seelie-Unseelie divide. Basically, he said that what we were facing was more important than politics, than the past, than any other excuse the average Fae could come up with. I didn't put much stock in it at first, though I admit his passion on the topic did snag my attention. But I've come to see that he's right."

I could feel Oliver's attention on me, and I half-turned so I could look up into his eyes. "If someone like me, who wanted nothing more than to escape Faerie politics and drama, can see the sincerity and truth in Jasper's motives, do you think that maybe you could give him the benefit of the doubt?"

I said it without a shred of impatience or judgment. I just put the question out there and watched my father's face. The muscles of his jaw tightened and then released.

"I suppose I could do that," he said finally.

I nodded. "As far as Drifte goes, I know he's an odd character. But I believe he and Jasper are similarly motivated, different as they might appear on the surface."

Oliver tipped his face my direction, and his eyes met mine. "You've changed so much, Petra."

My lips parted, but I didn't speak because I wasn't immediately sure if his statement was meant as a compliment or criticism.

"I knew you had this potential in you," my father continued. "I knew you had *greatness* in you. It started to come through when you took up Aurora and defended the Stone Order in Oberon's arena. But still, I knew there was more. I saw another glimpse when you took the throne. And yet I knew there was even more to come. I always knew you had greatness in you."

His voice began to falter, and I had to break eye contact as my throat began to close with the pressure of welling emotion. I stared at the floor and took a deep, slow breath before I dared look up.

"I don't think I deserve all that. I'm an absolute shit queen, for starters." I let out a quiet, rueful laugh. "But I appreciate your faith in me."

"You survived the coronation. You achieved some level of peace in the fortress. You've done it under extremely difficult circumstances. There's more to do, sure, but don't forget to give yourself a bit of credit."

My heart seemed to cramp in my chest as I once again remembered that Oliver wasn't my blood father. For a fleeting moment, I wished more than anything that he was. But with the next breath I realized that our lack of blood connection didn't truly mean anything. He'd raised me, loved me, and believed in me. What else mattered?

Vera bustled through the door, giving us a welcome excuse to focus elsewhere. Dark garments were heaped over both of her arms. She walked around the room, handing hooded cloaks to each of us.

Drifte wordlessly lifted his hand, declining Vera's offer of a cloak. She edged away, her eyes wide. Bryna sidled over to where I stood as the rest of us arranged our cloaks over our respective weapons. I braced myself for animosity, but she seemed subdued.

"You can't really tell what he's looking at," she murmured to me without moving her lips. "Kind of freaks me out."

I glanced at Drifte. "Yeah. It's a little unsettling. You've never met him before, I take it?"

She gave a subtle shake of her head.

The door opened again, a page arriving with Eunice. The former consort had already come to our meeting room so we could explain what we had planned. She'd agreed to aid us and gone back to her quarters to change. Vera helped her with a cloak.

The page and Vera both departed, leaving only Maxen and the party that would set out for the Daoine realm.

"I believe we're ready," Jasper said. His hand shifted to the sheath that hid Gae Buide, though I guessed he wasn't even aware of the movement.

"Before we go, I need a brief moment alone with Maxen," I said.

I turned to the door and then looked back, beckoning to Maxen. His brows arched in curiosity, he followed me. We went into the small anteroom that adjoined the meeting room where we'd spent the last few hours. I shut the door and turned to him.

"We don't have time to mince words, so I'm just going to be blunt. I wrote up a document that makes you the Carraig Sidhe head of state," I said. He started to speak, but I held up a hand to stop him. "I know I can't step down from the throne, but I'm not fit to lead a kingdom. Not as a true queen, anyway. I'll lead in other ways, ones that allow me to use my sword. I understand the spirit of Oberon's order, but he made a mistake. You need to be in charge. I'll be queen in name only. I'm a warrior, not a royal. And I sure as hell am *not* any kind of politician. In spite of what Oberon has said, we do still have need for leaders with political savvy in Faerie. If I try to be a head of state, I'll only screw things up even more for us. That much has become obvious over the past few days."

"Petra—" Maxen halted, his mouth snapping shut, opening, and then closing again. Finally, he let out a long breath. "If it's an order from the throne, you know I can't refuse it."

"That's right," I said.

I'd known exactly what I was doing in drawing up the official document. And unlike the other appointments I was making to fill positions in my court, where I wanted sincere buy-in from each candidate, Maxen was going to have to serve where I wanted him whether he loved it or hated it. I felt a small stab of guilt, knowing that I was taking advantage of his sincerity, of his track record as a faithful servant to his people. But I was putting him was where we—his people—needed him, within the confines of Oberon's order that I wear the crown.

"Then I won't argue," he said with a grating edge to his voice.

"I know you'll hold things together while we're gone, and I truly appreciate it. More than you know, Maxen. We'll work out the details after I return."

Part of me wanted to apologize, to tell him I knew it was unfair that he wasn't Marisol's successor. Despite his humble service, I knew that was what he'd wanted, to eventually take the throne. His mother had been grooming him for it, had probably whispered in his ear since birth that someday he would be king of the realm she created. But did anyone's life ever turn out exactly as planned? Mine sure as hell had taken a sharp turn off the course I'd foreseen for myself.

He gave me a tight nod, and my heart sank a little. It'd felt like Maxen and I had just started to take tenuous steps toward being on better terms, but my order had clearly set us back. I wasn't surprised, and it couldn't be helped, but it saddened me all the same.

"One more thing," I said. "Morven told me to tell you that the answer to our questions about the Fomoire power running through our blood lies in some caves. He seemed to think you'd know exactly what he meant."

Maxen squinted. "Caves?"

"Does it make any sense to you that the supposed god power running through our veins has something to do with caves or mines?"

"Maybe. I'll look into it immediately."

We rejoined Jasper, Oliver, Bryna, Eunice, and Drifte, who'd gathered at the back of the room where a doorway's arch was painted on the wall.

"We'll go to a remote spot of Drifte's choosing first," Jasper said. "There, we'll be met with Great Ravens who will take us into the Daoine Sidhe kingdom."

Eunice watched him with round eyes. She swallowed hard as Drifte stepped in front of the arch. Remembering what I'd said to Jasper about not taking anyone who couldn't defend themselves, I tamped down my concern about dragging Eunice into this and gave her what I hoped was a reassuring smile. Then, I placed my hand on the shoulder of the raven shifter. She only hesitated for a second before doing the same. Once the whole party had made physical contact with Drifte's arms and shoulders, he raised his hand and began tracing sigils in the air.

Just before we stepped into the oblivion of the netherwhere, I glanced over my shoulder at Maxen who stood alone a few feet away. His sapphire blue eyes held my gaze for a fraction of a second before everything gave way to the void.

We all shuffled out of the netherwhere into the dark night of a realm with no artificial light. Stars glittered overhead, and I could see the plume of my own breath against the dark sky in the chilly air. Something about the place rang with familiarity. When I spotted the lazy curls of smoke rising from small, rustic abodes, I knew we'd come to Drifte's settlement. Jasper and I had been there once before, when we'd been desperate to rescue Oberon from the Tuatha.

"Oh, my," Eunice murmured. She shivered visibly and pulled her cloak tight around her shoulders.

"Wait here," Jasper said. He and Drifte strode several feet away, and a moment later I heard the strange whistle Jasper used to call Great Ravens.

We were in a region so remote it wasn't part of any civilized kingdom. My chest went icy when I remembered the snow-peaked mountains. I looked off to the horizon, and even in the dark of night, I could see the white tops of the distant ranges. It appeared the snow line had descended considerably since my last visit.

Snow in Faerie. I pulled my cloak tighter. More snow than before meant the Unseelie had gained a greater foothold in the balance of power. The reign of Oberon and the Summer Court had lasted for seemingly endless generations, and the Fae had basked in the warmth and abundance of eternal gentle breezes, blooming flowers, and warm sunshine. But this place was crisp and cold. Summer was over, here.

"There they are," Bryna whispered. She pointed over the treetops of the forest to our left.

Just above the tree line, dark shapes were winging toward us. We all stood silently and watched the Great Ravens approach. Five of them, one for each in our party minus Drifte, landed in the clearing fifty yards off and then flapped and hopped toward us.

Oliver was shifting his weight and clenching and unclenching his hands. I moved to his side.

"I've ridden them several times," I said in a low voice. "Great way to travel. You'll get used to it."

"I'm not wild about heights," he said after a second's hesitation.

"Keep your eyes on the horizon, use your thighs to stabilize your position, and hold those feathers for all your worth," I advised.

Eunice had edged over to us and heard my suggestions.

"I've always dreamed of riding one, Your Majesty," she said, her voice awed. "You have my gratitude for making this dream come true and for trusting me with such a vital mission."

I suddenly wanted to hug her, even though I wasn't the hugging type. "We are lucky to have you."

"You're a brave woman." Oliver's words came out gruff and ended in a grunt. I peered at him, surprised. The stone man wasn't one to cast compliments around.

Eunice tittered with pleasure. "Oh, dear me, I do appreciate that coming from one such as yourself, my lord." Her fingers came up to smooth her hair.

"It's time," Jasper called.

Bryna, Eunice, Oliver, and I joined Jasper. Drifte turned and headed off into the shadows of the trees. Jasper assigned each of us a Great Raven, and when I approached mine, a grin spread over my face as I recognized the spiky feathers poking up on top of the creature's head.

"Hey, Mohawk," I whispered, petting the bird's sleek neck. I'd ridden this Raven a handful of times before.

Jasper got everyone else situated, and I mounted my bird, settling into the soft feathers and positioning my knees between the wings.

Something burst from the nearby treetops, and I swiveled around with my heart in my throat. Jasper raised a hand to the bird circling overhead, and I realized it was Drifte in his raven form.

Jasper climbed on top of his bird, and it hopped around to face us.

"They'll take us through the netherwhere into the Daoine realm," he said, his voice low but carrying in the quiet of the nearly deserted land. "The birds know to be stealthy. Just stay quiet in the air, keep low to your Raven's back, and wait until they land before speaking."

He whispered something to his bird, and the great creature hopped three times, flapped its wings hard, and took flight. The rest of the birds followed. Exhilaration blazed through me as Mohawk gained altitude. I lay over her neck, keeping my weight forward so I wouldn't tumble back. A glance to either side revealed that Bryna, Eunice, and Oliver had managed to navigate the takeoff.

Freezing air streamed past my face, numbing my cheeks and bringing tears to my eyes. We continued to climb for another minute or two, and then Jasper and his bird winked out of existence. A few seconds later, Mohawk plunged us into the void, using one of the Great Raven doorways that were invisible to Fae.

We materialized back into the world, and Mohawk quietly winged through air considerably warmer than that of the realm we'd just left. Ahead, I spotted three identical pointed pinnacles, the tops of the tallest towers on each of the three Daoine palaces, jutting up past the horizon line to loom higher than the distant range of foothills. The palace towers were lit with spotlights that highlighted their golden sheen. As we drew nearer, small explosions burst in the air around Palace City. Mohawk dipped a wing in alarm, but the glitter of fireworks showered down harmlessly a mile in front of us.

Jasper's Raven angled off to the right, toward a dark area of rolling hills that bordered one side of Palace City. The rest of the birds followed. We landed behind a low hill, except for Drifte, who continued to circle overhead.

Jasper tipped his head back, raised his hand, and then blew a couple of short bursts into his whistle. Drifte took off toward the palaces.

"He's going to scout the area for us," Jasper explained, sliding to the ground. "He'll let us know which way is best for us to enter. Then, Bryna will help us navigate Palace City."

The sounds of music, laughter, and revelry drifted to us on a gentle updraft of warm night air.

"I hope that Elvish wine is making everyone lose their minds," I muttered and began hiking up the small rise so I could get a view of the palaces.

The rest of my party trailed after me. I stopped before the crest so I wouldn't be fully exposed on the chance anyone was looking our way. We were about a half mile from the nearest edge of Palace City. The three strongholds were surrounded by an octagon of battlement walls, and guards patrolled the parapet walks between towers. But even from our current distance I could see that several of the gates were thrown open. Revelers were streaming inside, with a few coming out. It didn't look like a particularly locked-down situation from the outside, but if Finvarra was in there somewhere, there was certainly tight security surrounding him.

I turned to my half-sister, whose pale-blond hair glowed like spun silver in the light of the moon. "Where do you think they're hiding him?"

She pursed her lips and frowned for a moment. "Probably in the most luxurious guest accommodations they have. That'd be between the avian palace and the reptilian palace." She pointed between two of the three tall pinnacles.

"Is that Drifte?" Oliver asked, pointing at a dark shape darting toward us.

Jasper peered over the hilltop. "Aye, it's him."

My pulse quickened at the thought of finally getting some action, even if it was just walking the short distance to Palace City.

We set off in the direction Drifte took us. I walked next to Jasper and Eunice kept close behind us. Oliver and Bryna brought up the rear of our party. We moved quietly through the darkness shadowing the land that surrounded the brightly lit Palace City. Drifte led us by flying ahead a short distance, returning, and then darting ahead again. It appeared we were aiming for one of the main gates.

As we neared the bridge leading to the gate, I slowed and then halted before we reached the loose stream of people still flocking inside.

"It's time to split up," I said. "Jasper and Eunice will go ahead. The rest of us will trail you. Don't look back. We'll keep track of where you are." The last part was for Eunice, as I could tell she was nervous about what was about to happen.

"Once we're inside, you'll want to start making your way to the left," Bryna said. "There's a public garden area where I know of an entrance to a passage that will get us close to the luxury guest quarters. Go there and linger until we catch up."

Jasper brushed the back of my hand with his fingers. "We'll see you in there."

He was armed only with Gae Buide, as his Duergar short sword wouldn't have blended with the persona he was attempting to portray. I'd also had to leave my primary weapon at home, and instead of Aurora, I carried a generic broadsword.

Eunice fell into step beside him, and the pair made their way out of the shadows, joining the line of people flowing toward the footbridge leading to the gate. I waited until a dozen guests filled in behind them.

"Okay, let's go," I said to Oliver and Bryna.

To cross the bridge, we had to pass under three arched barbicans, each of them uplit and flanked by guards posted on either side. The soldiers' eyes roved the people moving toward the gate.

Most of the people ahead of and behind us appeared to already be in some state of inebriation, singing, joking, or laughing raucously. Our silence was making us stand out.

"We're too quiet," I muttered to my companions.

I threw one arm around Oliver's waist and the other across Bryna's shoulders. She shot me an irritated look but didn't push me away. I pasted on a big smile and listed a little as I walked.

To my surprise, Bryna started singing a drinking song in a strong, clear voice. I managed to dredge up the words by the time she got to the chorus, and I joined in. By the time we reached the gate, most of the people around us were singing, too.

I kept the back of Jasper's reddish-blond head in my sights and let out a little relieved breath when I saw that he and Eunice had made it inside. The guards at the gate didn't seem concerned about weapons, as a woman with two short swords on her back sauntered right by them. It didn't surprise me. The royal families and their courts would be tucked away in their palaces at their own private parties. They didn't care if drunken commoners carved each other up. It was characteristic of many Unseelie kingdoms to expect and even revel in violence as part of their celebrations, something that harkened back to the days when the Unseelie tribes were more primitive and wild. Before Finvarra had stepped in to civilize them and unite them into kingdoms.

We spilled into the wide-open space of a bailey. Most of the guests veered to the right, toward the loud music, voices, and occasional holler or crash. I spotted a sign for the public gardens that pointed to the left. Jasper and Eunice were heading that way. They disappeared into a corridor.

I said a silent prayer to keep them safe and steered Oliver and Bryna that direction.

Chapter 19

WE EMERGED INTO a large open courtyard dimly lit with the dancing flames of torches. We weren't alone—pairs of guests roamed the gravel paths that wove between flower beds, trees, and shaped hedges. It seemed to be the place for couples to look for a bit of privacy to steal a romantic moment. One couple leaned against a tree, their lips locked together and their arms twined around each other in a passionate embrace. Lusty moans and cries from behind some of the hedges indicated others had progressed beyond kissing.

Jasper and Eunice sat on a bench next to a tall, tiered fountain.

Oliver, Bryna, and I moseyed over to stand near them.

"Bryna, you're up," I whispered.

"See that structure over there?" She lifted her chin to the left. "It's a public restroom. In the end stall of the women's side, there's a trapdoor. It leads down into the service tunnels. I'll go in first and wait for you."

She broke off and strolled to the path that led to the small building, and a moment later she disappeared inside.

"The two of you should go next," I said to Jasper.

He and Eunice rose and traced Bryna's steps. I waited until they were in before nodding to my father. As our boots scuffed over the gravel, I looked around for Drifte, but the shifter was out of sight somewhere. I was just about to reach for the door when a man and a woman stumbled around the corner, the man plowing into Oliver. They smelled of alcohol, and they both wore broadswords on their belts. My insides tightened.

"Hey, watch it, mate," the man said. He shoved Oliver's shoulder.

The woman leaned forward, peering at us. "That's the ladies' room. You can't go in there," she said to Oliver, slurring just a little. She turned to me. "Honey, is this man trying to get you to do something you don't wanna do?"

"No, I'm fine," I said impatiently.

The man was still focused on Oliver. "I said you need to watch it." He punctuated every other word by jabbing his finger into my father's chest. Dumbass.

"Back off," Oliver growled.

That was all the man needed. He reached down and drew his sword.

Oliver nudged me toward the door. "Go, I'll be right behind you." He drew his own sword and nimbly tossed the handle between his two hands, obviously relishing the thought of taking the drunk man down a notch.

With a grumble, I pushed through the door, hoping Oliver would quickly knock out the man and catch up. But the clangs of metal outside indicated there might be more of a fight than I'd hoped.

I got to the last stall and found Bryna waiting. "Oliver got waylaid," I said.

She cursed under her breath. "You might as well go down." She pointed to a square opening in the floor where a tile had been removed.

I sat on the edge, let my legs hang through, and then dropped into the darkness. My feet hit a rough surface, and the stale and slightly rotten smell of standing water filled my nostrils. Eunice and Jasper stood off to the side. The unfinished ceiling was only about a foot and a half over my head.

"Someone tried to pick a fight with Oliver," I said and huffed an annoyed sigh.

"Damnit," Jasper muttered.

I looked up, hoping to see my father appear. Half a minute passed.

"Can you hear them out there?" I called up to Bryna.

"Shh!" she hissed irritably. She paused for a moment, listening, and then shook her head. "It sounds like the fighting's stopped. Hang on, I'm going to look."

She left and then reappeared several seconds later. "He's not out there," was all she said.

My heart dropped as I watched her lower herself through the opening.

I knew Oliver could handle himself, but I'd already lost him once. It made me edgy to not know what'd happened to him.

"Others may have noticed the fighting," Jasper said. "He probably had to hide to avoid more trouble. Next time we cross paths with Drifte, I'll see if he can locate Oliver."

I nodded, but my jaw worked as I tried to squash the uneasy sensation growing in the pit of my stomach.

"Boost me up?" Bryna asked Jasper.

He interlaced his fingers to create a step and then lifted her so she could reach through the opening and slide the tile across, plunging us into semi-darkness. Faint light leaked from far ahead.

Bryna landed back on the ground and brushed off her hands. "This way." She pointed in the direction of the weak light.

Plumbing conduits hissed and thumped above us as we followed her, and every so often water splatted on my head or shoulders or ran down the walls to form puddles. Widely spaced caged bulbs saved us from complete pitch dark.

My boots crunched on the gravel of what looked like an in-ground drain, and Bryna's head whipped around. "Try to keep it down, will you?"

I lifted my hands and shrugged. I was being as careful as I could, and I didn't think I was any louder than Jasper or Eunice. Bryna had always enjoyed criticizing my lack of stealth.

When we reached a crossroads in the tunnel, she stopped and looked both ways, hesitating for several long seconds.

"We're not lost, are we?" I finally asked.

She shot me a glare. "No." Then she stalked off to the left.

After a couple more turns, the tunnel dead-ended at a metal ladder. Bryna put one hand on it and turned to us.

"This'll put us out into a mechanical room," she said.

I tipped my head to look up at the rusted ladder. "How far will we be from the luxury quarters you were talking about?"

"About half the distance we were before," she replied.

"That's fantastic progress. Where to after the mechanical room?" Jasper asked. I cast him a quick, grateful look. I'd wanted to ask for more details, but Bryna was more likely to be helpful to him than to me.

"There's a stable nearby," she said. "We'll go outside and regroup there."

She reached for a rung over her head and nimbly made her way up. I went next with Eunice behind me, and Jasper climbed up last.

The air in the mechanical room was heavy with steam that immediately condensed and clung to my skin. Loud chugging of pumps drowned out all other sound. There was no sign of any workers, and again I was thankful for the Unseelie style of revelry that meant everyone was allowed to abandon their work to join in the party. Well, everyone except guards, soldiers, and servants who supplied the food and drink.

Bryna wove us through the machinery to an exit that spilled us into a corridor. By its plainness and the white-clad servants scurrying around, it was clearly a service hallway. And we most definitely did not fit in. Servants cast us odd looks, and one man gave us a dark frown, turning to watch us as we passed him.

"We need to get out of here," I muttered to Bryna.

"Yeah, I know."

She cut to the right, then left, and we came to a door that was propped open by a chair. We stepped through it and were once again outside. The smell of hay and manure indicated Bryna's memory was good—there were horses nearby. We skirted the wall of the building we'd just exited, following her as she speed-walked.

Behind me, I heard Jasper's reverberating low whistle, probably calling our location to Drifte. Half a minute later, it sounded again.

Avoiding the brightly lit open doors where attendants stood chattering and laughing, Bryna took us around the side and to the back of the horse barn.

She pointed to a keep, a rectangular building smaller than the one we'd just left, with a pointed roof that featured a glowing jeweled orb at the peak. "That's the luxury quarters."

The structure stood about half a mile away. Not a challenging distance to cover, except for one thing. Between where we stood and the luxury quarters, the place was thick with guards. We were within the outer wall of Palace City, but there was another layer of wall to get through in order to access the luxury quarters. A gate to that area was open, and horse-drawn carts loaded with bulky items concealed under tarps were lined up, ready to go through. Soldiers swarmed each cart, inspecting everything from the bottoms of the horses' hooves to the wheel cogs to the pockets of the cart drivers. I watched as guards peeled back a tarp to reveal a cart bed full of barrels. Elvish wine, if I had to guess.

"Between the supplies and the level of security, I'd say we're headed in the right direction," I said.

Jasper spared a quick glance at the carts, but his attention was trained on the sky. He stepped away from us and raised his fist.

"That's Drifte," he said.

It took me a second to pick out the shape of the dark bird against the night sky. Drifte swooped down toward us, and something landed with a soft ping on the dirt in front of Jasper's boots. The raven shifter banked away and then circled back.

Jasper bent to retrieve the object. "It's a key." He tipped his head back to watch Drifte. "Give me a moment. I'm going to speak to him."

Jasper darted away toward a spindly hawthorn tree and blended with the shadow of its trunk. A moment later, I saw a bird alight on the ground near the tree. The bird blurred, the blur expanded and shimmered, and then Drifte was there next to Jasper.

After a few seconds, Jasper and Drifte appeared to be finishing up their conversation. The raven shifter crouched and then sprang up to catch one of the hawthorn tree's lower branches. He swung up and blended into the foliage. As Jasper walked back toward us, a bird took flight from the top of the tree.

I saw the spark in Jasper's golden eyes, and I knew he'd gotten something useful from Drifte.

"See that door?" Jasper leaned around the corner of the barn and pointed.

Bryna, Eunice, and I peeked out to look. It took me a second to identify what he was talking about—a plain door that was almost completely obscured behind a trellis with decorative climbing plants threading up about twenty feet. It stood about halfway between where we were and the line of incoming carts getting inspected by Daoine guards.

"Yeah?" I said, scooting back into the shadows.

"Apparently it's the entrance for, ah—" He skirted a glance at Eunice. "Companions who've been granted entry to the luxury suite."

I moistened my lips as my pulse jumped in anticipation. "The key?"

Jasper nodded. "That's our way in."

Suddenly, I knew I couldn't allow Jasper to go in with only Eunice. There was simply no way I was going to stand around smelling horse shit while he went after the Unseelie High King.

"I'm going in with you," I said. "Not all the way to Finvarra, if that won't work, but I want to be nearby."

Bryna snorted and muttered under her breath.

Ignoring her, Jasper's eyes tightened as his gaze remained trained on me. "We don't know what's on the other side of the door. Eunice and I have a cover, but how would we explain your presence when we're questioned?"

"I'll say I'm offering myself to Finvarra as well," I said.

He peered at me doubtfully. "Petra, you don't do subservient. Plus, that's not the truth, and we both know it's not possible to tell such a lie. I really think—"

"No," I interrupted, my voice pitched low. I stepped close to him. "I'm sorry, but hanging back while others jump into the fray is not who I am." My hand went to my hip, where I drew my broadsword a few inches. "*This* is what I do. This is who I am—a fighter. It's the best I have to offer. And if something went wrong in there—and let's be honest, there's a very good possibility of something going wrong, and I was standing out here with my thumb in my ass while it was happening—I'd never get past it. So I'm going with you. Deal with it."

His gaze shifted back and forth between my eyes for a moment, as if he was reading something in my face. "Okay," he finally said.

"Good luck with that," Bryna said, the sarcastic edge to her tone making it clear enough what she thought of my little speech.

I turned to her. "Where'll you be?"

"I'll be looking for another way through the wall surrounding the luxury suite," she said. "No guarantees, but I'll try to get close. And more important, I'll be looking for a good escape route for all of us."

"I appreciate that," I said sincerely. I turned again to Jasper. "Did Drifte have anything to say about Oliver's whereabouts?"

I was trying not to think too hard about my father's vanishing act, but my throat tightened a little when Jasper looked down and shook his head.

"I'm sorry, he didn't."

I nodded and tried to keep my focus on the task at hand.

"I'll keep an eye out for Oliver," Bryna offered.

I gave her a tight smile of thanks and then drew a deep breath and set my sights on the door hidden behind the trellis.

"There's one oddity of the door," Jasper said. "Apparently it's charmed to only allow one person in at a time. So the first person unlocks it and goes in, and Drifte will come for the key and bring it to the next person." He shrugged.

"A form of security, I guess," I said.

Jasper, Eunice, and I crept around the other side of the barn and waited until the attendants were occupied. Then we scurried silently to the wall and kept to the deep shadows until we reached the trellis. Crowding behind the foliage gave us decent cover from eyes that might happen to peer our way.

Jasper stuck the key into the lock, and the mechanism shifted with a soft click. I elbowed the door open a few inches and peered inside. There was a carpeted hallway with candle sconces on the walls. The hallway dead-ended to the left, so there was no choice of direction to make. The ceiling was open to the sky. I spotted Drifte perched above.

"The two of you go in first," I said.

The vines jostled a bit as Eunice moved past me and slipped inside. The door closed, and several seconds later the soft swish of a birds' wings above was followed by the plink of the key hitting the ground. Jasper retrieved it and followed Eunice.

I tipped my head back and watched as Drifte appeared high above. He swooped my way, but instead of dropping the key, he bobbled it, let out an alarmed caw, and darted away. Confused, I leaned around the vines and craned to see where he'd gone. Drifte disappeared over the wall at the same time the drawstring of my cloak snapped against my throat as a strong hand violently hauled me backward.

I threw one elbow back at my attacker and reached for my sword with my other hand, but fingers clamped over my mouth and my sword hand. I quickly summoned armor.

"Not so fast, Your Majesty," a male voice hissed in my ear.

Before I could try to peel the hand away from my face, it released and something smacked my temple, right in one of the areas stone armor didn't protect. The world reeled, and I fought to cling to consciousness.

Chapter 20

I WON THE battle to stay conscious, but just barely. Stars and dark splotches danced across my vision, and for several seconds I couldn't muster the strength to fight whoever had grabbed me. He got both my arms behind my back and pinned them painfully high with one strong hand. His other arm snaked around my neck, and I felt the press of a knife edge under my left ear, the blade poised to slice across throat.

A male voice let out a dark, triumphant chuckle near my ear. "I knew it was you."

I carefully twisted my head around and looked up, and my mouth dropped open at the sight of my blood father's tall, bulky brother. "Darion?"

"That's right, *niece*." He punctuated the last word by kneeing me hard in the kidney.

I grunted and my knees weakened. My mind whirled as I focused on summoning enough strength to draw magic. After a second or two, my power flooded me in a warm wave and pushed to the surface of my skin, where it formed a thin layer of rock armor. A little flash of victory surged through me. With my neck protected, Darion couldn't cut my throat. But my success was short-lived. With a growl, Darion let my arms go. I stumbled at the sudden release of pressure, and before I could recover, he boxed me violently in the ear with a roundhouse punch.

My legs went weak, and I pitched forward to my knees, my ear ringing and my head screaming. If I'd had my full reflexes, I might have spun quickly enough to dodge the punch, but Darion was a career military man of large stature. And he hated me with the passion of a thousand suns for nearly killing him in the Battle of Champions.

My lungs labored as I tried to breathe through the pain and keep from passing out. By the grace of the gods, he didn't attack me again. I slowly tipped my head back to peer up at him. Everything swam as I fought to bring Darion's face into focus. The eye on the side he'd hit seemed to be spasming. I blinked hard a couple of times.

"Periclase isn't going to be happy to find out you're abusing one of his blood daughters," I said, my words a little slurred.

Darion sneered at me. "You'll *wish* I'd taken you back to Daddy's palace."

I pulled my right hand back on the dirt, slowly, intending to go for the sword that hung from my belt. I wasn't stealthy enough.

"Oh no you don't," Darion said.

I tried to scuttle out of the way, but I was too slow. His boot stomped down on my hand, which wasn't protected because stone armor didn't extend all the way down my hands. I screamed as bones crunched and white-hot pain took over.

He roughly pulled me up by the armpits, pulled my broadsword from its sheath and flung it away, and hauled me over his shoulder like a sack of flour. My breaths came out as wheezing moans. I wanted to struggle, but I had to give myself a moment to recover from the fog of having my head bashed and the excruciating pain radiating from my crushed hand. I looked down, trying to gauge whether I could reach any of Darion's weapons. I was slung over his left shoulder, and he wore his short sword on his right hip. I stretched my fingers toward it, but it was out of reach. I couldn't get to the karambit in my boot without his notice.

Then I realized he was taking me through the gate in the wall that protected the luxury suite, the one where carts were being stopped for searches. I squinted, trying to make sense of my surroundings from my upside-down viewpoint. Not far away, a hooded figure stood near one of the cart horses, petting the animal. When she turned my way, she tipped the hood of her cloak back a bit and met my eyes. I caught my breath. It was Bryna. She'd surely seen what'd happened.

She placed a finger against her lips, a signal for me to stay quiet. Then she looked beyond me to the gate, pointed to her chest and then to the gate, and nodded. I was pretty sure I understood what she meant—she was going to follow and, I hoped, help me escape Darion's clutches.

I flipped my fingers at her in acknowledgment and sent up a prayer that I was interpreting her signals correctly.

"Eh, what's this, Lord Darion?" a male voice called.

Darion's boots scuffed to a halt. "Too much drink and she's injured herself," he said. "Horse crushed her hand. She needs a medic."

I watched through slitted eyes as a guard came around to inspect my mangled hand. He sucked a breath in through his teeth. "Aye, she does need medical attention. Carry on, my lord."

Darion was on the move again, taking me through the gate. Bryna wasn't far behind as she pretended to be part of the cart caravan the guards were waving through.

"Don't try anything, princess," Darion hissed at me. "I won't hesitate to stab you through the eye. Just try me."

I grunted in response. My hand was already tingling intensely as my stone blood began to speed-heal my bones. It'd probably take half a day to heal completely, but I was banking on the fact that Darion didn't know how fast I could get better. I stayed limp over his shoulder and moaned a couple of times for effect, wanting to seem worse off than I was. Not that it was a huge stretch. My head was pounding like a bass drum, and I was pretty sure the punch to my ear had somehow damaged my eardrum because my inner ear was tingling like crazy, too.

I focused on gathering my strength and trying to figure out where the hell we were in relation to where Jasper and Eunice had entered. Not far behind, I spotted Bryna peeling off from the carts to tail me.

I let out a low moan and then coughed for good measure. "Where's my father?" I asked in a raspy, weak voice. "I demand to see Periclase."

"Daddy had to go oversee things at the Summerlands."

I let out a sad little noise for effect as my thoughts spun. Darion was walking with purpose. Where was he taking me?

We started up some stairs, and I lost sight of Bryna. I wasn't sure whether she was trying to stay back so she wouldn't be spotted or she'd gotten held up. Either way, I didn't want to wait for her. I flexed my injured hand, and my knuckles cracked as bones realigned themselves. It was weak and tender, but I could use a two-handed grip if I had to. I just needed a damn weapon.

I thought about taking my chances and pitching myself over Darion's back, but if I landed on my head, I wasn't sure I could stay conscious through another blow.

I awkwardly peered around for anything that could assist me in my escape from my blood uncle's huge hands. It was extremely inconvenient to be in a position where I could only see things after we'd already passed them. Not that there was much around that I might've used. We stopped climbing stairs, and Darion hauled me down a hallway with numbered doors, like a hotel. I guessed we were in the apartment section of the luxury accommodations, where the guest of honor's entourage stayed.

Darion stopped at a door. I had to make a move. I couldn't risk getting locked up somewhere. There was the sound of a latch releasing. As soon as Darion took a step, I swung to the side, curled my fingers around the doorjamb, and kicked for all I was worth, hoping my boot heels would find Darion's face.

He cursed and clamped his hand around my ankle, but I managed to slide off his shoulder. With one foot on the ground, the other locked in his grip, and my hands desperately clinging to the molding around the door, my body became the prize in a tug-of-war.

"Let go of me, you asshole," I ground out through clamped teeth. My injured hand was quickly losing strength and punishing me with white-hot pain as I tried to force it to grip the doorway.

Darion responded by yanking my leg hard enough to rip my fingers off the doorjamb. My upper body fell to the floor, and I flopped and kicked, trying to force him to let me go. But I was losing the battle as he began to drag me into the room.

"Help me!" I screeched, hoping nearby guests might be alarmed enough by my cries to investigate. "Help!"

"Hey, you stupid Duergar! Look over here, ass hat!" The female voice sounded familiar. I looked around but didn't see the source of the voice.

Darion glanced up but then went back to trying to pull me around the half-open door.

"Darion! I'm talking to *you!*" came the voice again, this time sounding as if it were only a few feet away.

He paused at the sound of his name, straightening to look up and down the hall. Suddenly, he roared and dropped my leg. I pulled my feet under me and hopped to a crouch. A knife handle stuck out of his shoulder, blood already staining his shirt. I sprang at the short sword on his belt. He tried to bat me away, stiff-arming my attack. I turned my head, and his arm smacked into the stone armor protecting my shoulder. He caught a handful of my hood, and I twisted out of the cloak to the sound of ripping fabric. Strands of hair got yanked from my scalp as my wig was torn away.

Still crouching, I curled my left hand into a fist and rammed it up into his crotch. Cheap shot, yeah, but I was in a pickle and wasn't above fighting dirty. Another knife appeared out of nowhere, whizzing past

211

my face and burying itself in his thigh, and his roar of pain rose in pitch. He listed sideways, crashing into the doorjamb. I stole the second of distraction and ripped the short sword from the scabbard on his belt.

"Petra!"

I whirled. "Bryna?"

The hallway was empty. Then I saw a shimmer like a heat mirage half a dozen feet away, and my half-sister materialized. A ball of silver sparks balancing on her palm sputtered and winked out, leaving only a rising wisp of smoke and a small chunk of metal in her hand.

"I was saving that obfuscation magic for our escape," she said irritably, tossing the metal away. "Let's get the hell out of here."

She didn't have to tell me twice. With the short sword clutched in my good hand, I raced after her. Bryna's feet seemed to barely touch the floor as she flew down the stairs, her long pale hair swinging out behind her. We reached the ground floor, and she took a sharp left.

"Jasper and Eunice are somewhere this way, I think," she said.

I wasn't sure how she knew where to go, but I followed her with blind faith as she turned through the corridors. We got some strange looks, but most people we encountered were too inebriated to be very concerned about a couple of young women racing past. At some point I realized my disguise had been destroyed in my struggle with Darion. My cloak and wig were both on the floor where he'd tried to drag me into his room. I reached up and plucked the Sylph-long fake eyelashes from my upper lids. No point in subjecting myself to their discomfort at that point.

Bryna steered us into a corridor that was open to the sky overhead, and just as I was about to remark that I thought it was the area where Jasper and Eunice had come in, we rounded a corner and nearly crashed into them.

Eunice screeched and then slapped her hand over her mouth, her eyes bugging as she silenced herself. Jasper caught me by the shoulders before I could go sprawling. After the blows to my head, my balance was a little off.

"Darion tried to kidnap me," I said breathlessly. "Bryna pin-cushioned him with a couple of daggers, but they're not mortal wounds. He's pissed."

"Here," he said, taking off his cloak and throwing it around me. "Put the hood up. It's better than nothing."

I gulped air, my heart racing. "We need to get deeper in before Darion alerts someone."

Jasper nodded grimly and then tipped his head back, scanning the sky. A black bird swooped toward us and glided down the hallway, back the way we'd come.

"Drifte will lead us to where we can find Finvarra," Jasper said. "Let's go before anyone tries to detain us."

With my heart in my throat, I nodded and we set off at a swift pace, following Drifte as he disappeared around a turn.

Chapter 21

THE RAVEN SHIFTER darted ahead and out of sight. I started to speed up, but Jasper held out his arm. "Not too close. He's going to make sure the way is clear."

We slowed to a fast walk, and I tried to calm my thumping pulse.

"Darion said Periclase isn't here," I said, flipping a look up at Jasper as he strode beside me. "He's at the Summerlands, and Darion made it sound like Periclase is in charge."

Jasper grunted. "Finvarra is probably still calling the shots."

Grim anticipation stole through me in a cold shiver. Taking out Finvarra would be a triple victory: it would weaken the Unseelie bid for power in Faerie if their revered figurehead was out of the picture, it would upset the military effort to take the Summerlands, and it would disrupt the Tuatha De Danann's plans. I hoped, anyway. But first we had to get close enough to him for Jasper to have a chance to use Gae Buide.

I frowned as something occurred to me. "It's odd that Darion is here. He's one of the highest-ranking officers in the Duergar forces. Doesn't really make sense for Periclase to send him to a big old hedonistic bash in Palace City."

"It's true," Bryna said. "This kind of party is definitely not Darion's style."

I nodded. "And from what I could tell, he isn't partaking of the festivities. There was no alcohol on his breath."

I scowled at the memory of his mouth near my ear as he'd held my arms at my back. Yeah, I'd definitely been in a position to smell drink if he'd had even a swallow that evening.

Jasper squinted down at me and then gazed off, his golden eyes losing focus. "Aye, that is a bit odd. Perhaps Periclase felt the need to make the gesture of sending his brother here as a liaison to the battlefield. Or as part of Finvarra's protection here."

I snorted. "Darion was doing a shit job of security detail, if that's why he's here. He was a long way from Finvarra when he caught me outside."

Drifte reappeared down the hallway, darting toward us and then banking sharply back the way he'd come.

Jasper pointed. "Let's go."

We all started jogging again, ignoring the stares of the revelers we passed. Fortunately, it was late enough that the majority of the guests were three sheets to the wind, or simply not in a frame of mind to be curious about four cloaked figures hurrying through the hallways after a bird.

I glanced at Bryna, who was running along to my right as Jasper dropped back a bit to make sure Eunice wasn't having trouble keeping up.

"Any idea how close we might be?" I asked my half-sister.

"Close," Bryna said crisply. She lowered her voice to a whisper. "I overheard some of the soldiers when I was loitering around the carts. They didn't call Finvarra by name, but their not-so-subtle gossip indicated he is in the large festival chamber of the luxury accommodations. The raven is taking us in the right direction."

I gave a curt nod. "Good."

"I'm going to peel off soon," she said. "I want to find an alternate way into the festival chamber. Are you really going to try to get inside with Jasper and Eunice?"

I pressed my lips into a grimace. "Yes. Unless it looks as if that will seriously jeopardize their chances of getting in the same room as Finvarra."

"You sure about that?" she asked, doubt painted all over her face. "That hood isn't much of a disguise. Someone's bound to recognize you."

I blew out an exasperated breath. She might be right. It was probably stupid of me to try to force my way into the plan we'd already set, especially now.

"Okay," she said loud enough for Jasper and Eunice to hear. "I'm off to the shadows. I'll be as near as I can manage and will do what I can to assist. Watch for me."

I nodded, and she slowed to a walk, letting the three of us go ahead. My heart dropped an inch in my chest. We'd come in as five. Now we were down to three. Worry over Oliver tried to rise up, and I did my best to squash it.

I peered ahead, trying to see into the distance of the dimly lit corridor. "Where's Drifte?"

When Jasper didn't respond right away, I flicked a sharp look at him.

"I think he took a left about a hundred yards—oof—" Jasper's sentence ended in a grunt as a large form stepped out from a side hallway and nearly clotheslined him with an arm. Jasper threw his hands out to catch his balance, nimbly ducking past his attacker.

Eunice shrieked as she slipped in her effort to avoid plowing into the fray.

I skidded to a stop, shoved Eunice behind me, and reached for the stolen short sword on my belt. But before I could get properly into position, we were surrounded by at least two dozen Duergar soldiers, all with swords aimed at our throats.

I whipped around, looking for anyone who could help, but partiers within view were all scuttling away. Two hulking figures were coming our way. I recognized both of them.

"Oh no." The words came out a bare whisper as sudden fear choked off my air.

One of the men was Oliver. The other was Darion, not even limping a little from Bryna's dagger to the thigh. He must have had a very skilled healer nearby.

When the two men got close, I blinked, sure I was imagining things. Oliver walked freely next to Darion. I scrutinized my father's face, looking for any signs of violence, or even just consternation at having been taken prisoner. He looked grim, but that was pretty much status quo for my father.

"Oliver?" I called out.

He raised a hand in acknowledgment, but his expression didn't shift.

My eyes flipped back and forth between Oliver and Darion, my confusion mounting by the second.

The soldiers made an aisle for the two men.

My blood uncle went to Jasper, whose arms had been restrained behind his back by two Duergar men. Darion reached for Jasper's belt and drew Bae Guide. Darion could hold the knife, but it was still linked to Jasper, so in Darion's hand it couldn't be used to harm anyone else.

Darion's lips parted as he held the weapon up to his eyes. "It's true," he breathed. He turned to my father. "I'm one step closer to believing you." His eyes still on Oliver, Darion flipped his fingers in a signal, and the soldiers began muscling us around the corner and through an open door.

All of us crowded into what looked like a guest apartment. The soldiers took my short sword, which was actually Darion's. Darion carefully set Jasper's yellow knife on an end table. I noticed Oliver had been relieved of his sword, too.

The soldiers all filed out, leaving me, Jasper, Oliver, Eunice, and

Darion alone.

My gaze locked on Oliver's face. "What in the *hell* is going on?"

Oliver's jaw muscles flexed as he ground his teeth. "I'll let him explain." He tipped his head at Darion.

My blood uncle strolled toward me and stopped less than two feet away, peering down at me with an icy gaze.

"What are you here for, Petra Maguire?" He spoke the words so suddenly and forcefully, I startled a little. But I held my ground.

My hands tightened into fists at my sides and glared. "I don't have to tell you sh—"

"Tell him the truth," Oliver cut in.

I looked past Darion at my father. "What?"

"Tell him why we're here. Tell him what that knife is for."

Had he lost his damn mind? I squinted at Oliver, but my father just nodded calmly.

I gave my head a slight shake. "Fine. We're here to kill Finvarra. Jasper is—was—going to do it with that knife, Gae Buide."

Darion's eyes gleamed. "Where did you get the knife?"

I held his gaze. "Oberon gave it to Jasper."

"Why?"

"Why what?"

Darion looked like he really, really wanted to slap me. "Why did Oberon give it to Jasper?" he ground out.

I let out an exasperated breath. Surely my father didn't think it was a good idea to reveal the truth of our trip to Palace City.

"Because . . ." I flicked a glance at Oliver, but he nodded at me to continue. "Oberon knows that Jasper is Finvarra's blood son. The Unseelie High King can only be killed by his own blood."

Darion blinked a couple of times, and he just stared at me for a long moment. Then a smile began to stretch the corners of his mouth. He finally stepped back and turned to look at Oliver.

I crossed my arms. "Someone needs to start explaining. *Now.*"

Oliver's lips twitched. "Turns out your uncle here has the same goal we do. Only, he didn't know he wouldn't be able to succeed."

I frowned, trying to make sense of it. Then I turned on Darion. "You mean you're here to kill Finvarra?" In my surprise, the words came out a little loud.

"Shush, woman!" Darion snapped.

Jasper moved toward Darion, his hands fisted. "Don't speak to her that way. She's a queen. Show some godsdamned respect, you Duergar—"

Darion puffed his chest. "You're one to talk, you deserter."

Oliver moved in between them, holding up his arms. "Calm down, gentlemen," he said, his tone much too mild, his face too deadpan, for the situation we were in. "It just so happens we're on the same team."

I peered at my father. "What are you talking about?"

"We're all on the same team. At least in this matter."

I squinted at him, as if that would clarify things. Then I snorted. A laugh burbled up my throat. Everyone turned to stare at me.

"I'm sorry," I said, snickering. "This is just . . ." I gave my head a shake and looked at Darion. "So, let me get this straight. You came here to kill Finvarra. You only found out just now that he could only be killed by his own blood. And then we happened to come along, also aiming to kill Finvarra but with a weapon and more importantly the person who could actually do it."

Oliver gave me a withering look. Darion let out an impatient breath. Even Jasper had a warning look on his face.

"Come on," I said, spreading my hands. "You have to admit this is *quite* the twist of fate. I mean, not that long ago, Darion and I were trying to kill each other."

Jasper folded his arms over his chest. "The question is, what are we going to do about it?"

"I can get you inside," Darion said. "I can get you right up to him."

My brows inched up, and I gave my uncle a curious head tilt. "But why? Why do you want Finvarra dead?"

"So Periclase can take his place," Oliver supplied.

I narrowed my eyes at Darion. "But if the Unseelie knew you killed their beloved banished High King, they'd never accept Periclase as a replacement."

"I'd planned to make it so no one would know it was the Duergar," Darion said grudgingly. "And even if it was discovered at some point, what choice would the Unseelie have? No other Unseelie ruler has the power Periclase has. He's the obvious successor to Finvarra."

I wasn't so sure the Unseelie would see it that way. Finvarra was a legend, a hero and almost godlike figure to the Unseelie. Periclase was just a king.

That devious smile returned to Darion's face. "But now, I don't have to worry about that. I've got my assassins."

I exchanged a look with Jasper. We were there to take down Finvarra regardless of the Duergar plans. And if we had a chance to accomplish the mission, we had to take it. But we couldn't let Darion get us killed in the backlash.

"If you can get us in, you can make sure we get out, too," I said to my blood uncle. "In fact, we're going to insist on it."

He let out a bark of a laugh.

My arms went stiff at my sides. "If you refuse, then you'll just have to find another blood relative of Finvarra to do the job." And good fricking luck with *that*.

He waved a hand through the air. "Fine."

"I'll need a specific promise in the form of an oath."

He snorted derisively. "No oaths."

We stared each other down for several seconds. He was the one to break the standoff.

"Petra, I could have all of you except Jasper killed, force Jasper to knife his blood father, kill Jasper, and wash my hands of all of you," Darion said with something almost resembling patience. "Don't be greedy. Take what I'm offering."

I lifted my chin, giving him a defiant look. "Jasper doesn't have to do anything at your command. You don't have Eldon anymore. You can't force anyone to do shit."

He sighed. "This is what you came to do, and I can all but guarantee you get the chance to do it. My people will stay clear after. You have my word that none of the Duergar will raise a weapon to any of you."

I clenched my jaw and looked off to the side. He was right. We'd come to kill the Unseelie High King. And this was probably the best we were going to get. My gaze slid to Oliver, and he gave me a subtle nod. *Take it*, he was saying.

"Okay." I covered the short distance between me and Darion in a couple of strides and stuck out my hand. "No oaths, but we can at least shake on it."

His gaze lifted in a quick eyeroll, but he grasped my hand and then released it.

I let go and stepped back. "Now, how will you get us close enough to Finvarra to slit his throat?"

A crafty little smile crinkled the outer corners of Darion's eyes. "It turns out our plans dovetail nicely with each other."

He started talking, and ten minutes later we were ready to go. My pulse quickened as I stepped out into the hall. I shot Jasper a glance as I realized something that nearly made me smile.

"What?" Jasper whispered.

"Here we are, Seelie and Unseelie, enemies who had reason to kill each other, working side-by-side for a common goal. This probably wasn't how you had envisioned it, but you're getting your wish. Fae coming together for the greater good of Faerie."

He gave me a quick grin, his golden eyes sparking.

"Ready?" he whispered to me.

I nodded. "Let's introduce Finvarra to Gae Buide."

Chapter 22

DARION'S PLAN REQUIRED us to allow his soldiers to restrain us. The only manacles they had handy were, unfortunately, made of cold iron. The cuffs were closed but not locked, so we could slip out of them when we needed to. The metal burned even through my stone armor.

Surrounded by Duergar soldiers, Oliver, Jasper, and I allowed ourselves to be marched from the apartment to a set of double doors that were literally thumping with the sound of the club music inside. It was obvious we'd reached some sort of inner sanctum by the number of Daoine guards on duty. Most were in their human forms, but a pair of large and unfriendly-looking monitor lizards waited like sentries on either side of the door. I swallowed hard and peered at the reptiles, knowing how unpleasant their bites would be. A flicker of movement overhead drew my attention to a perch mounted high above the door. On it rested a vulture so huge I froze in a split-second of primal fear when its beady gaze paused on me.

Darion was at the front of our group, speaking to the Daoine guard who appeared to be in charge, a man well over six feet tall with a large hooked nose. He beckoned to another Daoine, a muscular woman with tendons popping on either side of her neck and said something in her ear. She opened one of the doors, and deafening music blasted us for the second or two that it took for her to slip inside.

I shifted my weight and glanced over at Jasper, who was standing to my left. His jaw muscles were working and his eyes were tense, but he gave me a little twitch of one corner of his mouth, the ghost of a half-smile.

After what seemed like an eternity, the Daoine woman emerged and spoke to Hook Nose. He exchanged a few words with Darion and then signaled to the other guards. Two of them moved to open the double doors.

The bassline of the music bumped through my body as the Duergar shuffled us into the festival chamber. It'd been decked out to look like a high-end Vegas club. The lights were low, and the air was full of billowing mist that gave the place an ambiance of mystery. Blue pinpoint lasers drew dizzying random patterns in the fog. Small stages featured gyrating dancers of both genders and many different Fae races, and the large dance floor that surrounded a raised DJ station was packed. A balcony featured VIP groups nestled into the privacy of the shadows.

Some of the partiers paused to gawk when they spotted the stern contingent of Duergar guards escorting us around the edge of the dance floor. A few drew back as we passed, but no one on the floor seemed terribly concerned. I peered around, searching for Finvarra, but it was difficult to make out the faces on the balcony above.

Revelers scooted out of the way when we got to a crowded area, and once we'd neared the back of the room, I spotted something I'd missed in the chaos of the chamber: private balcony at the back entirely enclosed in dark-tinted glass. Finvarra had to be there. He'd probably been watching us since we entered. A shiver started at the crown of my head and cascaded down my skin, leaving goosebumps in its wake.

Our group halted at the base of the staircase that led up to the Unseelie High King. The Daoine guards moved aside to let us pass. A few of Darion's soldiers peeled off to either side of the staircase, probably because all of us wouldn't comfortably fit in the balcony.

At the top of the stairs, a thick glass door was pushed open by a beefy bouncer with darting, birdlike eyes. Darion threaded us between a pair of long sofas where a handful of beautiful women with glazed eyes lounged. A handful of Daoine guards lined the walls to either side, fully armed.

The glass door closed behind us, almost completely blocking out the sound of the music except for the bump of bass that vibrated through the floor. Finvarra sat in a low-backed upholstered chair, his back to us. His posture was one of a man at ease, a man who felt in control of everything and everyone around him. I couldn't help wondering how long Periclase had been working to not only gain Finvarra's trust, but also make the Unseelie High King believe the Duergar posed no threat.

The chair began to turn, Finvarra swiveling slowly around to face us. As we'd planned, I stayed at the back of our group and kept my head down and my face deep in the hood of my cloak, but I peeked ahead. Finvarra's elbows were propped on the armrests, one arm ending in the stump my sword had left when I'd sliced off the tip of his wing as he'd tried to attack me in his avian form on the grounds of the Summerlands. My mouth hardened with satisfaction. Too bad for him that he wasn't a reptilian shifter. They could usually regenerate limbs.

Something glinted against Finvarra's chest, a sparkling object revealed by his shirt which was unbuttoned partway down his chest. My eyes widened. It was the Stone of Fal. The Unseelie High King was wearing it on a chain around his neck. He'd already tried to invoke the stone twice without success. Oberon believed Finvarra was saving his third and last invocation for after the Tuatha descended on Faerie. It would be the final step in Finvarra's bid to take control as the High King.

As planned, Eunice approached the front of the group with Jasper trailing behind. He kept his head ducked as if in deference, to hide his face. Darion had liked our original plan of sending in someone Finvarra had history with, so that was what we went with.

Eunice dropped into a deep curtsy, made somewhat awkward with her hands bound behind her.

"Your Highness," she said, at once humble, emotional, and eager. "I am so deeply honored you agreed to allow me to see you. Please, I beg you, tell these men I speak the truth when I say you and I have been previously acquainted!"

He regarded her coolly for a moment. Then he lifted his gaze to Darion, and Finvarra seemed annoyed with my blood uncle. "I do know this woman."

Darion bowed. "My apologies, Your Majesty. I didn't want to make assumptions about what she said."

Finvarra flipped his fingers dismissively and looked past her at Jasper and then at Oliver and me. My blood seemed to freeze in my veins. But Finvarra's eyes merely roved over our disguises.

"I was told you come with an offering, an object so surprising I would not believe it without seeing it for myself," Finvarra said, his attention once again on Eunice. "Lord Darion said he saw it with his own eyes and trusts in its authenticity."

Eunice nodded quickly several times. "Oh, yes, Your Highness. My companions and I, we have a very, *very* special object for you indeed. I dared not travel alone, due to the importance of this object reaching you."

It was a tricky game, as we couldn't lie outright so we were forced to use pieces of the truth to gain audience with Finvarra. Eunice was doing a bang-up job of dancing around the truth on the fly. We were extremely lucky that he was intrigued enough to allow us to be brought to his private balcony.

Finvarra leaned forward a bit.

Jasper's arms flexed, his cuffs dropped, and he snatched Gae Buide from his belt. Elbowing Eunice out of the way, he sprang at Finvarra, momentum carrying them back to crash on the floor.

Eunice shrieked, covered her head, and ducked.

Everything seemed to speed up. I watched the flashing yellow blade as I shouldered past the Duergar men. Oliver was right there with me, both of us throwing off our shackles, but I was faster. I kept a hold of my restraints, the cold iron burning a stripe across my palm.

"Keep the guards from aiding Finvarra!" I shouted back at my father.

I reached down and drew the karambit hidden in my boot, a weapon Darion's men had missed, and charged through the chaos.

In a strange déjà-vu-tinged scene, Jasper and Finvarra wrestled. Jasper's cap and wig fell off in the struggle.

I was acutely aware of Gae Buide glinting in the blue laser lights coming from the dance floor, but this time I wasn't going to hesitate. If Jasper accidently nicked me, I'd be dead, but we couldn't let Finvarra get away again. Morven's words flashed through my mind. We had to kill Finvarra now. It was our last chance.

I rushed around to Finvarra's head and fell to my knees, drawing magic to form full armor.

Jasper was straddling Finvarra, both of them grunting and straining to overcome the other. Finvarra had an iron grip on Jasper's hand that held the yellow blade, but Jasper was pummeling the High King with his other hand, and there wasn't a lot Finvarra could do to fend Jasper off with a stump of an arm.

I reached into the fray with my cuffs, struggling to wrap the cold iron around Finvarra's wrist to force him to let go of Jasper's arm. But the old man was *strong*, and he barely seemed fazed by the burn of the iron. He let out a growl, and his face began to change shape.

"He's trying to shift!" I shouted at Jasper.

Finvarra seemed to gain strength as his body morphed. He kicked his feet up and threw Jasper off. Jasper flew over me, did a half-somersault, and landed sprawled on his back. Gae Buide bounced away. I dove for the knife, sliding across the polished wood floor on my chest. My fingers wrapped around the handle, and I scrambled back toward Jasper.

Instead of finishing his metamorphosis, Finvarra's form snapped back to humanoid. He'd risen to his feet and reached up to his neck. With his remaining hand, he grasped the Stone of Fal and yanked viciously, breaking the chain. Light began to emanate from his fist and white mist leaked through his fingers. The last thing I saw before my vision whited out in the blinding burst of Stone light was the glint of Gae Buide as Jasper dove at his blood father.

For a wild moment, I was once again in the body of the female warrior who wore ancient armor. My mind thrashed, as if it were a dream that held me under. I stood in that other woman's body, surveying a battlefield where endless lines of skeletal riders sat on horses. I wasn't alone. To my left and right were dozens of soldiers dressed like me, men and women alike.

I thrashed with frustration. This was no time for a vision driven by god blood!

When the light faded and my sight began to return, I crawled, squinting, toward where two figures lay limp on the floor. Jasper was face down, sprawled over Finvarra. Both men were still.

Chaos was rising around me, as everyone without New Garg blood was reacting to Finvarra's invocation of the Stone of Fal. If he lived, any second the entire place would turn against us. If not, I wasn't sure exactly what would happen.

I screamed Jasper's name, my voice ringing harshly in my ears. I grasped his shoulder with both hands and heaved him over, dragging him over onto his back. His eyes rolled under his lids, and then he was peering up at me with his golden gaze.

"Thank Oberon," I choked out.

"Is he dead?" Jasper asked.

I looked over at Finvarra. In my fear that Jasper had been mortally wounded, I hadn't even bothered to check Finvarra's status. His eyes gazed blankly past me. Dark blood flowed from a deep gash across his neck.

Jasper sat up and looked, too. He still gripped Gae Buide, the yellow blade swathed in dripping crimson.

"He's dead," I whispered. I turned to Jasper as a bolt of reality seemed to shake my entire being. "You did it. He's dead."

We stared at each other for a moment and then both seemed to have the same thought.

"The Stone!" I whipped around, looking for the magical object. "We have to find it!" I shouted the words so forcefully, my voice broke.

Jasper and I both scrambled on all fours around Finvarra's lifeless body, desperately searching for the Stone of Fal.

Someone was tugging on my arm. I tried to shake them off, but then Oliver's voice barked my name. I looked up, dazed.

"Petra, we've got to get out of here," Oliver said. He had a hold of Eunice's wrist with his other hand. Her eyes were wide with shock. "This place is going to erupt. We have to go."

"No, we must find the Stone of Fal!" My voice pitched high with urgency.

"We can't stay," Oliver roared, a vein popping out on his forehead.

He took me by the upper arm and yanked me roughly to my feet. Once I was standing, I realized what he meant. Down below, Daoine were shifting into their animal forms. They were clawing at each other as terror and confusion reigned. Finvarra had used the Stone, which would have brought everyone in the immediate vicinity under his command. But the sudden death of the holder of the Stone seemed to have plunged the whole process into pandemonium.

Jasper had dragged Finvarra's body several feet and then rolled him over to his side, looking for the Stone under the corpse.

"It's gone," Jasper said with a helpless shake of his head.

"No, it can't be," I said.

Oliver pulled at me again. "Petra, let's *go*."

I twisted around. "Where's Darion?"

"I don't know," Oliver said, dragging me toward the staircase that led down from the private balcony. "But if we stay up here, we're going to be trapped in this cage."

True to Darion's word, the Duergar soldiers didn't try to interfere with our escape. Darion himself was nowhere to be seen, but Finvarra was dead. We'd done it.

Chapter 23

I POUNDED NUMBLY down the stairs after Oliver, silently cursing myself for allowing the Stone of Fal to slip away. We'd played right into Darion's hands. We'd done his dirty work, eliminating Finvarra and clearing the way for Periclase to take his place. Darion would take the Stone to Periclase, and in the hands of a new owner, the Stone would reset. Periclase would get three chances to use its power. He'd take up right where Finvarra left off.

"We don't know Darion took the Stone," Jasper said, as if reading my thoughts. "For all we know, when the owner dies, the Stone disappears into the ether to emerge somewhere else."

It was tempting to comfort myself with Jasper's suggestion, but my gut told me that wasn't what'd happened.

We reached the bottom of the staircase and emerged at the edge of the chaos of the dance floor. It was a massacre scene, with Daoine shifters battling each other and much worse, tearing into Fae of other races who were unable to defend themselves.

I peered around wildly, suddenly realizing just how poor our position was. There were no exits nearby. We were unarmed, except for Gae Buide and the small knives Oliver and I had.

"How the hell are we going to get through?" I asked.

Oliver pointed off to the left. "That's the nearest way out."

Eunice whimpered, and I gulped. In between us and the door was a trio of enormous vultures viciously pecking and ripping apart anyone who stumbled too near. I watched, horrified, as a crocodile tried to scuttle past the birds. One of them grabbed the croc with its clawed talon and flung it against the wall about a dozen feet away from us. The reptile hit so hard, it broke clear through.

"That's our new exit," Jasper said. He held up Gae Buide. "Follow me and stay close."

We huddled at his back as we skirted along the wall toward the hole. Jasper jumped through first, and I was right on his heels brandishing my karambit. We burst into a hallway. I threw out my arms, struggling to keep my footing on the chunks of wall that littered the area in front of the hole.

"Look out!" Eunice screeched behind us.

The croc was still alive, and it was pissed. Moving faster than I would have imagined possible for such a bulky creature, it scuttled straight at us, its powerful tail whipping and its massive jaws snapping.

We all piled back through the hole into the festival chamber. With the croc bearing down from one direction and the fifteen-foot-tall vultures blocking the other way, we had nowhere to go.

"Petra, up here!"

I tipped my head back in confusion, looking for the source of the voice. It was Bryna, leaning over the balcony above us. I had to look away as the croc charged through the hole in the wall. Jasper was ready with Gae Buide. Narrowly avoiding getting an arm crunched off, Jasper slashed at the ancient-looking creature. It was only a glancing slice off the tough hide, but it was enough. The croc's roar melted into a terrible human scream. The shifter sagged, dead halfway into the room.

"Let's go," Jasper said.

I didn't have time to look for Bryna. Jasper grabbed my hand and jumped up onto the croc's body. Oliver had a hold of poor Eunice, and they were right behind us. We scrambled over the dead creature and tumbled into the hallway.

I whipped my head back and forth, trying to figure out which way to go.

A black blur was darting straight toward us from the left.

"That's Drifte," Jasper said.

The raven shifter passed us in a rush of wings and zipped on down the corridor. We all turned to follow. Running full-speed, we raced through and around groups of confused, drunk people reeling through the hallways. The worst of the chaos and violence seemed to have been contained to the room where Finvarra was, but it was only a matter of time before word spread and Palace City became thick with soldiers and panic.

Drifte got us out of the labyrinth of the luxury accommodations. I had a momentary sensation of relief when the cool night air hit my skin, but it was short-lived. We were still about three layers of walls from getting free of Palace City, and the nearest gate had just slammed closed.

I turned to Jasper. "The Ravens. We need them to get us out of here."

He already had his whistle in his hand, but he was hesitating. He pointed up. Daoine soldiers already lined the open walkways between towers, many of them armed with high-powered bows. Others were shifting into their bird forms—huge hawks and other birds of prey—and beginning to take flight.

"I can't bring Great Ravens into the middle of this," Jasper said. "We've got to at least get beyond the walls."

My heart plummeted.

Oliver let loose with a string of curses. I turned to see what he was reacting to, and a flurry of movement twisted my stomach and made my pulse speed. Daoine soldiers were rounding the corner ahead. The entire area was filling with Daoine rushing in like a flash flood of bodies.

"What are we going to do?" Eunice wailed.

I whirled around, looking for escape, but the Daoine were bearing down on us from all sides, lining the walkways above and filling the air in their shifter forms.

We couldn't fight. We couldn't run. We were trapped.

"Petra!"

I turned. It was Bryna standing in the doorway through which we'd exited a few moments before. She was waving furiously at us.

"Come on! Hurry, you idiots!" she screeched at us.

We sprinted back inside. I skidded to a halt. The corridor was thick with bodies running every which way. We followed Bryna around a corner. She stopped and yanked open a door I might not have even noticed, as it blended almost completely into the wall. We went through and found ourselves in a smaller, plain corridor that ran parallel to the one we'd just left. It was a service hallway. It wasn't empty but was considerably less crowded, and there were no soldiers in sight.

I had no idea where she was taking us, but I had to trust she knew a way out.

She made a sharp turn and pushed through a set of swinging doors. Steam and the fragrant smells of cooking meat and baking bread hit me in the face. We scurried through the kitchen, following Bryna. The cooking stations had been mostly abandoned, so there wasn't anyone to protest our presence.

She skidded to a halt in an area where partially plated dinners sat abandoned on a counter. A wide-open compartment gaped in the wall.

"Get in," Bryna snapped.

I blinked.

"It's a dumbwaiter," she said. "Get *in.*"

We piled inside, forced to crouch by the low height of the little elevator car. Bryna reached out and slapped the button on the wall next to the dumbwaiter. A door dropped down, plunging us into darkness, and we began to move up. The contraption groaned under our collective weight, the mechanics seeming to strain and struggle to lift us. The painfully slow, stuffy ride seemed to go on for an hour.

We finally stopped, and Bryna forced the door up. She hopped out into what looked like a small staging area. Linen-covered carts lined one wall. Pleasant music played through speakers. No one was around.

"What now?" I asked.

She pointed at one of the two doors. "We go out there, find a window to bust out, and he"—she jerked her thumb in Jasper's direction—"makes sure Ravens will be there to catch us before we go splat down below."

We piled out of the dumbwaiter and followed her out one of the doors to a small vestibule. A floor-to-ceiling window revealed a view of two of the three palaces of the City. Bryna reached into a pouch on her belt. On her palm she carefully balanced what looked like a steel marble. It jumped up, and a dozen inch-long spikes shot out of the surface. She winced as it landed back on her hand. Then she drew her arm back and hurled it at the window. The spiky little object exploded on impact in a burst of shattering glass and neon-yellow magic.

Jasper leaned through the opening and blasted his whistle. He stood there with his eyes on the sky.

"We're going to have to jump," he said. He glanced at me. I'd done this before.

I went to stand next to him and peered down. We were maybe eight stories up, putting us barely above the height of the walkways with the Daoine bowmen and women.

I shook my head. "It's a mess out there."

"I know," Jasper said curtly. "We'll need a bit of luck on our side."

With my lips pressed into a grim line, I watched with Jasper as five Great Ravens appeared low on the horizon. The birds flew higher as they approached, and then they disappeared overhead.

"They're circling around," Jasper said. He beckoned to Eunice.

She looked terrified as she stepped to the edge of the broken-out window.

"Jump as far out as you can when I say the word. Feet down, knees apart. Grab on tight when you hit the bird," he instructed.

She whimpered and nodded.

"Ready . . . now," he said.

A large black bird swooped in from the right. She leapt and landed on the bird, who zoomed away and out of sight. I devoted a second or two to admiring her bravery.

"Oliver next."

My father stepped up and jumped to his bird. Then Bryna. When I stepped up, Jasper squeezed my hand briefly.

"See you on the other side," he said. "*Now.*"

I jumped, hit a bony body covered with slick dark feathers, which I grasped in handfuls to keep from sliding off as the bird banked hard.

My Raven pumped her wings, and we gained altitude. Something whizzed past my ear, and my blood ran cold as I realized it was a Daoine arrow that missed me by mere inches.

The bird—I recognized Mohawk—sped away from Palace City. We cruised over the tops of trees for about five minutes and then plunged into the void of the netherwhere.

We rejoined the world in a place where the night was silent and peaceful. Mohawk tipped a wing and began a descending spiral. Slanting my gaze downward, I caught sight of two other Ravens below us. And beyond, I recognized the layout of the fortress. We were home. I watched the sky above until I saw two more Great Ravens appear and then let out a relieved breath, closed my eyes, and lowered my forehead into the bird's soft feathers.

It wasn't until we were almost on the ground that I wondered how Jasper had decided to have the Ravens take us to the stone fortress. I didn't have energy to devote to the thought. This was as good a place as any to come.

The birds were taking us to the fortress's training yard, and Carraig soldiers were running in from all directions. My heart jumped. That was all we needed—make it out of the Daoine Sidhe realm alive, having killed Finvarra, only to be mistaken for the enemy by my own people. I heard Oliver's voice calling out to the soldiers, telling them we were friendly. They halted and then approached more slowly, thank the gods.

Mohawk landed with a few light hops and then tipped a wing to let me down. I patted her neck and jogged to where my father and Eunice stood.

A loping figure in regular clothes—no armor or weapons—was coming through the soldiers. Maxen. The soldiers had begun to recognize me and bowed with mumbled greetings of "Your Highness" and "Your Majesty."

"Stand down," Oliver called. "There's no threat here. All of you, return to your posts."

The soldiers began to disperse, though they cast curious looks as Maxen joined us and the last Raven, carrying Jasper, landed.

Maxen was looking at us expectantly, hands on hips and panting lightly from his run to the yard.

"Well?" he finally said.

I waited a moment for Jasper and Bryna to join us.

"We got him," I said. "Finvarra's dead."

Maxen let out a whoop, grabbed me around the waist, and twirled me around. I couldn't help a brief grin, not just at his reaction, but also at how he'd let down his guard. I couldn't remember the last time he'd done that with me.

"There's bad news, though," I said, catching my balance as he set me on my feet. "We didn't recover the Stone of Fal. It may be in Periclase's hands now."

That sobered him up. He nodded. "Okay. You'd better tell me

everything. Let's go where we can have some privacy."

"My apartment?" I suggested.

We trooped quietly through the corridors of the fortress—empty except for workers with late-night duties and patrolling soldiers. It had to be late, probably closer to dawn than midnight.

Once we were behind closed doors, we recounted the entire adventure to Maxen. Eunice's head began to nod toward the end, and I called a page to escort her to her quarters.

I knew Maxen was concerned about the Stone, but he kept asking questions about what Darion had said. He seemed troubled.

"What is it?" I asked.

He gave a couple of slow shakes of his head. "I truly didn't see this coming. I wouldn't have guessed Periclase would try such a thing, no matter that he wouldn't have succeeded in killing Finvarra on his own. The mere fact that he planned the assassination has caught me seriously off guard. I don't like these kinds of surprises."

We were all quiet for a moment, and then Bryna's mouth stretched into a jaw-cracking yawn.

"You're welcome to stay the night here," I said. "We'll find quarters for you."

She nodded. "That'd be good."

I picked up my house phone and asked for another page. When he arrived, I stood and went with Bryna to the door.

"You were invaluable in getting us in and out," I said.

"Just doing my part for the betterment of the realm," she replied lightly.

"But you're Unseelie," I said. "In principle, you shouldn't have wanted to help us."

"I'm Unseelie like Jasper is Unseelie. I don't want to see Faerie destroyed."

I quirked a half-smile at her, which she returned before slipping out.

Not long after, Oliver and Maxen departed as well, leaving me and Jasper alone.

I went to him and took his hands in mine. "Stay with me?"

His golden eyes sparked. "You don't need to ask twice." Then he glanced down at himself. His clothes were torn, dirty, and blood-spattered. I wasn't in much better shape.

I turned toward the doorway leading deeper into my quarters and then twisted and beckoned to him. "I have an idea."

He followed me into the master suite, where I went to the bathroom and began filling the giant tub. Fifteen minutes later, I sat in the deliciously hot water with my back against his chest and steam rising around us.

"I can't stay long," he whispered, his lips at my ear. He threaded the fingers of one hand through mine. His other hand began to rove my body, starting just beneath my earlobe and working downward.

I sighed. "I know."

I shifted in the water, turning to face him, and pressed a kiss to his lips. I started to draw back, but he pulled me in, closing his arms around my waist as I straddled his muscled thighs.

"We'll just have to make the best of the time we have," he said, a hungry, growly edge to his voice that sent shivers spilling down my back.

We spent the next hour lost in each other, and then I fell asleep with my head on his chest, the beat of his heart like a lullaby.

I woke only a few hours later, but he was already gone.

I'd barely dressed when the house phone began ringing. I answered, expecting one of my attendants on the other end, perhaps announcing when breakfast would arrive. But it was Maxen.

"I need you to come to the foyer right away," he said, his voice strained.

My chest tightened. "What's wrong?"

"The hidden ones have begun to return."

I blinked, silent for a beat as I tried to process the news. "Okay. I'll be right there."

Chapter 24

I SLUNG AURORA onto my back and hurried from my quarters. A couple of guards followed behind me. I wanted to shoo them away, but I was too concerned about the tone of Maxen's voice to bother.

By the time I arrived in the foyer, a crowd of curious onlookers had already started to gather around the edges. But the middle of the expansive space was crowded—no, packed—with unfamiliar faces. Maybe eighty of them, by a quick visual estimate. Maxen was speaking with one of the men, a tall muscular guy about Oliver's age and with nearly my father's wingspan. The strangers were peering around, about half of them looking confused and the other half varying flavors of upset. All of them looked dazed. The space filled with the loud murmur of many conversations running together.

One of my guards jogged ahead of me. "Make way for the queen!" he barked.

People scooted aside and began to bow and curtsy as I passed.

I strode through the throng and halted next to Maxen. He bent in a hasty bow. The man Maxen had been talking to shot me a tight-lipped, suspicious glare.

"You're not Marisol Lothlorien," he said, his tone accusing.

"No, I'm not. Are you all New Gargs?" I'd nearly said Carraig Sidhe but used the old terminology instead. If these people were all stone bloods who'd been hiding themselves in the Earthly realm, they might not even know we'd been given kingdomhood and an official name.

"Aye," the big man said. "I demand to see Marisol."

I groaned internally. I recognized the way he said Marisol's name. It was the same tone Oliver used to have when speaking of our former leader while I was growing up. My thoughts spun as I quickly did the mental math. This man and Marisol had been close. Probably very close. He'd made a grave sacrifice at her request, abandoning his homeland and everyone he knew to conceal himself, to help Marisol hide our true numbers. Last he'd known, she was the New Gargoyle sovereign who was going to lead us to independence. Everything he'd done, all of his suffering for the past many years, had been for Marisol Lothlorien.

And I'd killed her and taken her place.

"Angus, we should go somewhere to speak in private," Maxen said, using his most reasonable diplomat voice.

Angus peered at him. "I can tell you're her boy, even if you hadn't said your name. You have her eyes."

Maxen reached up to steer the big man's shoulder. "Let's just go—"

He shrugged away from Maxen's grasp. "I'm not going anywhere until someone explains just what in the name of Maeve is going on here."

Maxen and I exchanged a look. I supposed I could have called in guards to forcibly escort Angus to a less public place. But that probably wouldn't have improved his mood or his reception of me.

I leveled my chin and gave him a hard look. "Marisol Lothlorien is dead. My name is Petra Maguire, Champion of the Summer Court, wielder of Aurora. And Queen of the people formerly known as New Gargoyles, now the Carraig Sidhe."

He peered at me dumbly. Then his eyes narrowed. "Marisol was supposed to rule. You're not *my* queen," he growled.

In the corner of my eye, I saw someone threading through the crowd. Oliver joined us, facing me and bowing. Angus glanced at him, back at me, and then did a double-take, his eyes widening as he took in my father.

"Angus," Oliver said. "It's been a very long time." He stuck out his hand.

Angus blinked several times and then grasped my father's hand and shook it firmly. "Oliver Maguire. She is a relation of yours?" His gaze flicked to me.

Oliver leveled his chin, his gaze direct. "Yes, Petra's my daughter. And though she may look more fighter than monarch, she is indeed our queen."

For a moment, Angus seemed to have warmed at the sight of Oliver, but his face hardened again. "I need to know what happened to Marisol," he said, his voice low and pained.

Oliver nodded. "We'll talk about that. There's much to discuss."

"Indeed," I said. I faced the crowd of newcomers. "We'll start finding places for all of you immediately. This is your home now, and you're welcome here."

My words didn't seem to warm the crowd much.

Amalie had arrived just after my father and was standing at a respectful distance. I went to her and we had a quick, whispered conversation about finding quarters for everyone.

When I rejoined the men, Oliver and Angus were deep in conversation. I watched them for a moment and quietly blew out a long, slow breath. If my father hadn't appeared in the foyer, I might have ended up in a replay of my confrontation with Raleigh. Thank the gods there'd been no fight.

But I couldn't relax. Angus didn't yet know I'd killed Marisol.

I looked over the crowd behind Angus. There were dozens of men and women, mostly my father's age or older, and a handful of teenagers and younger children. The adults all had the same sunken-eyed, haggard look to their faces, borne of too many years away from Faerie that had affected them like a wasting disease. As much as I'd wanted to get away from the fortress when I was a kid, I couldn't imagine a continuous exile of decades. It would have felt like a slow, excruciating starvation, cut off from the source of Fae power, vitality, and magic. And all of these people had voluntarily subjected themselves to the torment of it for Marisol Lothlorien, because one of her visions had demanded it.

Part of me wanted badly to hand off the leadership duties to Maxen. He'd already been appointed a role that gave him as much power as I had, and the new additions to the fortress would probably be more receptive to him, as Marisol's son. But I couldn't just be an empty figurehead and walk away from these people, leaving them for Maxen to deal with. Not after what they'd sacrificed. They deserved more from me.

Emmaline arrived, coming to me and curtsying, offering something she held in both hands. She'd brought me my crown.

"Your Majesty," she said. "You left in such haste, you forgot this."

As much as I didn't want to, I knew she was right—I needed to wear it. Without a word, I bent so she could position it onto my head. The weight of it seemed to settle over me.

As we began to make arrangements for the newcomers, my mind was jumping ahead to the conversations and possible confrontations I'd have to face. It would only be a matter of time before these people—our people—discovered that Marisol Lothlorien had died by my sword.

I took a deep breath and squared my shoulders. "Angus, won't you join me, my father, and Maxen in the Ruby Room? As Oliver said, we have much to discuss."

His eyes hardened as he regarded me for a long moment. Then he nodded. "That we do."

Maxen and I turned to walk through the foyer, giving Angus and the others a full view of Aurora on my back. I resisted the urge to look over my shoulder but heard Oliver and Angus in conversation behind us.

"Petra," Maxen whispered, leaning toward me. "Word came from the Summerlands that Finvarra's death hasn't slowed the Unseelie attack at all. If anything, Periclase seems to have held back before, and now he's really unleashing the full force of his weapons. Oberon thinks he's trying to make a show of his might to erase any Unseelie doubts about who should be Finvarra's successor."

My pulse thumped uneasily. "Damn," I muttered.

"That's not the worst of it," he said. "There is a rumor that the Dullahan were spotted in a remote region of Faerie. Oberon is working on confirming it. And . . ."

When he trailed off, I cut a swift look up at him. "What?"

"The Giants' Causeway has started to tremor."

I squinted at him. "The Tuatha?"

Maxen's gaze met mine, his eyes strained and his face pale. "Oberon believes so."

My mouth went dry, and a cold shiver swept over me. "We've got to get our hands on the Chalice of Dagda. And even more important, we need to figure out how to tap into the power of the Fomoire blood that runs through our veins. Our so-called god blood may be the only true weapon we have against Tuatha De Danann."

Maxen gave me a tight nod, but we couldn't speak of it further. We'd reached the Ruby Room.

I turned to face Angus, and my thoughts were a torrent. I felt pulled in half a dozen different directions. There was so much work to do in the fortress to unite the Carraig and get our kingdom running smoothly. But with Periclase closing in on the Summerlands and the Tuatha awakening under the mountain of the Causeway, kingdom business almost seemed a luxury. All I knew was that I'd have to do everything in my power to make sure the Carraig Sidhe and everyone in Faerie had a future to look forward to.

**Look for *War of the Fae Gods by Jayne Faith*,
the next book in the Stone Blood Series!**

About the Author

JAYNE FAITH WRITES fantasy set in the real world. She's a meditator, dog lover, TV addict, clean eater, homebody, sun baby, and Sagittarius. Her superpower is her laugh. She owns way too many colored pens and pairs of jeans. Visit her website at www.jaynefaith.com, where you can sign up for her VIP list and get free books.

Also by Jayne Faith

Ella Grey Series
Demon patrol officer Ella Grey beat death after an accident on the job, but something followed her back from the grave. Will it eat her soul or become her greatest ally?

Stone Cold Magic (#1)
Dark Harvest Magic (#2)
Demon Born Magic (#3)
Blood Storm Magic (#4)

Tara Knightley Series
Between paying off a debt to a Fae mob boss, working as a professional thief, and keeping up with her busy three-generation household, Tara Knightley barely has time to eat and sleep. But now she's going to have to choose: her family, love, or her freedom.

Oath of Blood (prequel)
Edge of Magic (#1)
Echo of Bone (#2)
Trace of Fate (#3)
more to come

Stone Blood Series

When vampire hunter Petra Maguire discovers she has a secret twin who's been kidnapped, she's determined to rescue her. But it could spark a magical war.

Blood of Stone (#1)
Stone Blood Legacy (#2)
Rise of the Stone Court (#3)
Reign of the Stone Queen (#4)
War of the Fae Gods (#5)
The Oldest Changeling in Faerie (#6)

Sapient Salvation Series

An innocent young woman fighting to survive in a foreign land. A powerful overlord longing to leave his dark past behind. The moment they meet, worlds clash as forbidden love ignites.

The Selection (#1)
The Awakening (#2)
The Divining (#3)
The Claiming (#4)